PRAIS[E]

'It is hard to believ[e ...]
Plot, pacing and charact[er ...]
that it feels more like [...]'
The Times

'My crime novel of the year ... Intense and evocative,
it tears at the heart-strings'
Daily Mail

'We devoured this stunningly drawn,
deeply compelling mystery in one day'
Crime Monthly (UK)

'Burr brings a piercing psychological acuity,
creating a nuanced examination of the emotional and
reputational stakes of a murder investigation'
Canberra Times

'There is a complexity and depth to the characters.
WAKE will appeal to fans of Jane Harper,
Christian White and Chris Hammer'
Books+Publishing

'Effortlessly accomplished, astonishing, sharply observed ...
A voice that will make you sit up and take notice'
DINUKA McKENZIE

'This is Australian crime fiction at its very best'
MARK BRANDI

PRAISE FOR *RIPPER*

'Will have you hooked from start to finish ... Exceptional ...
An amazing and addictive plot loaded with numerous brilliant twists'
Canberra Weekly

'A masterclass in pace, plot, character and creeping unease'
The Bookseller, Book of the Month

'Tantalising ... A glimpse into a small town that cannot
shake the ghosts of its past'
Weekend Australian

'Gripping, surprising ... fascinating ... Ripe for devourers of
Sarah Thornton, Jane Harper and Sarah Bailey'
Books+Publishing

'Filled with lots of twists and turns. I won't be surprised if this
becomes somewhat of a classic in the years to come'
Mamamia

'Startling, filmic and haunting'
ALLIE REYNOLDS

'Shelley Burr proves herself a master of the
modern Australian crime novel'
ROSE CARLYLE

'Unveiling one richly layered character after another,
RIPPER has plenty of tricks up its sleeve and crackles
with tension throughout'
JACK HEATH

VANISH

Also by Shelley Burr

WAKE
RIPPER

SHELLEY BURR

VANISH

hachette
AUSTRALIA

hachette
AUSTRALIA

Published in Australia and New Zealand in 2025
by Hachette Australia
(an imprint of Hachette Australia Pty Limited)
Gadigal Country, Level 17, 207 Kent Street, Sydney, NSW 2000
www.hachette.com.au

Hachette Australia acknowledges and pays our respects to the past, present and future Traditional Owners and Custodians of Country throughout Australia and recognises the continuation of cultural, spiritual and educational practices of Aboriginal and Torres Strait Islander peoples. Our head office is located on the lands of the Gadigal people of the Eora Nation.

Copyright © Shelley Burr Pty Ltd 2025

This book is copyright. Apart from any fair dealing for the purposes of private study, research, criticism or review permitted under the *Copyright Act 1968*, no part may be stored or reproduced by any process without prior written permission. Enquiries should be made to the publisher.

A catalogue record for this book is available from the National Library of Australia

ISBN: 978 0 7336 5215 8 (paperback)

Cover design by Alex Ross Creative
Cover photograph courtesy of Alamy (roof)
Author photograph by Yen Eriksen Media
Typeset in 12.5/19.5 pt Adobe Garamond Pro by Kirby Jones
Printed and bound in Australia by McPherson's Printing Group

MIX
Paper | Supporting responsible forestry
FSC® C001695

The paper this book is printed on is certified against the Forest Stewardship Council® Standards. McPherson's Printing Group holds FSC® chain of custody certification SA-COC-005379. FSC® promotes environmentally responsible, socially beneficial and economically viable management of the world's forests

To my love, my joy and my star

HE WASN'T SURE how long he'd been unconscious. There were no windows down here. Time slipped away from him. It didn't feel like something he was part of anymore. Like he was a rock and it slid past him like water. No, water wasn't right. That was too clean, too fast. Time glugged around him, like soup going cold.

His stomach turned and he sucked in a deep, desperate breath, worried he was going to throw up. That would sap the scrap of energy he'd gathered and he would have to sleep again before he could make the attempt to leave.

He couldn't sit up. He'd learned that the hard way. The last time he'd tried, a white flash had crashed over him, followed by black. He'd passed out and woken up seconds, minutes, hours later with nothing left to draw on. He'd had to sleep, and sleep hurt now.

Awake hurt too.

CHAPTER ONE

LANE WORRIED AT the cuff of his shirt, rubbing it between the fingers and thumb of his other hand. All the prisoners had been issued new shirts that week, which were stiff and nasty and smelled peculiar. They'd probably saved Corrective Services ten per cent on a budget line item and won some white collar in Sydney a promotion or bonus. Meanwhile, it had made everyone in the Special Purpose Centre edgy and jumpy. In a place like this, the tiniest thing could get tempers rising. The prisoners were already bored and lonely and unhappy as a baseline – add a fresh irritant and the Tin became dry tinder waiting on a spark.

It had been a pleasant surprise when his sister Lynnie let him know she was planning a visit, but it left him uneasy. Since he'd moved to the Special Purpose Centre in Bowral, her visits had gradually dwindled to Christmas and birthdays. He understood – she was finishing a university degree in Canberra, and the round trip was a long one. Long enough that she needed to budget for petrol, a motel room and takeaway. He also knew that still made him one of the lucky few – statistically most prisoners received no visitors at all after the first year of their sentence.

'This shirt is new,' he told her, since that counted as news in his world. There was something he wished he could tell her, information he'd discovered that left him fizzing with the urge to share, but visits were monitored. He couldn't tell her what he knew without telling her how he knew, and that would not end well for him.

'It's nice,' she said.

'It's hideous,' he said.

She grinned. 'Like your own taste was any better.'

She had him there. Money had been tight during the years he'd spent raising her, turning him into a champion op-shopper. If a shirt was in good condition and fit his broad frame, he would buy it – style barely factored into the decision.

She folded her hands on the table between them. She'd had her nails done, he noticed – tidy little ovals painted pale pink. 'I'm considering leaving my job so I can go full-time at uni. If I did that, I could graduate at the end of this year instead of next year.'

Lane tried to keep his face neutral. It hurt whenever she mentioned the compromises she'd had to make because of his decisions. He was in here, unable to support her the way he'd promised, and so instead of doing a full-time English degree like she'd wanted, she'd started an accounting cadetship – six years of part-time work and part-time study.

'The main downside is that, if I did that, you wouldn't be able to come to my graduation ceremony.'

'If that's the main downside, you should definitely do it,' he said. 'Just because I'm eligible for parole next year doesn't mean I'll get it. I might not be able to come next year either and you'll have lost a year for nothing.'

'You *will* get it,' she said. 'Your record is pristine.'

'I know,' he said. 'But there's plenty of people who think my sentence was too lenient. If I get one of those on the parole board …'

'There's plenty who think you shouldn't have served any time at all,' she said, her voice heated.

'They're wrong,' he said, trying to keep his tone mild. He pulled at his cuff again. Some of the men on his block hated them so much they'd taken to going about shirtless, even though it was winter, but Lane could never be comfortable like that.

'Please don't be defeatist,' Lynnie said. 'You can't show the board you're ready if you're acting like you don't think it will happen.'

Screw it. He needed to tell someone, but it was still too tenuous to get the governor's hopes up. Still, after months of quiet, painstaking work, if he didn't talk about it, he was going to end up developing the third man delusion – creating an imaginary friend because the pressure of being alone was too much.

'I've got some news,' he said.

It stung how completely Lynnie lit up at hearing something positive from him. 'Oh?'

'Do you remember what happened a couple of years ago, with Jan Henning-Klosner?'

Governor Patton Carver, who ran the prison in which Lane was currently a guest, had offered him a lifeline – a chance to work a case from prison. He'd asked Lane to try to befriend and surreptitiously interrogate Jan, also known as the Rainier Ripper, and prove that the Ripper's unidentified female victim had been Matilda, Carver's daughter, who had disappeared while backpacking nearly twenty years ago, during the period when Jan was active.

What Lane had actually learned from Jan had been beyond anything he or Carver could have imagined. It had brought a lot of answers to light, but not the one Carver had hoped for. Matilda was not one of Jan's victims.

Once the dust settled, one painful fact remained: Matilda was still missing, and Carver was no closer to finding her.

The light in Lynnie's face dimmed immediately. 'It's not something I would forget.'

'I think I've got a lead on Matilda,' Lane told her. He glanced over at the guard who was supervising the visiting room. Sweeney – a tall skinny man who'd only been working at the SPC for a few months – seemed focused on a prisoner who was talking to his girlfriend at the far end of the room, but Lane dropped his voice anyway. 'She disappeared during her gap year, while working at a farm in the Kiewa Valley. I realised I was getting nowhere focusing on Matilda's case. I was looking at the same information again and again and never seeing anything new. I needed to try from another direction. I started looking for other open Missing Persons cases from the region and –'

'Looking how?' Lynnie interrupted. 'I know you're not doing this on the LeapFrog laptop toys they give you in here.'

She was right. He'd complained to her often enough about how the tablets the prisoners had access to were more trouble than they were worth. If they weren't glitching, they were out of batteries, and inmates weren't even allowed to have the charging cable; guards took the devices away at night to charge. When they did work, the list of blacklisted sites was so long that the only topics he could research were how to file an appeal and how to do a self-check for herpes.

'I can't talk about that. It doesn't matter how I found it.'

'It very much does matter how you found it, Lane. You're eligible for parole next year, and William says you've got a really good shot.'

'William Magala? When were you talking to my lawyer?'

'Don't change the subject. Do you know how many infractions you can have on your record and still be granted parole? Zero! Zip! Duck egg!' She affected a deliberately bad Eurovision judge accent. *'Nul points!'*

The guard looked their way, and both of them fell silent. Lynnie's cheeks were flushed red, and Lane suspected he looked similar.

'If you've found something, you can pursue it when you're on the outside,' Lynnie hissed. 'She's been missing for twenty years – what's one more?'

'When I'm on the outside, I'll have a parole officer breathing down my neck. I'll have a job to do and rent to pay.'

More than that. There was a risk that a particularly motivated parole officer who caught on to him searching for Matilda could spin it as him acting as a private investigator without a licence. It was a minor offence, punishable by a fine, but still enough to see his parole revoked. He needed to wait ten years after his conviction before he could even apply for a licence again, and the law had carve-outs to deny applications where it seemed prudent – such as in the case of a former private investigator who'd served time for kidnapping and murder.

He'd searched for loopholes and hit a brick wall every time. He could not act as a private investigator. He could not set himself up as a consulting detective, Sherlock Holmes-style, and support other investigators. He couldn't even teach the training courses. He might be able to work in reception or office admin, answering phones and filing papers for another PI, but to be that close and not even able to do the dreariest and most dull investigative tasks would be worse than nothing.

Matilda Carver, however it turned out, was going to be his last case. He needed it.

'You can live with me,' Lynnie said. 'I won't charge you rent.'

'I'm not going to sponge off my baby sister,' Lane said. 'But I don't understand; when this came up last year you were all for it. You said it was the most alive I'd seemed in years.'

'Look how that turned out,' Lynnie said. 'You made a serial killer your best friend.'

'He wasn't a serial killer. You need to kill three people to be considered –'

'He killed more than zero people and you went to his funeral.'

'Someone had to.'

She sighed. 'I just don't think you know where to draw the line. I've put so much on hold waiting for you to come out of here …'

'What have you put on hold?'

'Nothing.' She put her hands over her face. 'That's not the point. It feels like I care more about your parole prospects than you do.'

'Everything alright over here?'

The guard, Sweeney, had stepped up to their table without Lane noticing. He mentally replayed the last few seconds of their conversation, wondering what the man might have heard. It would have been bizarre, he decided, but not incriminating.

'Everything's fine, officer.' Lynnie flashed him a smile. 'You know how siblings squabble.'

Out of the corner of his eye, Lane saw the couple the guard had been watching originally. The other prisoner had his hand palm up on the table, and his girlfriend put her hand over his. She cut a glance their way and, seeing the guard now focused on Lane, let something drop out of her sleeve into her boyfriend's palm.

Lane looked away quickly. Whatever it was would be trouble, whether they were caught or not, and what would spell the most trouble for Lane was if the prisoner clocked him witnessing the exchange and then the guards found contraband. Being labelled a snitch had landed him in sticky situations before, and he didn't want to go through that again.

'Have you ever thought about changing your name?' Lynnie asked.

Lane backtracked through their conversation, trying to figure out how that connected to anything they'd said, and came up blank. Perhaps that question was the reason for her unexpected visit, and her nerves had got to her before she'd found a natural segue.

'Occasionally,' he admitted. His name, Lane Holland, was also their father's. Lane Holland Senior had been a psychopath, and he had murdered at least two young girls, and probably more. Lane was in prison for killing him. 'But it's my name. I can't imagine being called something else. And if I changed it, you and I wouldn't share a family name anymore.'

Her expression tightened. Ah. Now they were getting to the heart of it.

'I would understand if you wanted to change, though,' he said.

Lynnie's legal name was Evelyn Holland. It had never appeared in the press; she was a victim in their family's history, not a perpetrator like him. But one of the trashier newspapers had let a sordid fact slip, which made her name easy to figure out: Evelyn had been named after one of their father's murder victims.

'If I was going to do it,' she said tentatively, 'it would make sense to get it sorted before I graduate. Then my degree would be issued in my new name.'

'That's smart,' he said. 'What are you thinking?'

'Evangeline,' she said. 'So my friends who call me Eve don't have to learn something new. And you can still call me Lynnie.'

'I'll call you whatever you want,' he said. 'Will you keep Holland? We could pick out a new family name together. Or maybe use Mum's family name?'

The more he thought about that the more he liked it. A clean break.

Lynnie was silent for a beat, and then she took a deep breath, the way she had as a kid when she was trying to fight tears.

Oh shit. Of course Lynnie didn't want to keep sharing a family name with him. She was about to start her real life, her brilliant career. Staying entangled with him wouldn't be a clean break for her.

'There's something else I need to tell you,' she said. 'You know, if I don't want to be going around with a different name on my degree …'

Oh.

Reflecting on what name she wanted. How she could suddenly afford to study full time. The beautiful manicure.

He was losing his touch.

He was abruptly, painfully, aware of how much time had passed in the real world. Part of him still thought of Lynnie as eighteen and barely out of high school. Twenty-three was still young for this, but not absurdly so.

'I didn't even know you were seriously dating anyone,' he said.

'It was casual for a long time,' she confessed. 'I just wanted to focus on school, and work, and have fun and make friends. I didn't want any major life stuff to happen without you there.'

'I would never ask you to put your life on hold,' he said.

'Oh, don't be a drama queen,' she said. 'I mean, they say the brain hasn't even finished forming until you turn twenty-five. It wasn't a sacrifice. So, when I dated it was always casual. And most things fizzled out or blew up anyway. Then this one didn't.

And calling it casual began to feel like a pantomime around the time he added me to his car insurance as a second driver.'

'I feel like you're deliberately skirting around telling me anything about this guy. It is a guy, right?' At her nod, he continued. 'Does he live in Canberra? Where do you know him from?' He grimaced. 'He isn't your boss, is he?'

'No, he isn't my boss – and he lives in Sydney.'

Sydney. That explained the hurry to graduate university, if she planned to move to be with him. Sydney was closer to the Special Purpose Centre than Canberra, so he might see her more often. And it solved a problem he'd been studiously ignoring: that if he did manage to get parole, he might not be allowed to live in Canberra while still under the control of the New South Wales corrections system. But he would never be able to afford to live in the country's most expensive city, even without the dire employment prospects of a parolee.

'He travels to Canberra a lot for work, though.'

'Oh god, is he a politician?'

'He's a barrister. He appears at the High Court sometimes.'

A barrister who lived in Sydney but sometimes worked cases at the High Court. That wasn't a fresh graduate she might have met in the Hancock Library or at a house party.

'Lynnie,' he said, trying to sound calm, 'are you engaged to my lawyer?'

'Maybe a little bit?' She grimaced, and clapped her hands over her face. 'Sorry, that makes no sense. I'm a lot engaged to him. *Maybe a little bit* was my go-to answer when people asked if we were seeing each other.'

That ached. There were people in Lynnie's life who saw her every day, every week, and not always in the same room. They saw things, and put the pieces together, and asked. All he got was what she was ready to tell him.

And it made sense that she should fall for William Magala. He was good looking, well dressed, whip smart and making waves professionally – in no small part due to his role in Lane's defence, a headline-grabbing case that had opened doors to more. Lynnie was smart too, and building her own career, and – to his very biased eyes – beautiful. Not to mention young.

'There's quite an age gap, isn't there?'

'Seven years,' she scoffed. 'I get the odd side-eye at his work functions, but in a decade no-one will notice.'

'He's always been very … generous with me when it comes to billing,' Lane said. 'He hasn't –'

'Are you seriously asking if I've been trading sexual favours for your legal work?' Lynnie asked. Thankfully she looked more amused than offended. 'No. And he's not going to work for you for free after we get married.'

'I'm not planning to commit any more crimes. Look, I'm just trying to …' He didn't know what he was trying to do, really. He was in no place to play the wise older brother sizing up her choice of partner. 'You have to admit there's a power differential.'

'What's going on here?' a voice boomed across the visiting room, and Lane flinched. For a beat he thought the guard was yelling at them.

Instead, Sweeney walked up to the table of the couple Lane had noticed earlier. He thrust out his palm. 'Give me what she handed you.'

Lane's heart sank.

'She didn't give me nothing,' the prisoner protested. 'We were holding hands.'

'I think you should step out,' Lane said to Lynnie, dropping his voice low.

Lynnie nodded, looking regretful, and slipped out of her seat. This happened sometimes, and they'd learned a short visit was much better than trying to hang on while tensions in the room boiled over.

'She passed you something, and you put it up your sleeve,' Sweeney snapped. 'Give it to me.'

'He told you I didn't give him anything,' the girlfriend said. 'Are you some kind of fucking re –'

'Don't!' The man she was visiting slapped her forearm.

It succeeded in getting her to bite back the slur, but hitting a visitor was way out of line and Sweeney was on the prisoner like a shot, locking an arm around his neck and dragging him off the stool. 'Hands off!'

Lane glanced over to the door and was relieved to see Lynnie on the other side, watching through the window with a pale face. He gave her a rueful wave, and a female guard ushered her out to the foyer.

He doubted this was how she'd always dreamed her engagement announcement would go.

Two more guards barrelled through the second door, the one that led to the main body of the prison. 'Everybody out!' the guard on the left shouted. 'Visiting hours are over.'

'Prisoners on the rear wall,' the other one added, her voice quieter but firm.

Lane and the others lined up and then filed out of the room, grumbling among themselves. The offending prisoner was whisked away, presumably to be searched.

Instead of directing them back to their cells, the female guard marched the line through to the quadrangle, the SPC's supposed recreation area, where other guards were bringing in the rest of the centre's population, arranging the scowling men in neat rows like schoolchildren waiting for assembly.

A muster. Lane hoped it would be a brief exercise, a flexing of the guards' power to bring them all to heel before the incident in the visiting room could set off a chain reaction.

The minutes dragged on, turning into fifteen, then thirty, then a full hour while the men stood in their lines and the guards took occasional headcounts and conferred among themselves. Sounds floated in, audible even through the thick walls. Clangs and thumps and the low groan of the hinges of heavy doors.

They were tossing the whole place. Whatever that prisoner had slipped up his sleeve must have been bad, because from the sound of it every cell was being searched. All Lane could do was stand in his assigned spot, clench his fists and wait, hoping they wouldn't find what he had hidden and knowing they would.

CHAPTER TWO

IT WAS SWEENEY who came to escort Lane to the governor's office. The guard walked silently beside him, eyes ahead, and so Lane was free to practise maintaining a neutral expression. Jaw relaxed. Eyebrows down. Mouth in a soft line.

Governor Patton Carver was seated behind his broad desk. The previous times Lane had been in this office the desk had been decorated with the clutter of ordinary life: family photos, stationery, a lunchbox and cutlery. Today it had been cleared off, so the only three items on the desk stood out. A small stack of papers covered in Lane's handwriting, a torn A5 envelope and a mobile phone.

Lane didn't let his gaze rest on them. Instead, he focused on Carver's face, keeping his lips pressed gently together. The biggest possible mistake would be to start speaking unprompted. Blustering denials, pretending to be confused about what was going on, making excuses or casting blame elsewhere – no matter what he said, Carver could use it to let him walk himself into a trap.

'Sweeney, you can go,' Carver said, making no effort to acknowledge Lane.

The guard nodded and stepped out, pulling the door closed behind him. Lane remained standing. Jaw relaxed. Eyebrows down. Mouth in a soft line.

Carver waited until a full minute had ticked by on the clock on the wall. Then he stood, walked to the door, and opened it a crack to look out. Satisfied that Sweeney had actually left, he closed it again and turned the lock.

'Sit, Holland,' he said, returning to his own seat.

Lane sat in the chair opposite Carver. He didn't slouch into it, nor did he sit bolt upright. Imagining himself in a front-row seat at a theatre, he tried to look respectful and interested but not nervous.

'What the fuck is this?' Carver pointed at the phone.

Lane looked at it properly for the first time. Of course, he knew exactly what it was: a black Samsung – an older model but decently functional. He was probably its third or fourth owner; he hadn't been the one to smuggle it into the Special Purpose Centre but had received it from another prisoner. Whatever happened, he needed to avoid naming that man. If Lane turned someone in for smuggling, he'd have a knife in his kidneys before breakfast.

When not in use, he'd kept the phone hidden in the envelope, tucked away with his legal papers from Magala. Lane kept himself out of trouble and went out of his way to avoid annoying the guards, so that was a reasonably safe place to keep it.

Guards didn't mess with those papers without a good reason. But today they'd had a good reason.

'Looks like a phone, sir,' Lane said.

Lane's relationship with Carver was complicated. For his first few months in the centre, Carver had been a distant figure, a signature on the bottom of forms. Then he had come to Lane with the bizarre proposal that Lane go undercover in the medical unit to elicit a confession from fellow inmate Jan Henning-Klosner.

In the two years since then, their relationship had returned to an uneasy distance. Lane already found it difficult to persuade other prisoners to leave him alone; because he'd once made his living solving crimes and turning people in to the police for rewards, a lot of them assumed he would be willing to do the same thing from the inside if they let anything incriminating slip. For that reason, he wasn't willing to be Carver's pet private investigator – but at the same time, he'd been unable to leave the question of what had happened to Matilda Carver alone. With nothing else to distract him from the grinding monotony of prison life, the mystery had continued to occupy him. But to conduct any kind of investigation, he'd needed a lifeline to the outside world. The internet.

'Don't be a smart-arse,' Carver said. 'Do you have any idea how hard I've been working to get your security classification changed to C?'

Lane blinked. 'You have?'

Prisoners in New South Wales were classified A through C, depending on their security risk. A was reserved for those who were hardest to handle – the men who tried to escape, or started fights, or worse. C prisoners required a bare minimum of supervision, and qualified for privileges like day leave, or the chance to work or attend training outside the prison.

Lane had been classified B for most of his term. If Carver had been working on getting his classification changed – not a simple process for a serious offender – then he must have some plan up his sleeve to get Lane access to the outside world.

'I asked you to get me out of here so I could look for Matilda. You said no.'

'Because I'm the governor of this prison, not the bloody Governor-General. This is what I had to do to make that happen. Excuse me for not wanting you to spend months walking around this place thinking the rules don't apply to you anymore.'

And Lane had just ruined it.

He had really hoped to have this conversation on his own terms, when he was ready to present it to Carver in full. Most of all, he'd hoped to be able to present Carver with a still-smoking gun to support his theory, something compelling enough to make his method of uncovering it an afterthought.

Alas.

Lane picked up the phone and unlocked it. That was a risky move; if he refused to enter the passcode, there was no way Carver could force him to give the prison access to the contents of the phone.

'I've been using it to search for Matilda,' he said.

Carver raised his eyebrows. 'How convenient for you.'

'You can look at the browser history,' Lane said. 'You'll see the government's Missing Persons database, ancient social media pages, the National Library, the Wayback Machine. You won't find any porn sites or betting pages or even the news. I don't use it for anything other than pushing the case forward.'

Carver took the phone and opened the browser history as suggested. 'That's actually pretty sad,' he remarked.

Every minute Lane had that phone out was a risk. He couldn't waste the time, or the battery power. He couldn't exactly ask the guards if they'd pop his phone on to charge while they were powering the prisoners' permitted devices overnight. Power banks were one of the hottest items in the prison, and he'd often had to leave the phone dead for weeks while he saved up enough cash or favours to buy a bit of charging time. Not to mention what it was costing him to keep the SIM card working. He couldn't afford to waste it.

'I think I've found something,' he said.

That got Carver's attention.

Lane continued. 'You see, at first I tried looking for Matilda the way I'd work any of my cases. I looked at her social media and that of her friends at the time.'

That had been tough, because back when Matilda disappeared, nearly twenty years ago, social media meant Myspace, Friendster, even LiveJournal. Photos were linked from hosting sites, many of which were long gone.

People said that once something was on the internet, it was there forever, but that couldn't be further from the truth. Most things disappeared, and quicker than you would expect. Websites winked out when their hosting expired, forums shut down, pictures were replaced by 'image not found' error messages.

On social media, people purged old albums, deleted accounts or locked them to friends only and then stopped visiting, leaving new friend requests forever unanswered. Still, Lane had painstakingly assembled a map of Matilda's friends and acquaintances, and their friends and acquaintances. If that had involved occasionally guessing a poorly chosen password on an abandoned account, Carver didn't need to know.

'I wrote to her friends, asking if they remembered anything. I'm sure you already know that nobody answered, since you would have seen their replies when you checked my mail. I tried every trick I know and got nowhere, slowly.'

Carver reached over the desk and slid the phone back towards him. Lane opened the gallery and scrolled until he found a good, clear picture. 'Do you know this man?'

Carver examined the photo. It showed a tall, rather ordinary man with brown hair and brown eyes, dressed in a blue flannel shirt and jeans. A girl of about twenty stood next to him, pouting to show off her plum lipstick.

'No,' Carver said eventually. 'But the girl rings a bell.'

'Her name is Kristal. You've probably seen pictures of her because she and Matilda worked together in the Kiewa Valley, right before Matilda dropped out of contact with you.'

'And the man?'

'His name is Reginald "Reggie" Karpathy. Or it was, rather. He died eighteen months ago.' Lane scrolled through the images, holding up another. 'Here he is with Caitlin Engeron, who was reported missing two years before Matilda.' He scrolled to a group shot, where Karpathy was just visible in the upper right corner, nursing a beer. Lane pointed to a young man in the foreground. 'This is Alain Serling, who was reported missing the same year as Matilda.'

Carver shook his head. 'I think I'd have noticed if there was a cluster of Missing Persons cases in the area.'

'True. You were certainly on the ball about finding matching cases of unidentified women's remains. But it would have taken more than a cursory search to connect these cases.'

'Oh? Why do I suspect I'm not going to like what your more-than-cursory search entailed?'

'How about we agree to stay light on the details and focus on the important part? In brief, I looked at every Missing Persons report in a hundred-and-fifty-kilometre radius from where Matilda was last seen, for the five years before she went missing and in the twenty years since, both open and closed. Ruling out those that were opened and closed within a few days, I found ten cases. And I worked them all. Their social media. Their friends. Friends of friends.'

It rolled off the tongue so easily. Months of work summed up in a few sentences. Months hunched over the phone, one ear straining for guards who would confiscate it or other prisoners who'd be willing to jump him for it. Crawling through ancient posts, ancient pictures. Connecting dots and drawing lines, until the place where they connected formed the face of a man.

'I narrowed it down to four with a definite connection to Reggie Karpathy: Caitlin Engeron, Alain Serling, nothing for a long time, then two years ago a new one: Brandon Roby.'

'That's three.'

Lane scrolled to the picture that was his one ace to play. 'Here's Alain with Matilda. That's four.'

Carver looked at the picture. Matilda had an arm hooked around Alain's neck, but their body language looked more playful than romantic. 'When was this taken? I've never seen it before.'

'I got it from Alain's profile. It was posted six months after Matilda was reported missing.'

'It might be an old picture,' Carver said.

'It might be,' Lane agreed. 'But do you see those hills behind them?' He traced the shape with a fingertip, hovering above the screen so he didn't accidentally swipe the picture away. He'd spent countless hours on Google Maps, looking at satellite pictures and uploaded photos, until he finally found a hill formation that matched. 'Those hills are located in a farming community near the Hume Weir. About an hour from the Kiewa Valley – where Reggie Karpathy owned a farm.' He added, 'The farm still exists. According to the local papers, his son Samuel took over and "intends to carry on his father's vision". The article didn't specify what that vision was.'

The fact that Reggie had passed away could be a sticking point. Lane was painfully aware that if Karpathy was responsible for Matilda's fate, that secret would have likely died with him. But it could also mean that now was the best time to get answers – with Reggie beyond the reach of justice, the people who knew him might be more willing to talk.

'You think this Karpathy was a serial killer?' Carver asked.

'That's the interesting thing,' Lane said. 'Caitlin Engeron?

Her Missing Persons file was closed after five years, marked found. She's alive and well.'

To another audience, that might not have been a particularly interesting fact. But to someone like Carver, who had spent decades imagining the worst possible fate for his only daughter, it was a carrot so enticing it bordered on cruelty.

'According to Caitlin's Missing Persons report, one day she left her parents' home to go to work and never arrived. She worked as a receptionist and hadn't said anything about going to work on a farm. But there was an election the year her file was closed. She enrolled to vote, giving an address on Hill Road in Georges Bridge. That was Karpathy's address.'

'Do I want to know how you got her voting information?'

'Voter rolls are public,' Lane said, leaving out the part where he had posed as a relative putting together his family tree to get a librarian to pull that 'public' information for him. 'Alain's story is similar,' he continued, subtly changing the subject. 'He told his family he was going to look for harvest work. He took several months' worth of his asthma medication with him, so clearly he planned to be gone for a while. He dropped all contact with his parents once he was on the road. The photo suggests he made his way to Karpathy's. Brandon Roby's family reported he left their home after a short stay in the hospital. He's autistic, and they're very concerned for his wellbeing. He was friends on social media with Reggie's son, Samuel.'

'So Karpathy was harbouring runaways?'

'Only minors can be runaways; these are all adults.'

'Still.' Carver stared down at the photo of his daughter. 'Matilda wouldn't do that to us.'

'Brandon Roby also had an excellent relationship with his family.' According to them, Lane didn't add. 'Alain might have chosen to drop contact with his family. But the Serlings make a post every year on the anniversary of the day he left. Even all these years later, it gets dozens of comments from Alain's friends and extended family about how much they miss him. Alain had a huge network of people who loved him, and he's never reached out to a single one to put their minds at rest. It's not proof, but it says to me that something happened to him.'

'We do the same thing,' Carver said. 'Matilda's schoolfriends miss her too.' He looked away, his gaze going to the empty spot on the desk where he usually kept his family photos. He took a deep breath and, clearly uncomfortable with Lane seeing him get emotional, asked, 'Have you talked to this Engeron woman?'

Lane shook his head. 'She owns a dress shop in Adelaide, and I've tried calling the shop. So far she has failed to accept a call from a prisoner of the Special Purpose Centre. I've avoided making calls from this phone in case someone complains and I get caught. She put up an Instagram picture last week of a book she was reading. It was called *Adult Children of Emotionally Immature Parents*, so I don't think that relationship has improved any.'

'I could try calling her,' Carver said.

'You could.'

Carver paused and Lane stayed silent, letting the man get his thoughts in order.

'What about this farm, then? Is it some kind of commune?'

'If you want to call it that.' Lane clicked on the tab for the farm's website, which he'd had open for months. The header was a group of people, all dressed in identical work pants and button-down shirts in a variety of colours but the same style. Carver studied the group, and his face fell when he didn't recognise any of them as his daughter.

'They don't have much of a public presence, but they sell some products online. You know, organic, artisan, locally grown. Goat cheese, soap, salami, pickles. They seem to grow vegetables for local shops.'

'Hippies, then.'

'Maybe when they were established, but it's all pretty mainstream now. From the photos it seems like a pretty white group, but I couldn't find any other red flags – no white supremacist symbols or tattoos or dog whistles in the site copy.'

In many ways, being in prison had made it difficult to keep his knowledge up to date, but it did give him ample opportunities to learn to decode those ever-evolving signs.

'Isn't organic farming a leftie thing?'

'You'd be surprised. There's "we have to grow our own food to save the world from climate change", but there's also "we have to grow our own food and stockpile guns because the World Economic Forum wants to force us all to eat bugs". I think these guys are the former, though,' he hurried to add. This conversation was not going to go the way he needed it to if Carver got spooked. 'There's an Acknowledgement of Country in the site footer, and this lady is wearing a Progress Pride pin.' He pointed to the middle of the largest photo. 'Plus, we're talking about Matilda here. Of the two, which do you think would have attracted her?'

Carver considered this for a moment, then nodded.

'Sir' – Lane knew now was the time to lay it on thick – 'I know I don't have much. I've been trying to look at an elephant one inch at a time. If you just let me widen my frame of view with access to a computer and some uninterrupted time, I'm sure I can find more names.'

Carver looked unimpressed. Lane knew the plea had been a long shot, but it was worth trying.

'I could go out to this farm myself, ask around,' Carver said.

'If they are connected to Matilda's disappearance, they'll take one look at your name and clam up so fast your ears will pop.'

Carver put his hands on his knees; Lane was sure he wanted to clench them into fists.

'You could pass the information on to the police, of course.' That was the worst possible outcome for Lane – to get the police to act on what Lane had discovered, Carver would have to disclose where it came from. Then Lane would be of no further use to Carver, and left with a prison smuggling charge on his record. 'But the police's help has been … less than stellar, so far.'

That was a delicate way of saying they'd caught a police officer fabricating official police files, including some related to Matilda, to cover up his involvement in another crime.

Carver actually cracked a smile, and Lane relaxed a fraction.

'A private investigator is your best option,' Lane went on. 'But they would need time. If this is a cult, say, or some kind of criminal org, finding information means getting on the inside and earning their trust. It would take months. The per diem –'

'Knock it off, you're not that slick,' Carver interrupted. 'You should go, I get it.'

Lane said nothing. There was nothing to be gained by stating the obvious.

Carver stared down at the phone for a long moment. Then he seemed to reach a decision. He opened a drawer in his desk and swept the phone inside, then shut the drawer firmly.

'What do you know about our work and study release program?'

'Not much,' Lane admitted. 'I'm in for kidnapping and murder; there's no way I'd qualify.'

'You'd be surprised,' Carver said. 'The system is supposed to be for rehabilitation.'

It would be a bad idea to scoff out loud at that, so Lane didn't.

'Your earliest possible release date isn't that far off.'

'This time next year,' Lane confirmed. 'If the parole board are persuaded.'

'That's exactly it.' Carver leaned forward and pressed his palms to his desk. 'What's the point of paroling you with no useful skills, no employment prospects, no connection to the community? You'd be back in the dock by Christmas.'

Lane would never willingly commit another crime, but it wasn't that simple. Prison was a pipeline built in a circle. Plenty of men and women before him had walked out the gates with the best intentions, only to be unable to find work or housing.

They came sliding straight back on charges of petty theft or trespassing or public nuisance, or because they couldn't make it to mandatory appointments or pass the drug tests. Lane had the advantage of his sister's support, and he didn't have a network of criminal associates to drag him back under, or addiction issues, but that was the end of the list of positives. He had no work prospects. His degree was in criminology and all his work experience in private investigation. He could never hold a licence for that work again. He could never own a firearm. He couldn't join the police. He'd be waiting tables or driving a delivery van, and that was if he could find an employer who wouldn't ghost him the minute he told them what was about to come up on his background check.

'It would look good for your hearing if you could show you're working towards some kind of realistic life on the outside. Some training or work experience. Hypothetically, that training or work could take place in the region of this Karpathy farm, and on occasion you might find yourself with spare time to nose around, meet the right people, ask some questions.'

'Hypothetically,' Lane said. 'If I could get approved for the leave.' He just didn't believe it.

'I understand your scepticism, but your record inside the prison is impeccable.' Carver's eyes cut to the drawer containing the phone, but he said nothing. 'And if I can be frank – you shot a man who murdered children. I seriously doubt there would be a public outcry if the press took an interest in the fact you'd been granted leave.'

'Well, I've got nothing to lose if I put in a request,' Lane said.

Carver's smile disappeared. 'There is one thing,' he said. 'If the Karpathy farm is near the Hume Weir, that's practically in Victoria. It would look deeply off for me to send one of my prisoners all that way for leave. I don't suppose you have family down there?'

Lane shook his head. 'My only living relative is in Canberra.'

'Then I think for this to work you'll need to be transferred to the prison in Albury. And this centre is getting close to capacity – it would be unlikely you'd be transferred back here after the leave. You'd serve the rest of your sentence down there.'

Lane's stomach dropped. The Special Purpose Centre was as close to pleasant as prison got. It housed prisoners who were frequently targeted in general population or were otherwise a headache for administrators. The inmates here wanted to be left alone, and so mostly left each other alone. In a normal prison he would be right back to constant worry that he was about to be jumped by prisoners convinced he'd been planted by the police to spy on them. It also meant a longer drive, or even a flight, for Lynnie to visit, especially if she moved north to be with her new fiancé. It could go from twice a year to 'oh, it's not that long until you're released anyway' in a heartbeat.

But he'd be outside the walls. Still a prisoner, still restricted and monitored, but outside. And he'd be working a case.

CHAPTER THREE

IN THE CORRECTIONAL system, time had to be measured in months, not minutes. Forms were lodged. Letters exchanged. Meetings scheduled and then rescheduled. Procedures proceeded.

As Hemingway would put it, things happened gradually and then all at once. The Serious Offenders Review Council approved the request to downgrade Lane's security classification, and his subsequent request for leave to undertake training was not just approved but hailed as a sign that he was finally showing some interest in self-improvement and rehabilitation.

Carver personally reached out to every business and farm within a ten-kilometre radius of the Karpathy property, seeking expressions of interest in taking on a prisoner as an apprentice. He included the farm itself in his list, more to avoid arousing suspicion by skipping it than with any expectation they would be interested.

Lane wasn't nearly as surprised as Carver when, among the very short list of positive responses, an offer came from Samuel

Karpathy himself. From what he'd learned about the way Karpathy operated, to him a prison release program would look like a goldmine. If the farm wanted to attract people who were rudderless, vulnerable and lacked strong connections to family and friends, prisoners checked every box. Lane couldn't help worrying, though: if something dangerous was going on at that farm, but he couldn't prove it, then he was putting every prisoner who came to the farm after him in harm's way. But he had to risk it.

With the necessary ducks now in a row, all that remained was to contact the victims of Lane's crime, to give them an opportunity to object to his release into the study leave program. The first part of this was easy. Because the man he'd killed was their father, Lynnie was deemed the victim's next of kin. She immediately responded with an impassioned statement of support.

That left Mina McCreery.

He'd met Mina when he set out to solve the disappearance of Mina's twin sister, Evelyn, when they were nine years old. More than that, he'd set out to prove a theory he'd secretly held all his life – that his own father murdered Evelyn. But when things didn't go according to plan, he'd taken his father hostage, determined to prove Lane Holland Senior was a murderer with a stark offer: show Lane where the body was buried, or Lane would kill him. With the benefit of many years distance and a cooler head, Lane now recognised that it was closer to a mental breakdown than a valid plan. He'd never wanted to hurt Mina. But she had stumbled across them, and Lane dragged her along with them rather than risk her ruining everything by calling the police. Or, as the justice system preferred to put it, Lane kidnapped her.

A letter was sent to Mina, offering her the standard twenty-one days to respond. As she always had, Mina answered with a silence that told Lane nothing – or perhaps everything.

•

The whole process dragged on so long that it was the last week of October before Lane found himself packing up his handful of belongings and turning them over to be searched and scanned, then submitting to a search and scan of his own self. He had no contraband to worry about this time. Carver might have made the phone disappear from his record, but Lane wasn't silly enough to expect it back.

He was fitted with some fancy new jewellery, in the form of a black ankle bracelet that would track his location twenty-four hours a day. The fence around him would no longer be visible to the eye, but it wasn't gone.

The busload of prisoners transferring out travelled under the watchful eye of Sweeney, the same guard who had delivered him to Carver on the day his phone was discovered. Lane filed that point away for consideration. There were only so many guards, but was that really just a coincidence?

Most of the passengers slept or played cards or read as the bus rumbled across New South Wales, bound for a facility outside the border city of Albury. Lane stayed glued to his window. For years his idea of a grand tour had been visiting the cafeteria, the exercise yard and the shower block all in one day. Sights that had bored him to tears as a kid – paddocks rolling past, other cars, signs and roadside memorials – thrilled him today. Around the halfway mark, though, tiredness crept in. He'd spent most of his life travelling long distances with his itinerant family, and then on his own as a private detective; it had never worn him out before. But no matter how seasoned he'd been, he'd lost condition, and eventually he had to close his eyes and let sleep take him.

It was late afternoon when they pulled into the prison that was now technically his home base. Ordinarily it would still be bright out at this time of year, but rain bucketed down so heavily it was difficult to see anything.

The other prisoners filed out, but Sweeney motioned for Lane to remain seated.

Sweeney stood in the open bus door and conferred with a woman in a Corrective Services uniform, shielded by a slate-grey umbrella. Whatever they were talking about was lost in the endless drum of rain, but it looked heated. Eventually the woman threw up her hands, snapped something and walked away.

'Is there a problem?' Lane asked, nearly hollering to be heard. He didn't know what he would do if, having come this far, his new prison then pulled his leave for some reason.

Sweeney looked irritated at being questioned, but walked up the aisle so Lane could hear him. 'The area we're supposed to head into is under flood warning.'

'Are they evacuating?'

'Nah, it's a watch and wait. The roads are open but expected to go under if the rain doesn't let up. Given their shitty condition they might wash away altogether.'

Lane went cold. That sounded like a weeks-long delay. Long enough for the whole idea to be called off.

'Lucky for you our ride is already here. If that yellow warning turns red before we get underway, the suits will get spooked and cancel your program. Which will be fine for you, because they'll assign you a cell, but I've got nowhere to stay. So don't dawdle.'

'You're coming to the farm?' With the ankle monitor on, Lane didn't need to be under guard. Carver hadn't told him he was getting a babysitter too.

'Something Carver worked out with the Albury governor,' Sweeney said. 'I'm assessing the farm with an eye to setting up a permanent program. Apparently it's going to be a real jewel on my résumé.'

So that was how Carver had made the phone go away. Bribe the guard who found it with a cushy six months of do-nothing work, and probably a pay bump. Which meant two possibly dangerous things: Sweeney was not averse to breaking the rules for his personal benefit, and he knew the situation with Lane, Carver and the Karpathy farm was not on the up and up. It didn't necessarily make him an enemy, but Lane wasn't dumb enough to assume it made him an ally.

●

Their ride was a late-model dual-cab ute. Lane looked it over. He wasn't a car guy, but it absolutely wasn't what he'd expected. He'd imagined he might be picked up in an old Kombi van, or a farm ute older than he was. This ute was obviously powerful, and even to his inexpert eye it screamed expensive.

Sweeney opened the rear door and ushered Lane inside, then climbed in after him. The cab interior smelled like it was straight from the dealership.

The man in the driver's seat turned around and smiled. 'Hi,' he said. 'I'm Dave Harrington – but Dave's fine; we're not big on formalities at Karpathy's.'

Dave was a reedy man in his mid-forties, with brown hair shaved close to his head. He was close to the right age to be Alain Serling, but Lane dismissed that possibility immediately. His ears were all wrong, and ears were difficult to change.

The ute's engine was so quiet that the rain drowned it out completely, and Lane hadn't realised it was on until Dave threw the car into gear and pulled out of the parking space. It was a stark contrast to the heavy rumble of the last ute Lane had been in.

'Is this an electric?' Lane asked, more to break the ice than out of real interest.

'I wish,' Dave said. 'Can't get those here yet. Maybe next year, though I doubt an electric ute will ever handle our hills. This is a hybrid.'

'You're into cars, then?'

'I was a mechanic before. Still am, I suppose, although I only work on the farm trucks and tractors now.'

'Before?'

'Before coming to Karpathy's.'

'Have you been there long?'

Sweeney shot him that irritated look, but Lane ignored him. A boring drive was the perfect excuse to ask as many nosy questions as he wanted, and he wasn't going to waste it.

'Ten years this Christmas.'

'Wow.' Not long enough to have been there when Matilda arrived, but it was a startlingly long time to live and work on someone else's farm. 'What made you give up being a mechanic? There's good money in that, isn't there?'

Dave gave him a tight smile in the rear-view mirror. 'Just so you know, if you ask people at the farm why they came, you might get an answer that's a lot heavier than you expect. It's not small talk.'

'Right. Sorry.'

'You're all good, mate, it's just I've seen some people get off on the wrong foot. Anyway, as for why I chose the farm over being a mechanic, I think you'll understand when we get there.'

•

After the five-hour drive from the Special Purpose Centre to Albury, the forty minutes to Georges Bridge felt like nothing.

The structure that gave the town its name was an old trestle railway bridge, crossing a creek that had burst its banks and turned either side into a swamp. The railway tracks were long gone, replaced with a wide cycling path which signs identified as the High Country Rail Trail.

The town was a small cluster of shops, most shuttered and barricaded against the water that rushed down the footpath. The independent grocer was open, as was a sandwich shop named Natalie's, both accessible via a bright yellow plastic ramp placed over a hill of sandbags.

'Alright if we stop?' Dave asked, pulling into a parking space without waiting for an answer. 'There's a strong chance we'll be cut off for a couple of days with these floods. We can fend for ourselves in almost everything, but there's a few bits people will riot without.'

'Makes no difference to me,' Sweeney said.

'What will happen if the farm floods?' Lane asked.

Dave laughed. 'No chance; it's high in the hills. But there's only one road, and the lower parts will be underwater by morning.'

Lane and Sweeney sat silent in the ute as Dave disappeared to do his shopping. There was a sense of unreality about the scene. The light was fading, and Lane was sure someone would rap on the window any moment and tell him there'd been a mistake, and he had to go back to prison.

Dave emerged accompanied by a solidly built woman in a bright orange jumpsuit. Her hair was tucked under a beanie. She spoke to Dave for a moment, then turned to close and lock the doors of the sandwich shop; Lane saw SEARCH AND RESCUE printed across the back of her suit, identifying her as a State Emergency Service volunteer.

'This is Natalie Matthews; she's going to ride with us for a while,' Dave announced, climbing into the driver's seat.

'Thanks a lot,' she said, taking the front passenger seat. She pulled her beanie off and wiped the rainwater off her face with it, revealing grey-streaked brown hair pulled back in a braid. 'There's a call-out on Hill Road, and my little Mazda won't handle it.'

'Someone caught in floodwaters?' Lane asked.

Natalie shook her head. 'A trapped driver. I'm not trained for water rescue. My specialty is high-angle rescue, so I'm usually on the alpine call-outs. We're not far from the snowfields here.' She gave him a nervous smile. 'Sorry for the prattle; I've been at this fifteen years and it still jangles my nerves.'

'Here in Georges Bridge?' Lane asked, aiming for casual.

'These gentlemen are Lane Holland and Rick Sweeney,' Dave jumped in, cutting off Natalie's answer. 'New arrivals at the farm.'

'I figured. Welcome. I run the sandwich shop in town. If you're ever hungry you should come find me.'

'I saw. Are you named for it, or is it named for you?' Lane asked, trying to steer back to the question of how long she'd lived in town and whether she'd known Matilda or Alain.

'Oh, neither. Would you believe it had that name when I bought it?'

'Buckle up, everyone,' Dave said as he flipped the headlights on. 'It's slippery out there.'

They sent up a spray of water as they left the town behind.

'How many have you got living at the farm these days, Dave?' Natalie asked.

'It's been a minute since we've done a headcount. About forty, I'd say.'

'Well, do me a favour and find out for sure. Disaster season's just around the corner.' She glanced around and, perhaps mistaking Lane's keen interest in the conversation for confusion, she added, 'We have a problem with people moving up into the hills without telling us. Campervans, tents, people living in sheds. It causes big trouble when a fire or flood comes through. We might get three times as many people as we prepared for turn up at the shelter – or, worse, someone calls from an area we thought was uninhabited, and we have to send our people into a red zone to help them. But Karpathy has always been good about it.'

The hill road, as its name indicated, was steep and winding. Soon the left side fell away, the rocky ground held together with stubby gum trees and prickly-looking bushes. The light faded rapidly, and soon the only opportunity to pick out new details came when they rounded each corner, as the headlights washed over the void and the windscreen wipers cleared a brief arch.

'Anyway, what brings you boys to Karpathy's?' Natalie asked. She had her phone in her hands, and it buzzed constantly with new alerts as the waters rose below them.

Lane hesitated, and looked at Dave. Had he warned Natalie who she was getting into a car with when he offered the ride?

It was unlikely Lane's name would ping for anyone but the most dedicated crime buffs. He hadn't been mentioned in the paper in years. He'd opted not to be named when the Rainier Ripper case blew up again two years ago, and public interest in the Evelyn McCreery case had faded quickly once it was solved. But there was no way he was going to get away with concealing his identity. Surely people still googled each other, looking for social media accounts and whatnot.

'I'm on education leave from Albury prison,' he said. 'I'm here to learn to be a farmer.'

If that shocked Natalie, she didn't show it. Probably the town rumour mill had already done its work, and she was only asking to be polite.

'How interesting,' Natalie said. 'What made you want to be a farmer?'

Lane hadn't actually prepared an answer to that question, but it didn't matter because Dave interjected: 'Who wouldn't want that?'

'Generations of farm kids who fled to the city at the first opportunity?' Sweeney muttered.

'And their kids are coming straight back,' Dave said. 'Regional returners are the new tree changers. I read that. They were sold a false bill of goods and they're waking up to it. Leave the farm, get a city job, and then what? Live with four flatmates in a one-bedroom apartment watching Instagram reels of people planting gardens and raising chickens.'

'Most of those "homestead" influencers are secretly rich people filming their hobbies,' Natalie countered. 'Like Marie Antoinette playing milkmaid.'

'Karpathy's is the real deal, though.' Dave smacked the steering wheel with his palm. 'Real food, real soil, honest work. I don't know where I'd be if –'

The ute slipped sideways, sliding over to the wrong side of the road. Lane grabbed the back of Dave's seat to steady himself, relieved that they had swerved towards the high side of the hill, not the side that would have sent them tumbling back down to the valley.

And relieved that no-one had been coming the other way.

Dave was sanguine, easing off the accelerator until the ute was barely crawling along. Lane was grateful he hadn't panicked and slammed the brakes, which might have spun them out.

'Sorry, folks,' Dave said. 'Bit of turbulence this evening.'

'All this rain on a dirt road, we might as well be driving in potter's clay,' Natalie said. 'The council ought to pave it.'

'Then we'd be dodging potholes,' Dave pointed out. 'You've seen the state of the highway.'

Gradually Lane's heartbeat returned to normal.

Natalie dug in her handbag and pulled out a metal lunchbox. 'Biscuit?' she asked, leaning around to offer it to Lane. Stickers covered the lid, most of them cartoon characters or watercolour fruit and vegetables, but one bore the name and phone number of a women's shelter and the other a men's crisis hotline.

Lane took out a biscuit, but Sweeney waved it away.

'Can't eat gluten,' he explained.

'Oh, I'm sorry,' Natalie said. 'I wish I'd known; I have gluten-free biscuits in the shop.' Her phone buzzed again, and as she read the message her upbeat demeanour disappeared. 'The call-out has been cancelled.'

'They got the driver out?' Dave asked, clearly not as skilled at reading body language as Lane.

'No,' she said simply.

Dave gave a tsk of sympathy. 'You want to ride to the end of the line with us? You know there's always room for you at the farm. It's the safest place in the area right now.'

'Thanks, but there'll still be work to do on site. I'll help them pack up and catch a ride back with another volunteer. Just drive carefully; we might meet the SES truck coming the other way.'

She hadn't given the offer even a moment's consideration, Lane noted. It might have been because she was focused on the accident, but there was an undercurrent to her interaction with Dave. They seemed friendly on the surface, but whenever one offered an opinion, the other immediately took a different position.

Flashing lights cut through the rain haze, and they all fell silent as they rounded the last curve and saw the accident site. Another ute had sliced through the underbrush like a knife, coming to rest wheels up in a gully below.

'Fuck,' Dave said. 'That's one of ours.'

HE SHUFFLED HIS *hips to the side, teeth gritted against how sore they were, until he found the edge of the mattress. He pushed his legs forward until they slipped off and hit the floor, then braced his feet on the side of the mattress, giving him enough leverage to push his torso off the edge. He flopped onto his belly, and let one cheek rest against the floorboards. They were cool on his skin, meaning it was night-time, or perhaps very early morning; by lunchtime the spreading heat would reach even in here, warming the wood almost like it had been touched directly by the sun.*

Night-time meant they would be asleep. That was good. If he was careful and quiet, he might just manage to slip away.

CHAPTER FOUR

THEY DROVE IN silence after dropping Natalie off, Dave's jovial demeanour replaced with anxious contemplation.

He pulled the car over at a farm gate only a few minutes later. If the driver of the crashed ute had started out from the Karpathy farm, they hadn't driven very far before they lost control.

A man who looked to be in his mid-thirties stood by the gate, wearing a headband with a torch. He opened the gate so they could drive through, then locked it behind them. Dave stopped just inside the gate, and the man climbed into the seat Natalie had recently vacated.

Dave turned to the back seat and said, 'This is young Sam Karpathy.'

'Just Sam,' the man said. He gave them all a wide grin, which vanished as he took in their faces. 'What's happened?' he asked.

Lane looked at Dave, waiting for him to answer, but watched Sam Karpathy in his peripheral vision. He didn't want to look like he was studying him, even though he was.

This was the first person he had met who would definitely have been at the farm when Matilda passed through. He might have been a teenager at the time – too young to have been involved in her disappearance, perhaps – but he would certainly be able to remember her.

'Who else had a farm ute tonight?' Dave asked.

'No-one,' Karpathy said. 'You were the only one with permission to take a vehicle.'

The phrasing stuck out to Lane. They were a long way from town, up a long winding road, and it seemed everyone but Karpathy needed permission to access a vehicle.

But he was jumping to conclusions. He needed to slow his roll. Dave had said it was a farm ute; of course those could only be used if Karpathy agreed. Maybe other residents had their own cars.

'There's been an accident,' Dave said. 'Bad.'

Karpathy looked around, like the crashed ute might reappear. 'No-one was out,' he repeated. 'Did it have a numberplate?'

Dave shook his head. Lane hadn't noticed if the plates were missing when they passed the car; he'd avoided looking too closely, out of respect for the driver.

'Roll past the big shed, we'll do a count,' Karpathy said. He turned around and once again flashed a P.T. Barnum smile. 'Sorry, guys, not the welcome I was planning for you.'

They rolled to a stop in front of a squat, rectangular building, the kind that could be loaded on the back of a truck and moved to a new site any time. It seemed permanent, though, as it was surrounded by a waist-high chain-link fence with a small gate. In the glow of the headlights, Lane could see it was the last of four identical buildings; everything beyond disappeared into the gloom.

'You'll be hosting the chickens come summer,' Karpathy said.

'What does that mean?' Lane asked.

'Shut up and get out of the car, Holland,' Sweeney said.

Inside the fence was a little herb garden. Lane wasn't good with plants, but he recognised parsley easily enough, and rosemary. Beside the door was something tall, with wispy leaves and half-moon clusters of yellow flowers. Another plant had blue stars for flowers and wide, flat leaves. He reached out and plucked a leaf, which prickled his fingers with fine hairs. He dropped it. Deeper in he saw something ominously spiky, and decided he was done touching plants for the night.

The building had two doors.

'You're on the left,' Sweeney said. He opened that door, and ushered Lane inside. The room was lit by a little oyster light, which Sweeney turned on by slapping a palm against it. It was affixed to the wall with a command strip. A thin green wire connected it to a solar-charging panel that had been taped onto the room's one small window.

'Is there no power in here?' Lane asked.

'Not like you've got a phone to charge,' Sweeney said, and snorted at his own joke.

'I do have to charge the ankle bracelet once a week.'

'The admin building has power. You'll go there to juice up.' Sweeney turned the light on and off a few times to check that it was working. Or possibly just to be obnoxious. 'While we're on the subject: ground rules.'

'Yes. Please.' Lane glanced around the rest of the room. Six bunks – three sets of two – lined the walls in a U-shape. The small remaining space had open shelves where he could store his belongings.

'You're going to have a lot more freedom here than you're used to. You're here because the department assumes you know misbehaving isn't worth the damage you'll do to your parole chances. Don't prove them wrong by doing dumb shit. Don't make extra work for me. Don't bother people, don't get into fights and don't try to run away. You're not to leave the boundaries of the property without an escort and you're not to use the farm vehicles. That includes the quad bikes. You are absolutely not to touch any of the firearms.'

'There are guns?'

He knew that a rifle or shotgun was standard on most farms, for pest control or to euthanise animals in an emergency. He'd learned that from Mina McCreery, who always carried one on her own farm. The same one he'd used to commit his crimes.

'Not as far as you're concerned. I sleep next door. Do not wake me unless you're on fire – and even then, try putting yourself out first. Questions?'

'Is there a bathroom?'

The only doors were the one that led outside and one in the adjoining wall, meaning that if there was a bathroom it was only accessible from Sweeney's room.

'There's a shared block; we'll find it in the morning. In the meantime, a bush wee isn't going to kill you.'

It might, Lane thought, considering the spiky plants he'd found. But he just nodded, and wished Sweeney a good night.

When he went to close the door behind the guard, he noticed the knob was perfectly smooth, like one for an internal door. There was no lock. He left the door open, letting the smell of fresh rain drift in.

He could pick any bunk he wanted, he supposed, like the first kid dropped off at scout camp. The mattresses were about hand-width thick and obviously cheap, but they looked far more comfortable than the beds in the Special Purpose Centre.

After an hour or so, Dave opened the gate, now wearing another head-mounted torch. He approached Lane's door with an umbrella in one hand and an insulated grocery bag in the other.

'I've brought you guys some dinner,' he said. 'Karpathy wants you to know he's really sorry, he hoped to have a proper welcome dinner for you, but …'

'Understandable,' Lane said. 'Have you, uh, resolved the ute situation?'

Dave's mouth twisted. 'There's definitely one missing. Karpathy's doing a discreet headcount now. It's not unusual for him to do the rounds and chat to everyone, so he can check if someone's missing without anyone else noticing something's off.'

Lane felt for Dave. Someone he knew was dead, and all he could do was wait to find out who. Lane couldn't offer anything but useless sympathy, which Dave accepted with a shrug.

Lane took his dinner – a bowl of vegetable soup, kept warm by a little clay lid – and ate it sitting cross-legged on one of the spare beds. The soup was made from spinach, basil and some kind of root vegetable he couldn't identify. Parsnips maybe, or turnips. Simple enough, but he was starving and it was fresh and warm and better than prison food by a country mile.

What he wanted to do right now was start making notes. Ideally he'd like to have a case board, somewhere to pin the pictures of the missing people and his notes, and see what connections he might have missed. But he couldn't risk writing anything down, let alone putting his work on display. Anyone could walk in here, and Sweeney might search his belongings.

The only thing he had felt worth the risk was bringing along a printout of the photograph of Alain and Matilda together. That was tucked inside a cut seam at the bottom of his bag.

So he had to keep his notes and his plans inside his own head. He was here now, and the next step was to identify who'd been here at the same time as Matilda, and glean what information he could without arousing their suspicions. That was going to require building a lot of trust, fast.

He also needed to figure out the power structures of the farm. Sam Karpathy owned it now, but he was new and young. Was he in charge, or did he only think he was? Who else had authority and influence?

Dave was an interesting guy – friendly, and clearly a true believer. Exactly the kind of person who would be chosen to pick up new arrivals. He'd come to the farm long after Matilda disappeared, so was unlikely to know anything about her, but he seemed to like Lane, and he might be able to leverage that when meeting the others.

Natalie Matthews had been intriguing. She was comfortable riding in Dave's ute with them but seemed wary of the farm. Was that because she knew something, or did all the townies view the farm that way? He was keen to talk to her again.

Sweeney obviously had nothing to do with the investigation, but he was still a wildcard Lane needed to consider. He had obvious contempt for Lane, but it was the sort of blokey disregard that almost circled back to being respectful. It was 'I don't like you, go away', not 'I don't like you, so I won't leave you alone'. He didn't seem like the sort of guard who wanted to put Lane in his place or subtly torment him. As long as he didn't cause trouble or create work for him, Sweeney would probably leave Lane alone.

It wasn't late, but it had been a long day. When he'd finished his soup, he stretched out on the bed. The rain on the roof was loud, but it was a comforting white noise. Beyond it, Lane was struck by the quiet. Back in the Special Purpose Centre, it was impossible to tune out the background noise of so many people packed into a cold, echoing space. Here, he heard only the occasional snatch of people chatting as they walked down the gravel road, and the bellowing of some animal off in the distance. Perhaps a cow unhappy about being stuck out in the wet.

Maybe it was louder on a normal night, when conversation didn't need to compete with the rain. Maybe they all usually stayed up later, but tonight there was nothing to do but wait out the storm.

•

Lane woke to the sound of doors opening and closing along the row of accommodation huts.

'Has anyone seen Hannah?' a woman asked, but if anyone answered, it was lost as the group walked away.

Lane dressed in his prison-issue pants and an undershirt. Someone had left a waterproof high-vis jacket hanging on the back of the door, and he pulled it on.

He hesitated for a moment before he opened the door, wondering if he should ask Sweeney for permission to leave, then decided the guard would be more irritated at being woken up than by Lane going in search of the toilet block on his own.

Outside, Lane got his first good look at Karpathy's farm in the light of day. It was hard to see much, with the rain still falling steadily, but what he could see was impressive. The road he stood on ran along the ridge of a hill, which fell away to the valley below. Across from him, not far away but separated by that void, stood a cluster of tiny buildings. They were painted in a riot of colours, and each had its own small verandah and flower garden. It reminded Lane of how he'd always pictured Hobbiton, in the Shire, when he read *Lord of the Rings* as a kid.

'Nice, eh?' Dave said behind him. 'Everyone will help you build your own, if you decide you need one. Of course, you can always stay in the accommodation huts if that's more your style.'

'Does Karpathy provide the materials?'

'No, but you'd be surprised how little they cost. Work a year or two and you'll have plenty saved up.'

Lane could see the appeal, especially to someone with few other options. Simply show up, and there would be a job, a bed and three meals a day waiting for you. He'd met men who had committed crimes to get that kind of security, without the promise of their own tiny house dangling in the future.

'And Karpathy can just put up as many houses as he wants?'

Dave shrugged. 'Under a certain size, it doesn't have to go through council. There's supposed to be a limit on the number, but Reggie worked something out way back when. I think the farm is technically registered as a caravan park.'

'Huh.' A very accommodating local government, Lane supposed. 'I don't suppose you could point me to the facilities?'

Dave pointed down the road, to a mudbrick building. 'Ever used a composting toilet before?'

'I grew up bouncing from showground to showground. Trust me: there's no set-up that can scare me.'

•

Emerging from the bathroom a few minutes later, Lane sheltered from the rain under an overhanging eave and did some people watching. The farm residents who were up and about all wore high-vis rain jackets, making this easy to do.

Something not quite human huffed behind him, and he turned to see a yellow lab, gone soft and grey around the muzzle. It wagged its tail and dropped into a play bow.

'Hello,' Lane said cautiously. He'd never been good with dogs, but this one seemed friendly. He held out a hand, palm down and fingers spread, and let the dog come over and give him a sniff.

'Who's a good dog then?' Lane asked. 'Is it you? Are you the good dog?'

This set the dog off in a full-body wiggle as it threw its whole self into confirming that yes, Lane had found the good dog, well done him.

Lane rubbed a hand over its head and scratched one velvet-soft ear. 'I knew another good dog who looked a lot like you, once,' he said. 'His name was Echo.'

The dog's ears pricked, and his eyes snapped up to fix on Lane's face. Something went cold in Lane's stomach.

'Echo?' a woman's voice called from the other side of the toilet block.

Two yellow labs with the same name wasn't that weird a coincidence, Lane thought desperately. It had been years, and he was a thousand kilometres away from where he had met the first one. Mina had once mentioned that she didn't even name Echo – he'd been a failed cadaver-sniffing trainee, and the program had given all puppies NATO alphabet names. Probably lots of breeders did that.

The woman rounded the building, and Lane could breathe again. The woman searching for Echo wasn't Mina McCreery.

She looked nothing like her, and was easily a foot taller, with spiky red hair.

'Oh, there you are,' she crooned when she caught sight of the dog. 'Deana, I found him!'

'Phew,' a familiar voice said, and Mina McCreery walked around the other side of the block.

Lane's first thought was of the letter sent to her by Corrective Services, notifying her of their plans to approve his leave. As a registered victim, she was informed of all his movements. She must have received the letter and used her three-week head start to get here before him. But why? Why not just send him an email?

Then, judging by the pale look of horror on her face, he didn't think that was what had happened at all. She looked as shocked and upset as he was.

This was a disaster. Unsolicited contact with one of his victims was a massive, *massive* violation of the conditions of his sentence. If she made a complaint, not only would this leave opportunity be yanked from him, but he could kiss his chances of parole goodbye as well. There was no way the department would believe this was a coincidence, but he wouldn't be able to offer any other explanation for why he had come all this way, to this specific farm – not without dumping Carver in it, which would have similarly dire consequences.

The other woman clapped Mina on the shoulder and headed into the toilet block. This was Lane's opportunity to speak to Mina frankly, before Sweeney made an appearance.

But without speaking to him or acknowledging him in any way, Mina clipped a lead on Echo and led the dog away, leaving Lane alone with his spiralling panic.

•

Breakfast was served in a wooden hall set up with trestle tables and bench seats. At one end was a table stacked with mismatched crockery, cups, a coffee urn and a large pot from which people were ladling something into bowls. Mina stood in the line, her back straight and shoulders tense, twisting a ring on her finger.

He glanced at the ring but didn't let his gaze linger. He was quite sure she hadn't worn a ring when they first met. It was a simple gold band with a small clear stone. It could be an engagement ring, but she wore it on her right hand, not the left.

It was none of his business.

Not wanting to stand right behind her in the queue, Lane scanned the room and saw Dave sitting at a table in the corner with Sweeney and a woman about their age. Lane had no intention of sitting with Sweeney, but Dave caught his eye and waved him over.

'Come sit here and I'll get your breakfast,' he said.

'We get table service, apparently,' Sweeney said as Lane slid onto a bench.

'Just for today,' Dave assured him. 'Once you're settled in, we'll show you where the kitchen is and you can collect your own.'

'Are we not eating from the pot like everyone else?' Lane asked.

Mina, having served herself, had found a seat at the furthest possible point from Lane's table. If she was planning to turn him in for violating the no-contact order, wouldn't she have done it immediately? Surely she wouldn't stop to eat an awkward breakfast in the same room as him first.

'It's alright, Dave, we've got it,' a girl said. She had a plate in each hand, both with the same type of clay lid that had covered the soup the previous night. Beside her another girl hovered with two bowls. They both looked to him to be about Lynnie's age or maybe a little younger.

'I'm Sarah, and this is Trish,' the girl said, putting one plate in front of Lane and the other in front of Sweeney.

'And I'm Gretel,' the older woman said. She had no food in front of her but was sipping something from a glass bottle. Lane thought maybe she was a few years older than himself, although he had lost the knack for telling a woman's age. It was always a surprise to recall that he himself was in his early forties now and not his mid-thirties, the age he was when he went to prison.

Lane introduced himself briefly, but Sweeney said nothing.

After an awkward pause, Dave chirped, 'And this is Rick.'

'I go by Sweeney,' the guard said.

'Oh!' Gretel exclaimed. 'If we got married we could hyphenate our names and be Sweeney-Todd!'

Sweeney looked at her blankly. 'Why would we do that?'

'It's an old story,' Sarah said. 'The Demon Barber of Fleet Street? There was a musical with Johnny Depp.'

'Not a big fan of musicals,' Sweeney said.

Lane lifted the clay covering from his breakfast: toast, eggs and a ham steak. 'These are cool,' he said, nodding to the lid.

'I make them,' Gretel said. 'I've got a little studio in my house, and a kiln.'

'Wow,' Lane said. 'One of those little houses fits all that?'

She shook her head. 'I don't live here, my house is next door, right up the hill. The storm knocked my power out, so I'm camping out here until it clears up enough for me to get up on the roof and see what's happening.'

Lane wasn't trying to keep an eye on what Mina was doing, but somehow he kept finding his gaze resting on her anyway. He looked away each time he realised he was doing it.

'You're the prisoner, right?' Trish asked. She stirred her breakfast, a soupy porridge, without eating any. 'Karpathy says we're not allowed to ask what you did.'

She looked at him like she was hoping he would tell her anyway, but Lane rather liked that rule.

'Just so you know, I believe in prison abolition,' Sarah added.

Lane wasn't sure what to say to that. He'd been rather pro-prison for most of his life. Since being in one himself, he'd met a lot of men he was glad weren't walking the streets. He'd met a lot more who needed a social worker, not a cell.

'Is the fancy breakfast some kind of special treat for new arrivals?' Lane asked, cutting up a square of egg and toast. The toast was oddly chewy – gummy, even. He glanced at Sweeney's plate and saw his toast was identical, so they must have both been served gluten-free bread.

'No, this'll be your usual,' Dave said. 'Until the ham runs out, anyway. Karpathy decided it would be easier to set you two a separate menu than figure out how to budget for what you'd eat as a regular farm resident.'

Sweeney laughed. 'You mean the farm would rather charge the department for five dollars' worth of ham and eggs than ten cents' worth of porridge oats. It's fine, you can say it.'

This sat uncomfortably with Lane. Prison food budgets were notoriously low, yet he was going to eat better than the farm residents did.

'They're eggs from our chickens and ham from our pigs,' Dave said. 'We're not paying supermarket prices.'

'You didn't kill a pig especially for us, I hope,' Lane joked.

'Oh, sure,' Dave said breezily. 'Her name was Pepper.'

Lane paused, and pointed with the fork. 'This ham had a name?'

'Uh-huh. Would you like to see a picture?'

'No, thank you.' That put Lane in an awkward position. He'd been eyeing the ham steak, unsure if he would be able to handle chewing it. He'd shattered his jaw as a teenager and had to have it surgically reconstructed. Some foods weren't worth the ache they would cause. But if he left it on his plate now, Dave would feel judged.

'Don't worry,' Dave said. 'A lot of people have trouble adjusting to that when they first come here. People know their ham comes from pigs who lived their whole life shoulder to shoulder in a feedlot, then got herded onto a conveyor belt to die. They're fine with it. But the idea that we knew Pepper, made sure she had a great life followed by one bad day, makes people queasy. They prefer the cruel system they can distance themselves from.'

'That makes sense.' Lane sliced off a tiny sliver of meat and put it in his mouth, chewing carefully.

'I don't know how you can stand to start the day with a heavy food like that in your stomach,' Gretel said. She took a sip from her bottle.

'Most important meal of the day,' Dave said, in the tone of someone used to this conversation.

'Are you intermittent fasting?' Sweeney asked, nodding at Gretel's water bottle.

'Oh, no. I get what I need at home. I love the company here but I never eat the food.'

Lane opened his mouth to ask why but was interrupted by Trish.

'Why is there only one of you?' she asked. 'When Karpathy mentioned prisoners coming to work on the farm, I was imagining, like, a bunch of you chained together.'

'Chain gangs are an American thing,' Sarah said.

'This isn't prison labour,' Lane explained. 'I'm on study leave. As long as I follow the rules, I'm allowed to live outside the prison while I do a TAFE course. It's supposed to help me reintegrate into society when I'm released.'

At the mention of his upcoming release, Mina turned to look at him, then immediately looked away. So she could hear them, even over the hum of normal breakfast conversation.

'But you're working on the farm?' Trish asked.

'It's on-the-job learning. I work on the farm, you guys tick off the competencies, and after six months I get an agriculture certificate.'

'Does the government pay for that?' Trish frowned, possibly thinking of her own study loans.

'Agriculture courses are free for anyone,' Dave interjected. 'There's a skills shortage. If you want to do it too, come to the office and we'll get you signed up.'

'Why do you keep looking at Deana?' Sarah asked.

It took Lane a moment to realise she was talking to him. 'Who?'

'At our three o'clock with the dark hair?'

Right. Mina. He'd heard the other woman call her 'Deana' outside the toilet block. Was she using a fake name?

Trish lowered her voice. 'She keeps giving him the stink eye; of course he's going to look if he sees someone staring at him.'

'I understand if people are curious about me,' Lane said, also sotto voce.

'Deana's a good egg,' Dave said, a hint of warning in his voice.

'Yeah, yeah, she's fine,' Trish said. 'But she can be a bit intense. She's worked on a farm before, so if you pull a ticket with her she acts like she's the shift supervisor.'

Lane had no idea what 'pull a ticket' meant, but set that aside for the moment. 'Has she been here long?' he asked.

He didn't like gossiping about Mina, but he needed some information if he was going to figure out what to do about finding her here.

'Like, seven months?' Sarah said. 'No, wait.' She started counting on her fingers. 'I've been here eight, and then Hannah arrived –'

Both Dave and Gretel flinched at the mention of Hannah's name.

'I remember because I gave her my gift exactly a month after I moved here. Then Deana came a few weeks after her, so maybe six months?'

Six months. Which meant she'd already been at the farm before Lane and Carver even hatched their plan.

'Where is Hannah, anyway?' Trish asked. 'Is she skipping breakfast again?'

Lane made eye contact with Dave, who confirmed his suspicion with a grim look. Hannah was the driver who had lost her life the previous night.

'I'm going to grab a cup of coffee,' Lane said, half to give Dave a bit of space to break the news and half because he was desperate for some caffeine.

'It's not coffee,' Trish said.

'You're in the Riverina, mate,' Dave said. 'We can't exactly grow it ourselves, and there are no sustainable or ethical ways to buy it.'

'There's no coffee here,' Lane repeated. He was going to die.

'We grow chicory root,' Trish said. 'Don't worry: two weeks and you won't know the difference.'

Sarah made a face that didn't fill Lane with optimism on that front.

'You mentioned yesterday that there are some things you buy in, though. You're not completely self-sufficient?'

'We don't aim to be,' Dave scoffed. 'That's every man for himself taken to extremes; capitalist individualism masquerading as sustainable agriculture. What we're aiming for is community. There are some things that it doesn't make sense for us to produce ourselves, so we connect with other local farms that can. What we can't get either way, well …'

They gave it up, like the coffee. 'So you trade with other farms in the area?'

'Karpathy – the senior, I mean – took care of all that. It was what he was good at. Young Sam handles it now.'

'He passed recently?' Lane asked. He knew this already, but it would look odd if he let on. If Lane really was there to learn to be a farmhand, he would have had no reason to have trawled through the family's public records.

'About a year and a half back. We're all still reeling.'

Lane glanced around the table at the others. Sarah, who had arrived after Reggie Karpathy's death, looked uneasy but not distressed. Trish seemed more bothered, while Gretel stared sadly into her glass bottle.

'It was unexpected?'

'Definitely,' said Dave. 'He was barely sixty, and I thought he'd live twice that. The way he lived, he's the last one I thought could have a heart attack.' Unlike the fervour he'd showed when he was lecturing earlier, Dave's expression now had a glaze of discomfort. Lane suspected Karpathy's sudden death didn't gel with the way Dave thought the world worked, and it was unpleasant for him to sit with that.

The conversation stopped. Not just at their table but at every table, all at once, like someone had thrown an acoustic blanket over the room. Sam Karpathy had entered the hall, and just like that, everyone had turned to look at him.

'Good morning, everyone.'

'Morning, Sam,' they all chorused back, like they were in a school classroom. Lane couldn't help looking at Mina, who had joined in the greeting.

'The weather report says the rains won't let up today or tomorrow, so all field jobs are cancelled. The bottom of Hill Road is underwater, so we won't be able to access the town for the indefinite future.' He drew a shaky breath and folded his hands in front of him. 'Some of you might have noticed Hannah isn't here this morning. She was in a car accident last night, and I'm sorry to have to tell you she passed away.'

A gasp went around the room.

'I understand this is difficult news. If you need some time off to sit with it, let me know. But I've found that the best thing to do in the face of tragedy is ground yourself in routine, so there are job tickets on the board for anyone who would prefer a distraction. You might also have noticed some new arrivals.'

Lane lifted his hand in a wave, although few people looked over. Most people still looked dazed from the news about Hannah.

'We had planned to do the welcome ceremony tonight, but instead we'll hold a memorial for Hannah. If anyone wants to talk, I'm here.'

A knot of people immediately gathered around him.

'I'm sorry,' Lane said, to the table at large. 'Were you close with Hannah?'

'Of course,' Dave said. 'We're all close here.'

'We were in the same cabin,' Sarah said. 'I thought … God, I noticed she didn't come in last night, but you know …'

'Who was out with her?' Trish asked. 'Are they alright?'

'She was the only one in the car,' Lane said, wanting to give a small bit of reassurance.

Instead, both Trish and Sarah turned to him with shocked expressions. 'What?'

'That can't be right,' Trish said. 'She didn't have a licence.'

CHAPTER FIVE

'YOU KNOW, LANE, you're a rather unique arrival,' Karpathy said, leaning back against the gate and putting one arm up on the cross bar. A deliberately relaxed posture, in Lane's opinion.

Lane remained standing straight, his arms loose by his sides. Not mirroring Karpathy's casual attitude, but not hostile. As neutral as possible.

'I imagine none of your other residents have a murder on their record,' Lane said.

If Lane putting it so baldly surprised Karpathy, he didn't show it. 'Oh, don't be so sure of that.'

That caught Lane off guard. 'There are people here who have killed someone?'

Karpathy answered like it was a perfectly ordinary question. 'Everyone comes to this farm for a reason. Sometimes those reasons are dark.'

'Sarah and Trish mentioned that you told people not to ask why I'm in prison. I really appreciate that.'

'I don't tell people what to do,' Karpathy said. 'I just reminded them that everyone here gets to share their story only when they choose to.'

Which meant that Lane needed to tread very carefully when it came to drawing information out of people. Even standard small talk might be deemed too invasive.

'I'm not going to pretend the fact that you were in prison –'

'I *am* in prison,' Lane interrupted. 'Present tense.'

'I'm not going to pretend that you being in prison doesn't matter. It's part of who you are. It's shaped the story of you. And the story of you matters, Lane.'

Karpathy looked so earnest as he spoke that Lane would have felt embarrassed for him, if he believed it.

'Everyone here understands that you are paying your debt. Nobody has the right to make you pay extra with cruelty or scorn or judgement. If you ever feel like that's happening, I want to know right away. You can come talk to me any time.'

'Thank you,' Lane said, biting back the urge to add 'sir'.

'You're welcome. Now, that's not what makes you unique. Plenty of our residents, past and present, have had run-ins with the justice system. Or the foster care system. Or have had trouble with their parents. Maybe they've even lost their parents. Myself included.'

Forced teaming, Lane noted. You and me, we're the same.

'Well,' he said, looking to defuse the conversation, 'I think in my case, losing my second parent can, as Wilde would put it, be considered carelessness.'

'I can see I'm making you uncomfortable, which is the opposite of my intention. I'll cut to the chase. You're unique because everyone else here chose to come. They learned about us and sought us out and they came here looking for something. A new start, a reconnection to the land, a family of choice instead of the one they got stuck with. But you've been sent here.'

Reading between the lines, new arrivals had usually been thoroughly worked before they decided to come to the farm. Showing up was stage two of the process, and Lane had skipped stage one. Possibly that meant Lane would be more resistant to their tactics, and Karpathy knew it.

'Even so, I don't want you to feel different, Lane.'

He kept repeating Lane's name. That was another strategy to build rapport quickly; Lane had used it on occasion himself. Now he wondered if this was how people felt when he was trying to warm them up to get what he wanted. Had they been onto him the whole time?

He suspected sometimes Mina had.

'To that end, I don't think anyone is best served by you getting about in a Corrective Services uniform. We've got a clothing pool, and I'm sure there'll be something that will fit you. Let's have a look, hey?'

Instead of opening the gate, Karpathy swung over the top in a single practised motion, a move that suggested familiarity with the space and remarkable athleticism. Lane put one hand on the cross bar and knew immediately that he wouldn't make it over.

He unlatched it and came through, then had to jog to catch up with Karpathy.

The admin building was a classic weatherboard farmhouse, with peeling yellow paint and a wide verandah currently covered in muddy footprints.

Seeing Lane look, Karpathy said, 'It had no internal walls when my parents bought the place. They added two bedrooms, a kitchen and a bathroom. The kitchen is gone now, we needed the floorspace for storage.'

The front door opened to a cramped hallway, with doors on either side, and one at the end.

'The farm office is here.' Karpathy indicated a door to the right. Lane noticed that there was no lock on the door, unlike the one on the left. Karpathy's living area? The door at the end also had a lock, a heavy deadbolt with no key in it.

'I understand you'll need to use a charging station in there. There's power in the office, the kitchen and the animal sheds, but you'll probably be underfoot if you try to use the last two.'

'There's power in the animal sheds but not the residences?' Lane asked.

He'd assumed that his was unpowered because it was new, or to cut costs for the prison program.

'We need power in the animal sheds to meet national standards for our meat and milk production. Cheese day is coming up at the end of this week, by the way; that's always fun. The residences are for sleeping, and you don't need electricity to sleep. Quite the opposite. I bet you'll get the best sleep of your life here, away from a million blinking LEDs and humming devices.'

'What if I wanted to read a book, or write a letter?' The little push light in his room had been too insipid for anything more than finding his way to bed safely.

'It doesn't really matter now we're headed into the warmer months. Come summer, you'll probably hit the hay before the sun goes down. There's a light in the dining hall, if you really need one. You won't get bored, though. When it's not so wet, we have bonfires most evenings, and there's always plenty of music. Do you play an instrument?'

'I can play "Hot Cross Buns" on the recorder.'

Karpathy laughed, although it was a piss-poor joke. 'Dave would love to show you how to play guitar. He's desperate for another guitarist to show up so he can switch to the bass.'

For a moment Lane thought they were headed for the locked door at the end. Karpathy noticed him looking and said, 'That connects to a shed in the back. Please stay out of there.' He switched to a much more cheerful tone as he pushed open the last door on the right. 'Here we are!'

The room was a narrow galley lined with the same wooden shelves used in the dining hall. 'Clothes are here.' Karpathy pointed to the back wall. 'Everything on that shelf over there is free for the taking – if you have anything you don't need anymore, pop it in here and it might be exactly what someone else is looking for. Leave the other shelf, though; that's where we keep things that were left behind. We don't want any legal issues, so we stash them there for a few months in case their owners come back for them.'

Lane wondered how often that was happening to need a dedicated space set aside.

'Speaking of legal issues!'

Lane's head was beginning to spin with Karpathy's frequent subject changes. This one felt forced. Clearly people leaving wasn't a topic he wanted to stay on for too long.

'If there's any paperwork you need to do now that you've moved here, we have copies of most forms in the office. Mail redirection, voter enrolment details, that sort of thing. There's going to be a council election in November, so we'd encourage you to get onto it.'

Ah. That explained why the voter rolls for this address had been so informative. Lane had been wondering. But in a place like Georges Bridge, the forty or fifty residents of this farm would be a significant voting bloc in a council election. The sort that could seek special concessions, or make the local government staff reluctant to poke into their affairs.

'I reckon this will fit,' Karpathy said, pulling a pair of jeans from a shelf and tossing them to Lane. He rummaged through a pile of folded shirts, apparently arranged in a way that was readable to Karpathy and looked like chaos to Lane. They were all variations on a theme – button-down collared flannel or light cotton.

When Lane had an armful of clothes, Karpathy took a moment to straighten up the folded stacks, then turned and looked expectantly at him.

Lane looked back. Was Karpathy planning to watch him change? The last several years had worn away any expectation of privacy – he'd been strip-searched less than twenty-four hours ago – but that didn't mean he'd forgotten what constituted normal behaviour.

But then Karpathy gave him that too-big smile again and left.

Lane dropped the clothes on the floor and turned to the abandoned goods shelf. Karpathy had said they only kept things for a few months, so any possessions belonging to the missing people would be long gone. Still, Lane doubted that the official Missing Persons list told the whole story. He gave himself thirty seconds max; any more than that and Karpathy could pop back in, and he needed to have made a plausible amount of progress towards getting changed.

First he took stock of where everything was—he needed to be able to put it back so it looked untouched. Judging by Karpathy's knowledge of the clothes, Lane was sure he would notice immediately if something in the room had moved.

Lane picked up a woman's purse with a gold Chanel logo on the clasp. Lane ran a thumb over it—it was plasticky, so likely a fake, which made it less suspicious that it had been left behind. He checked inside. No wallet, no phone. Just a copy of a book – *Erewhon* by Samuel Butler – along with a muesli bar wrapper and a piece of brown paper folded into a tight rectangle. He unfolded it and realised it was just a paper bag, brown on the outside and waxed on the inside, like the ones used by bakeries. He flipped through the book, looking for slips of paper tucked between the pages or significant annotations, but found nothing. He put the purse back.

The other items on the shelf were a single Ariat workboot, a blue tie and a small plush toy shaped like a pineapple. He didn't touch that.

His time was up, and he quickly stripped out of the clothes supplied by the prison and pulled on those Karpathy had given him. He was a little put out by how well the pants fit when he buttoned them up. Karpathy clearly had a good eye. There was something stiff and square in the front pocket, the corner scratching his upper thigh. He pulled out a photograph, an old one – old enough to be printed on glossy paper with the film brand printed on the back. It was slightly warped; evidently the pants had gone through the wash and been hung up to dry with the photo unnoticed in the pocket. The picture was the sort most families had on a shelf somewhere: a father and two kids, a girl who was maybe six and a boy a few years younger, in front of a Christmas tree. Their mother was presumably the one holding the camera. It took Lane a moment to recognise the man as Reggie Karpathy, the late owner of the farm, which made the little boy missing a tooth Sam Karpathy, who was probably standing right outside the door.

In his research, Lane hadn't come across any mention of a Karpathy daughter. He flipped the photo over, hoping to find a note with names or a date, but it was blank. He scrutinised the picture again. There were Christmas stockings lined up on the wall, he noticed, with names stitched on: *Mummy*, *Daddy*, *Sammy*, and a fourth, disappearing out of frame, cut off after *Na*.

•

Karpathy stood on the verandah, sheltering from the rain and watching something off to the right.

Lane stepped up beside him and saw that he was looking at a greenhouse. The walls looked like they were made of glass, but the inside was so clouded that it was impossible to see what it contained, beyond vague shapes moving around.

Karpathy turned. 'Looks good!'

'Yeah, but we're wearing the same outfit,' Lane joked. 'One of us is going to have to change.'

'Ha!' Karpathy said, not even pretending to laugh. 'I know it might feel odd at first, but because we use greywater on the farm, we do have to insist that everyone wears natural fabrics. Cotton, wool, linen.'

Karpathy kept using the word 'we' whenever he mentioned the farm rules, but as far as Lane could tell, Karpathy was the one setting and enforcing them. Was it a leftover habit from when 'we' meant Karpathy and his father? Was there some sort of collective decision-making process? Or was he trying to imply that one existed when in fact it didn't?

'Did you know that polyester and other artificial fabrics shed microplastics into the water when they're washed?'

'No,' Lane admitted.

'If we let residents wash their polyester clothes in our laundry, then spread that water on our gardens, those microplastics would build up in our soil. But we get that asking people to replace their whole wardrobe is a big ask, so we provide what we can. It's cheapest to buy in bulk from a wholesaler, so there's not as much variety as we'd like.'

Lane didn't know what to do with that. It was a reasonable rule, once Karpathy had explained it, and it was generous of him – or 'them' – to ensure people could comply easily. But that was the sticking point: compliance. Even if it wasn't intended to be a uniform, it was one. And uniforms usually went hand in hand with an expectation of obedience; they were worn by minimum-wage workers, schoolchildren, soldiers.

And prisoners.

'The rain's going to make the tour tricky, but I'll do my best. You might want to put some boots on.' Karpathy pointed to a row of identical black gumboots in various sizes, lined up against the wall. 'Should we go find Rick?'

'Rick?' Lane repeated, then realised that he meant Sweeney.

•

'It's beautiful here,' Lane said as they walked down the gravel road together. The farm had sweeping views of the valley below. Lane couldn't help noticing the familiar shape of the hills that had appeared in the background of Alain Serling's photograph.

'Thank you,' Karpathy said. 'My father worked hard all his life to make it a lovely place to be. There were no trees here when he bought it, and before we planted out the gullies the erosion was awful.'

'Have you had a fire there?' Lane asked, pointing to a spot down the hill covered with scorched black grass.

Karpathy laughed. 'In a way. We do a lot of cool burning in the autumn and winter to reduce the fire risk. That spot was part of a mosaic burn project. There's a local Aboriginal corporation that uses our land to run traditional burning workshops once a month.'

'At least you don't have to worry about fire this year,' Lane said. 'With all this rain.'

Karpathy chuckled. 'I wouldn't be so sure. In hill country like this, the excess water drains out of the soil fast. The wet means that we can't do our usual spring hazard reduction, and there'll be a whole flush of extra growth that will turn into kindling when it dries out. All it would take is two weeks of hot, dry weather to send us catastrophic.'

They found Sweeney in the first place they looked: the cabin. He was still wearing his guard uniform, and Karpathy didn't suggest that he change; presumably there had been some agreement on that front which Lane wasn't privy to.

'You've got bugger-all phone service up here,' Sweeney grumbled, pulling the door shut behind him. 'And no 5G at all. I can barely check my emails.'

Karpathy shrugged. 'For a lot of us that's a plus. We've got a landline for business and a satellite phone for emergencies.'

'Good morning,' someone called from a nearby garden bench.

'Morning, Winton,' Karpathy said.

Winton looked straight out of a vintage horror poster, in a long waterproof leather coat and hat with a dripping brim. Across his knees he had a scythe, and he was sharpening the long, curved blade with a whetstone. His steady strokes made a *shingk, shingk* noise.

'Bit wet to be cutting grass,' Karpathy observed.

'Too wet to move the goats, too, so I have to cut them some hay,' Winton explained.

'Are you guys Amish or something?' Sweeney asked, as they carried on down the road.

Karpathy laughed. 'No. The Amish have some good ideas, and I'm happy to borrow good ideas from anywhere, but they're a heavily Christian-based, patriarchal group. We're very committed to equality here.'

'And religion?' Lane asked. 'If I wanted to go to town for services –'

'Holland, that fucker's funeral is the only time I've seen you in the chapel,' Sweeney interrupted. 'You don't go to services and you're not getting a free weekly trip into town by pretending you do.'

Lane would have quite liked an excuse to go down to the town and start asking questions, but really he'd been trying to find out if anyone else went there regularly. The farm seemed very isolated – though perhaps being cut off by the floods was adding to that impression. He also wondered if Karpathy tried to prevent his residents from coming under the influence of other authority figures, like a minister.

'Well, I don't think anyone goes to town for that. A trip uses a lot of petrol.' Karpathy looked uncomfortable at the suggestion. 'I suppose if you really wanted to, you could hitch a ride when Dave takes the weekly harvest to the farmer's market. He does leave at four am, though.'

'You do have powered machinery, right?' Lane asked. 'The utes, and Dave mentioned a tractor?'

'Yes. We try to keep our use of machinery and fossil fuels to a minimum. We're not carbon neutral, if you don't count offsets, but we try our best.'

Which meant, Lane suspected, an awful lot of manual labour ahead for him. Even more if they didn't use pesticides or herbicides.

'And you're organic, right?'

'Yes, although that's not what's most important to us. We're magpies, really. We take a little bit from organic farming, a little bit from permaculture. A bit from the Amish, from Korean natural farming, from pre-war farming practices. Everyone has something useful to teach us.'

'What is most important to you?'

'Survival,' Karpathy said. 'Whatever it takes to keep this farm going and ensure everyone who lives here is safe and fed, without depending on anyone else. Speaking of! You've probably already noticed the gardens here.'

He pointed back towards the four blocks of housing and their neat little front gardens.

'We've got four blocks that house newer residents in a dormitory style. Each one has its own garden, which enables us to grow our annual vegetables using a super basic rotation system. Four gardens, four seasons. At the beginning of each season, one is planted, and whoever lives in that particular dorm is in charge of that garden. Once the plants are at the end of their growing season, we move the chickens in to clean it up, then we turn over the soil and get rid of any weeds and their seeds. Then it gets mulched and rests until its time rolls around again. Because you boys are new, and there's only two of you, we've given you an easy one. This garden's nearly finished, and there are just a few herbs to look after. You will have the chickens in summer, though!'

He said this like it was exciting news, so Lane said, 'Great.'

Out of the corner of his eye, he saw Sweeney put a hand on his stomach, his jaw tightening. Lane was about to ask him if he was feeling okay, when Sweeney caught his eye and shot him a look that made it clear he wanted nothing from Lane, least of all sympathy.

'These gardens feed us,' Karpathy explained, 'along with the orchards, and the animals, and what we can forage. Unfortunately there are a lot of rules we have to follow for the vegetables we sell, so there are separate market gardens over on the north face of the hill. Come on.'

'I think I'm going to check out here,' Sweeney said. 'I'm here to babysit, not farm, so I don't need the tour.' His tone was dismissive, but he looked miserable, and he still had a hand over his stomach.

'Is there anything that would help?' Lane asked. 'A cup of tea, maybe?'

'I've got what I need,' Sweeney grunted, and he disappeared back inside the cabin before they could say anything more.

Lane looked at Karpathy. 'He can't eat gluten. Is it possible there was something in breakfast?'

Karpathy shook his head. 'We don't grow wheat, so we don't eat it. He's alright, though.' He looked amused, an expression which turned to puzzlement when he saw Lane's blank look. 'Last night's soup?' he prompted.

'What about it?' Lane asked.

'It was made with sunchokes. They're incredibly nutritious, but some people can't digest them. Nothing worse than the occasional twinge and a bit of gas, though.'

'A heads-up would have been nice.'

'I'm sure Dave meant to warn you, but accidents happen. Are you feeling okay?'

'I grew up on the show circuit; I've got a cast-iron stomach.'

Karpathy brightened. 'The show circuit? That must have been interesting.'

'That's one word for it. Have you travelled much?'

'The US a few times, and the UK. Once to Bolivia.'

Lane paused. That wasn't the answer he'd been expecting. 'Doesn't flying so far clash with what you're trying to do here?' He took in the farm with a sweep of his hand.

Thankfully, Karpathy found that question amusing rather than offensive. 'That's a fair point. We try to weigh up the benefits and the cost. I learn a lot on those trips, make connections, and sometimes bring back things that I just can't get here. I wish there were better solutions. If we go back to wind-powered passenger ships crossing the Pacific, I'd be all over that. One time, Dave went to the United States on a container ship.'

'How'd that go?'

'Well, it was originally supposed to take forty days. Then a boat got stuck in the Panama Canal, and he ended up missing the event he was travelling there to attend. We decided to stick with flying after that.' He smiled. 'We keep it to a minimum, though. Who would want to be anywhere but here? Ask any of the residents.'

'Do you get a lot of newcomers on the farm?'

'It ebbs and flows. The tide is low right now, but we should see an uptick as the weather gets warmer. A lot of people spent the winter stuck inside, fantasising about spring weather and fresh air, and some of them will make their way to us. Of course, my father used to handle the recruitment, but I'm starting to get my head around it.'

'I'm guessing you get a lot through the harvest trail, or people on backpacker visas?'

Karpathy made a face. 'We probably could. But we're trying to build a community here. Someone trying to tick off their days worked on the land so they can go back to the coast isn't a good fit.'

That was interesting. Matilda and Alain had both been travellers, albeit ones who didn't need a visa. Matilda in particular had been travelling the country as a practice run before she went overseas to see Europe and her birth country, Czechia. She was the opposite of what Karpathy was looking for.

What had changed? The Karpathys' approach, or Matilda's plans for the future?

Lane wanted to ask how he found people, but Karpathy barrelled on. 'We keep a job board outside the dining hall. Some jobs need to be done every day, some once a week, and if you spot anything that needs doing, you can write out a ticket and put it up. Usually we let people pull any ticket they want, but given it's your first day, I'm going to start you in the wash-and-pack shed. I –' His face turned sombre. 'I had asked Hannah to show you how it's done.'

'I'm sorry for your loss.'

'Thank you. She was only here a few months, but she was important to us all,' Karpathy said, a little stiffly.

'Did you get to the bottom of why she had your ute?'

'She was going to town to get sandbags,' Karpathy said, his tone cooling.

That didn't make sense, given how Karpathy and Dave had responded the night before. Who other than them would decide the farm needed sandbags? If someone else told her to go, why didn't they raise the alarm when she never came back with them? And why, out of everyone at the farm, would they send an unlicensed driver in such dangerous conditions?

But it was clear Karpathy didn't welcome this line of conversation, and Lane had too much to lose to push at the wrong time.

'I'd show you how to wash and pack myself, but under the circumstances I really want to get around and check in on people, make sure they're doing alright.' Karpathy looked thoughtful. 'Maybe Deana can help you; she's pretty new but really knowledgeable about the state rules.'

Lane looked at him, trying to read his face. It struck him that if Karpathy had done any research on Lane, pictures of Mina would have come up. Did he know who she really was? Was he messing with Lane?

'Maybe it'd be better if one of the male residents did it?' he said. 'I don't know how comfortable this Deana would be spending the day shut up in a shed with me.'

He didn't get even a flicker from Karpathy. People who were being manipulative often let it slip with a smile, or seeming too pleased with themselves; it was known as 'duper's delight'. But either Karpathy was an exceptional actor, or there was genuinely nothing behind his suggestion.

'Of course she'll be free to say no,' Karpathy said. 'Let's go find her.'

•

Lane walked to the wash-and-pack shed, leaving Karpathy to find Mina on his own. He'd passed the point of no return. He should have pulled the plug as soon as he realised Mina was on the farm. He could have called Carver, or William Magala, and arranged to leave.

But for whatever reason, Mina was living here under a fake name, and it wasn't right for him to expose her. Maybe she had found some kind of peace here, living as 'Deana', away from the shadow of her past. He couldn't take that away from her simply to protect himself.

Or maybe that was just a very convenient story that allowed him to keep doing what he wanted. Allowed him to cling to this scrap of freedom.

The least he could do now was stay away and let her come to him. She could tell Karpathy no, and someone else would be sent to teach him. They could sit in opposite corners of every room, and sleep in different buildings, and he would wait for her to pull a ticket each morning and make sure he was somewhere else. Maybe that would work.

The shed was small inside, just a few square metres. A bench lined one wall, divided into four sections: one right in front of a window, with a wire basket full of lettuce leaves sitting on it; a sink; a section that looked like a giant metal dish strainer; and then a solid counter with an empty cardboard carton, in front of another window.

The door crashed open and Mina stormed in. If her goal had been to put him on the back foot, it worked.

She pointed to each section in turn. 'They push the harvest in through the window. Wash. Dry. Pack. Congratulations, you're now trained in the wash-and-pack shed.' She folded her arms and stared at him. 'You're violating your no-contact order.'

'Trust me, I am very aware of that. I told Karpathy not to send you if you weren't comfortable with it,' Lane said.

'What was I supposed to say? *No, I'd rather avoid Holland, he's the only person who knows about that time I fucking killed someone?*'

It had been Lane's idea. He'd taken the gun out of her hands. He'd helped her wash away the evidence. He'd told the police when they arrived that he'd been the one to shoot his father. He'd looked a judge in the eye and pled guilty.

And now this was how Mina thought of him? As someone who had the power to blackmail her?

'I've never told anyone about that,' he pointed out. 'Why would I start now?'

She pulled her arms closer to her chest, hugging herself. 'I don't know. I'm sure it would help with the parole board.'

'I need to show remorse to get parole. Suddenly denying a charge I pled guilty to years ago will absolutely not improve my chances of parole.'

'How about giving you a story to sell once you're out there needing to pay rent and bills again?'

'I've got a lot more to lose here than you. If you're worried, why didn't you say something when Corrective Services notified you I was being moved?'

She rolled her eyes. 'I never got that. Living under a fake name doesn't work so well if you have mail forwarded to you with your real name on it.'

It was hard to believe that the explanation could be so simple, but he did believe she was genuinely shocked and upset to see him. Her response didn't feel faked.

'Look,' she said, 'whatever you want, I'm not giving it to you.'

'I don't want anything,' he said.

Someone knocked at the shed door, making them both jump. Mina hustled over and opened the door. Lane hoped that the angry flush on Mina's face and their tense postures didn't seem suspicious.

Outside stood Gretel, the woman from breakfast. She was still clutching her water bottle in one hand, and in the other she held a square wicker basket by the handle.

'I see you've got the hang of it,' she said cheerfully. She peered past Mina, and her face fell at seeing only Lane in the shed. 'I was told you and Sweeney weren't feeling well. I've brought something that might help.'

Mina pushed past her and walked away without saying anything. Gretel turned and watched her go, but it didn't seem to trouble her.

'Uh, no, I'm fine,' Lane said. He wondered who could have told her that – if it had been Karpathy, he would have mentioned Sweeney had returned to his room. 'Sweeney's back at the accommodation block. What do you have?' He hoped it was something with caffeine. His mother had sworn by a can of Coke as a cure for stomach ache.

'Privet berry syrup,' she said. 'I make it myself. Obviously I don't grow privet myself, it's noxious stuff, but there are always berries overhanging back fences, planted before people knew better.'

'I thought privet berries were poisonous,' Lane said.

'It's medicinal,' Gretel said. She took the bottle out of her basket and offered it to Lane. It was a recycled minibar bottle, which in a previous life had held a shot of vodka. The syrup inside was thick and black. 'A teaspoonful will set you completely to rights.'

'I'm already fine,' Lane said, waving it away. 'But if you have any coffee or tea hidden in that basket, I can make us a cup.' He pointed to the hot-water boiler above the sink.

'Of course.'

Lane's elation was short-lived, plummeting when she pulled out a jar packed with something green and crumbly. 'Chamomile and blackberry leaf,' she said. 'Also great for the digestion. But I'll pass on the cup and pop over to see poor Sweeney. Have a good one.'

She put the jar on the edge of the bench and, with a jaunty wave, headed back up the driveway.

Lane didn't bother making the cup of tea. He sat down and laced his hands together, squeezing his palms tight.

He hadn't ever let himself imagine meeting Mina again. He'd put that in a box marked 'not going to happen' and never opened the lid a crack. It would have been deeply sad of him to sit in his cell for years, imagining that Mina was out there somewhere, thinking warmly of him.

So he definitely hadn't done that.

HE JUST HAD *to make it to the door.*

He forced his body up, only an inch. He put his weight on his knees and elbows, his forearms and palms still pressed to the floor. Crocodile pose, he thought. In another life he'd done yoga weekly in the ratty hall at his high school. He'd told his friends he signed up for it because it was what all the girls chose for PE, but really it was the only option he could handle with his asthma.

He pretended that the screaming in his muscles was just his body protesting at the end of a brutal yoga session. No pain, no gain. He slid his left forearm forward, then his right knee. Other arm, other knee. The room was not big, maybe two body lengths to the door. Forearm. Knee. Forearm. Knee.

CHAPTER SIX

LANE SERIOUSLY CONSIDERED hiding out in the shed for the rest of the day. The clock said it was lunchtime, but he had no appetite. If that changed, he could always have a nice lettuce salad and a cup of Gretel's weird tea.

But it was only his first day on the job, and if Sweeney had to drag himself out of his cabin to make sure Lane hadn't somehow dumped the ankle monitor in the shed and escaped, he would never hear the end of it.

•

He scanned the groups seated in the dining hall for lunch. He didn't want to keep going up to people to ask how long they'd lived on the farm – that would be off-putting and suspicious – but there were signs that some residents were more likely prospects than others. Age, for one thing; twenty-somethings like Trish couldn't be long-term residents, unless they'd been born here. But Lane had noticed that, despite the number of people living on the farm long term, he hadn't seen any kids running around nor any signs of their presence, like play equipment or bikes. He didn't know what to make of that.

Another sign of a long-time resident was what they wore. The clothes were all much the same, and Karpathy had told him that laundry was done communally – they threw dirty clothes in a pile to be washed by whoever volunteered, and then just grabbed anything in the right size from the clean pile. But between his youth on the show circuit and his time in prison, Lane had a good understanding of how people who lived communally behaved. He knew that the real long-termers probably had a favourite pair of pants or a shirt that fit just right and didn't itch, and they would fight to get it back each time. On top of that, their boots would be more broken in, better moulded to the shape of their feet. Same with their hats.

He took a helping of vegetable soup – served in a cup so people had the option to take lunch back to work with them – and made a beeline for a table in the corner, where two men and two women were sitting together.

They looked a little surprised when he approached the table. 'Room for one more?' he asked.

'Of course,' one of the women said, giving him a smile that didn't reach her eyes.

He introduced himself, and learned that they were Deirdre, Roni, Clay and Frank. Lane wished he could write that down. He was good at remembering names, but the curve was going to be steep with so many new people.

He ate a spoonful of soup, waiting for the others to resume their conversation, but they simply ate their lunch in silence.

'What's everyone working on today?' he asked, after an excruciating minute. He had expected that not everyone would be keen to buddy up to him, but knowing it didn't make it any more comfortable.

'Maintenance on the drainage ditches,' Frank said.

Lane waited for a beat, then said, 'Karpathy has got me started in the wash-and-pack shed.'

'That's wonderful,' Roni said. 'It's really important that gets done.'

Lane looked at the queue of people waiting for food, hoping to see someone who might bring a bit more ebullient energy to the conversation – Dave, or Sarah and Trish. Instead, he saw a strikingly familiar face.

It was Brandon Roby: his third missing person.

•

Lane followed Brandon out after lunch. The rain had thankfully slackened to a light drizzle. Lane waited until they were out of earshot of the dining hall before clearing his throat. Brandon turned around, obviously expecting it to be someone else, because he looked thrown to see Lane behind him.

'Do you have a moment?' Lane asked.

He thought he saw a flicker of something nervous in Brandon's expression, but it was quickly replaced with the standard sunny smile. 'Absolutely. Do you mind if we walk and talk?'

Lane had come up with a simple backstory for broaching this topic; there was no need to get complicated or give away too much. 'I know this might sound weird,' he began, 'but are you Brandon Roby?'

Brandon grimaced. 'People don't really bother with last names here.'

'It's just on our way here yesterday we stopped at one of those tiny towns where the cafe is also the general store and post office. They had a Missing Persons poster up, and I'm pretty sure you were on there.'

He thought that covered all the bases nicely – it wouldn't have been that odd to be reading posters while bored and waiting at a cafe on a long trip, and if it was only the day before it wasn't a stretch that he would be able to recognise Brandon today.

'Shit.' Brandon started walking faster, so that Lane had to jog to keep up with him.

Brandon led him up the hill to the greenhouse Lane had noticed earlier. When they reached the entrance, Brandon held up a hand. The door was propped open, but Brandon kicked aside the rock holding it and closed it to show Lane a sign on the door.

It was bright yellow with a bold exclamation mark, beneath which was printed: WARNING. DO NOT ENTER WITHOUT VENTING.

'Never go into the greenhouse without opening the door and all of the vents for at least five minutes first. It's a moot point right now because we can't run the biochar kiln in weather this wet, but when we do use it, the chimney directs the smoke into the greenhouse. That lets us recapture some of the CO2 we're releasing, and the plants love it.'

'But if someone forgot and went inside,' Lane said, 'they'd pass out. Maybe even suffocate.'

'Hence the sign,' Brandon agreed, re-opening the door.

Lane shook his head as he followed the other man in. They'd built a DIY gas chamber.

Lane pulled the door shut behind them for privacy, but noticed there was no way to secure it from the inside. There was a slide bolt on the outside, presumably to keep people out when the kiln was in use. He left it as it was, and hoped no-one would interrupt them.

Inside there was a ladder set up, with a bucket of soapy water sitting beside it. Obviously Brandon and some others had been working to clean the smoke residue from the ceiling. Roughly half the panels were clear, showing the heavy grey clouds above them, while the other half were waiting for the afternoon.

Brandon slumped against a bench, gripping the edge with his hands as he faced Lane. 'Whatever she's offering, I might be able to match it. I just need to talk to Karpathy.'

Lane wasn't even sure there had been a reward. If there was, it would only have been a few thousand dollars. Not the kind of money to make Lane take note. Matilda's case had a modest reward attached, offered by the Carvers, but Lane wasn't stupid enough to think he had a shot at getting it, even if he did crack the case.

'Why do you need to talk to Karpathy about money?' If Karpathy was offering loans to residents, Lane could imagine a multitude of ways that might have gone wrong.

Brandon looked puzzled. 'To draw down from my pay. Didn't he tell you how it works?'

Lane shook his head. 'I'm on a different system,' he said, gesturing to his ankle tracker.

'Oh.' Brandon pressed his lips together. 'I shouldn't explain it; it'll come out all wrong and make it sound bad.'

Okay. Lane made a mental note to follow that up. 'You said you can match what she is offering. Who's she?'

Brandon hesitated, looking wretched, then said, 'My mother.'

'I take it you're not surprised she's reported you missing?'

Brandon scrubbed his face with his hands. 'I'd hoped she hadn't, but no. It's not a big shock.'

'I'm sorry,' Lane said, genuinely regretting that he'd caused Brandon so much distress. 'But now that you know, you could have it taken down. Then this wouldn't happen again.'

'I can't.' Brandon pulled a chair out that had been tucked under a potting bench, and sank into it. Lane remained standing, but did lean against the bench so he didn't feel like he was looming over the other man. 'If I call the police … Look …'

'You don't need to explain yourself to me,' Lane said, but he got the impression Brandon wanted to talk.

'I'm an adult.' Brandon said the words like they held a heavier meaning. Maybe it was something he'd said a lot, or thought a lot but had held his tongue. 'I am autistic and I am an adult. I can live by my damn self.'

'Your parents don't agree?'

'My father's not in the picture. My mother?' Brandon chuckled darkly. 'I'm still wondering. Maybe she genuinely believes I can't. Maybe she knows I can and just doesn't want me to. What matters is that I can, and she won't let me.'

'And you couldn't just move away and tell her to get over it?' Lane knew firsthand that moving away without a parent's support was a terrifying, tenuous existence. But at least his parents had let him go. He couldn't imagine doing all that while also feeling like he was being hunted.

'It sounds simple, doesn't it? I was a legal adult, and I even had an engineering degree, despite her best efforts. Every time I had a big exam she would have a massive emergency the night before. Her car had broken down and I needed to come pick her up, or she was having chest pains and I needed to sit in the ER waiting room with her until two am. You know the worst part? If I tried to tell people I thought she was doing it on purpose, they'd act like I was imagining things. But if I applied for an extension on every single exam because I'd had a family emergency, the professors would have laughed me out of their office. It got so much worse in my final year, when we all got sent home and the classes went online. No matter how many times I talked to her about it, she would "forget" and pop in while I was doing an exam. To prevent cheating, they pay some guy in the Philippines to watch you over Zoom while you're doing the test. I got threatened with zeroes because there were so many reports of a second person in the room. I had to start barricading the door, so she switched to banging on it every five minutes, claiming to be confused about why it was locked.'

'But you managed to get your degree?'

'By the skin of my teeth. When it came time to find a job, she pulled the same shit with my phone and video interviews. If I did them at the local library instead, or had an in-person interview, she would go into my emails to get the contact details and call to give me a "personal reference". You know what hiring managers do with an application from someone whose Mum keeps calling them?'

'She had your email password?'

'Yeah. It was a condition of living with her. Her house, her rules, right? Except when you're doing your damnedest to stop the person from moving out.'

'Then it becomes financial abuse,' Lane agreed.

'Luckily that was the time when restaurants would give a job to anyone who could prove they have a pulse. I started waiting tables, and saving up my paycheque, and the manager didn't give a shit what she said or did.' He took a shaky breath. 'That's when it got really bad.'

'You don't have to tell me this,' Lane said again. 'I just wanted to make sure you knew; I'm not going to tell anyone else.'

'No, I do have to tell you. You know how many people have listened to this much of the story, made a bunch of understanding noises, and then started in on the "you only get one mother" routine?' He laughed without mirth. 'Thank fuck I've only got one mother; imagine dealing with more of her.'

'Trust me, I know better than you think.'

'Same hat, hey?'

'Not precisely, but close enough to understand.'

'Huh.' Brandon relaxed a fraction. 'Look, I've started the story and it's going to bother me if I don't finish. I mentioned I'm autistic, right?'

'Briefly.'

'For me that mostly means I struggle a lot socially, and the squeaking noise styrofoam makes enrages me. But it also means that when I get really stressed or overstimulated, I can have meltdowns.' He studied Lane for a moment, perhaps looking for some sign of judgement or disdain. He must have been satisfied with what he saw, because he continued. 'When it happens I need to go somewhere safe. Block out sounds and light. Scream into a pillow. One day my mother picked a fight with me right before I left for work. It got out of hand and I melted down. To be clear' – he slapped the potting bench with an open palm – 'I do not get violent. I do not get in people's space. I do not scream at people; I scream at myself. I was not a threat. But she called the police. You know what happens to autistic men having a meltdown when you add cops to the equation?'

Brandon took a moment to collect himself.

'They showed up at the door with guns at their hip and their hands resting on them. I feel lucky I didn't get shot. Instead I got a seventy-two-hour hold in the local psych ward. I think some of the nurses clocked what was going on – one even gave me some pamphlets for men's shelters and online support groups. But the doctor? He had her in his ear every day, sobbing about how much I'd struggled in uni, my terrible grades and dead-end job hunt. She described every moody conversation like I'd lashed out at her unprovoked. She fought against them discharging me, and let it slip she planned to apply for a conservatorship.'

'Do you think she would have been successful?'

'Probably not. But I had no money, a job way below my qualifications and now a history of involuntary hospitalisation. If someone was trying to take away your freedom, how sure would you need to be that it would fail?'

Lane didn't say anything. He didn't think that pointing out he had in fact lost his freedom would add anything of value.

'For me, any risk at all was too high. I did a midnight flit the second I saw an opening. I cashed out everything in my account in case she found a way to access it, and ran. I slept rough for a few weeks, terrified that the cops would grab me again any minute. I didn't even dare approach the shelters the nurse told me about, in case my mother had the same list. But I did visit the online forums, and eventually I met Karpathy there.'

'Junior or senior?'

'Junior. I was a bit confused when I got to the farm and found out that he had a great relationship with his dad.'

'Did he claim online that he was also an abuse survivor?'

'No, but he always popped into threads with great advice. I just assumed, you know? At first he was just a sympathetic ear, and we DMed for a while. One time he even paid for a pizza to be delivered to me at the library. After a few weeks he asked if I'd be interested in coming to check out the farm, and to be honest I thought there was a fifty-fifty chance I was going to be murdered. But I was in such a dark place by then that either option felt like a better solution than living the way I was. Or going back.'

'And you're happy here?'

Brandon nodded. 'I like it. It's quiet. The work is interesting. The food could be better, and I wish there was more than one TV. But yeah, I could happily keep hiding out here until either she dies, or I meet someone I want to marry. A wife would knock any chance of a conservatorship on the head. Karpathy helped me set up a medical power of attorney, so I don't have to worry about the hospital calling her if I ever end up in a coma.'

'Did you appoint Karpathy to make decisions for you instead?'

Brandon gave Lane a searching look. 'No. Would it be a problem if I did?'

'I'm just curious how it all works.'

'You should talk to Alessandra then. She was a lawyer before she came here – she's still registered. A lot of people here need help with paperwork. Name changes. Power of attorney. Divorces sometimes.'

Hmm. So the farm had a mechanic, an engineer and a lawyer. Quite impressive qualifications for basic farm labour roles. And he definitely did need to talk to Alessandra. It sounded like if anyone knew the who's who of the farm, it would be her.

'What about your degree? Nice as this place is, if you just wait here until you feel safe, you'll miss out on years of work experience.'

Brandon shrugged. 'Maybe I will. But honestly? When I started my degree, I wanted to save the world. But nobody's hiring for that position. I'd talk to recruiters, and they'd say, *Sure. Come talk to this firm that consults on aircraft design. You can make them more fuel-efficient and cut down on carbon emissions.* But you know what happens when you make planes more fuel-efficient?'

'Ticket prices go down and people fly more?'

'That's the best-case scenario. Worst case, the government takes that technology and can drop more bombs on the same budget. And that's just the positions they found a way to greenwash. Most were just great pay, great benefits, come help us build the torment nexus. You can work from home on Fridays.' He shook his head. 'I feel like I'm doing a lot more to save the world here than I ever could out there. And I do get to use my engineering skills.'

'Building things like this greenhouse?'

'Yeah.' Brandon lit up. 'Right from day one, Karpathy – senior, I mean; Sam Karpathy's dad – was super open to out-there ideas.'

Exactly what Brandon would have needed at the time – he'd been over-controlled, prevented from working to his full potential, stifled again and again.

'What about Karpathy junior? What's he like to work for?'

'Oh, it doesn't really feel as if I'm working for him. He's not the boss; he's just the one who has to deal with the tax office.' Brandon laughed, and Lane suspected this was something he was repeating, not something he'd come up with himself. 'He's not quite so, *Yes, have a go, what's the worst that could happen?* as his dad was, but that's normal. He didn't expect to take over so soon.'

'His father's death was sudden, right? He wasn't sick beforehand?'

'You ask a lot of questions.'

'Sorry. I'm new here; I think I'm a bit anxious at being in a new place after so long.'

Brandon nodded. 'You're a private investigator, right?'

Well, that confirmed for Lane that there had been some discussion about him among the farm residents. Which raised the question: why had Mina been so surprised to see him? Hadn't she heard that a private investigator-cum-prisoner named Lane Holland would be arriving soon? Why hadn't she left before he got there?

'Not anymore. But I guess the instinct to try to scrounge up whatever information I can hasn't faded.'

'You could do a lot of good here with a skill set like that.'

So far Lane hadn't seen much evidence that his skills were a good match to life on a farm. 'How so?'

'You could help Karpathy find people like me. The ones who need this place.'

The idea chilled Lane. 'It does sound like the sort of thing I used to do. Tracking people down online.'

'You've obviously still got it. You found me.'

'Well, you don't need to worry. I'm not going to tell anyone. But I might not be the last one to recognise you. One phone call could make you a lot safer.'

'Or maybe one phone call results in some police officer taking pity on a poor old lady who misses her son and letting something slip. It wouldn't be the first time police have given a victim's address to their abuser.'

Lane left Brandon to his cleaning work, feeling shaken. It was a heavy reminder that people most often disappeared by choice. Carver had occasionally hinted at fractures in his relationship with his missing daughter, Matilda. She'd been adopted at birth and planned to return to her birth country to reconnect with that part of herself, which her mother and father took as a rejection. Could that conflict have been more serious than Carver let on? He certainly couldn't ask Carver, even if he could figure out a way to contact him. If he'd lied once, he would lie twice, and be angry at Lane for asking. Was it possible that Matilda, like Brandon, had sought refuge here – and stayed?

CHAPTER SEVEN

LANE HAD ORIGINALLY planned to sit out Hannah's memorial. He'd never met the woman, and he risked overstepping by turning up to an event to which he had little emotional claim. But the memorial was a perfect opportunity to watch the farm residents while they were focused on more important things. What would a present-day Matilda look like, if she'd spent the intervening twenty years on Karpathy's farm? She'd been twenty-one when she vanished, so she'd be around forty now. Because she was adopted he couldn't look to her parents for any hints about how she might have aged, so he had to consider any woman who looked to be between thirty and fifty.

Matilda's hair had been blonde, but it might have become darker over time, or she might have gone grey or dyed it another colour. But perhaps that wasn't allowed; if Karpathy was so concerned about the greywater that he wouldn't let residents wear polyester, surely he wouldn't allow them to use bleach or boxed dye here either. Lane couldn't recall seeing anyone with an unnatural hair colour or visible regrowth.

Her eyes were green, and that wouldn't have changed, unless she was getting around the farm in contacts. Her weight could have gone up or down – probably down. He'd noticed that Brandon had slimmed down since the photo on his Missing Persons profile was taken.

Noses tended to stay the same, although their shape and size could shift through healed injuries or surgery. Ears, as well.

The most challenging part was that he had to work from memory. He couldn't very well carry around the picture of young Matilda and Alain to consult. He'd studied the picture often enough that he was confident, but there were no guarantees. After twenty years, people could change in staggering ways, unless they worked very hard not to. Any 'Where are they now?' magazine photo spread was proof of that.

The rain had cleared by the time the sun started to set, washing the hills to the west of them rose-pink. He followed the general drift of people to the fire pit. When he heard 'fire pit', he'd imagined a Bunnings special, a metal bowl maybe a metre across, so he was taken aback to find that the pit, which was dug directly into the ground and lined with old red bricks, was the size of a backyard pool. The actual pile of wood was small – probably because their usual sources were too soaked through to get a truly enormous fire going – but obviously they were in the habit of going big.

Big enough to burn a body.

Dave was sorting through the woodpile a few metres away from the pit, adding to a bundle of kindling tucked under his arm. He gave Lane a nod.

Karpathy stood beside the pit, where a white wooden folding table had been set up. It held a caterer's urn that Lane now knew not to hope was for coffee. Next to the urn, he was surprised to see a Bluetooth speaker and an older model iPhone. Lane didn't recognise the song that was playing – something gentle and folky, with guitars and a pipe. He normally didn't mind that sort of music, but something about this song put him on edge. His jaw ached.

'I'm really glad you came,' Karpathy said. He reached out and clasped one of Lane's hands in both of his, like they were meeting after a long absence instead of a bare few hours. He looked over Lane's shoulder. 'And you.'

Lane turned, and was surprised to see Mina not far behind him. Staying clear of each other was obviously going to be harder than it sounded in such a small community. He looked away, careful not to force her to make eye contact.

Mina took a small step back, as if to avoid Karpathy reaching for her, but he didn't. 'Hannah was a special person,' she said.

'This is nice,' Lane said. 'It must have been tough to pull together on such short notice.'

What he really wanted to know was whether impromptu memorial services were something the farm was practised at.

'It's important for us to be able to process things like this as a community,' Karpathy said. 'I'd rather put the effort in to "pull something together" fast than let things fester.'

Rings of benches surrounded the firepit, made from offcuts of gum tree trunks, most with the bark still on. Lane found a seat towards the back that gave him a good view of everyone, albeit some only in side profile.

The song changed, but still something felt off about the music. Lane wondered if the speaker was damaged and buzzing right at the edge of his perception.

Soon the sun had set completely, and the only light source was the roaring bonfire. The seated residents disappeared into the darkness, aside from those closest to the flames. Lane had come up with a shortlist of people who could not be immediately ruled out as Matilda and Alain, although none of them looked strikingly like the missing pair either. Out of the handful of men the right age for Alain, only one had blue eyes like him. There were two women who could possibly be Matilda.

Karpathy stood up, and lifted his voice to speak over the music. 'We're here to mark the passing of Hannah, who was with us for far too short a time, but long enough to take a special place in our hearts. We're going to start by talking about the facts of what happened, and then we'll hold space for anyone to share any feelings that come up. Then we'll make a plan together to support each other.'

Support each other? Or control their emotions?

'Many of you saw Hannah yesterday. She wasn't at breakfast, but by mid-morning she was working with the group setting up sandbags to protect the admin building from rainwater coming down the hill. If anyone wants to share the details of their last conversation with her ...'

'I'd like to,' Dave said, stepping forward from his spot tending the fire.

What was this? It wasn't a eulogy. It felt more like trying to cement an official version of events in place.

'I saw Hannah when I was on my way to the garage to grab a ute. I was headed into town – Albury – to collect our new residents.' He scanned the crowd, as if looking for Lane and Sweeney. Lane made no move to attract his attention. 'We chatted for a bit – about the rain, of course – and then I had to hustle because I was worried I wouldn't make it back before the roads closed. The best we can tell ...' His voice cracked, and he paused to pull himself together. 'The best we can tell, I was the last person ever to speak with her.'

Lane frowned. That didn't make sense. Karpathy had told him she was going to Georges Bridge for sandbags, which neither he nor Dave had known about at the time. If she never spoke to anyone else, who had told them why she was driving to town, and how had they known that?

Karpathy took back the floor with nothing more than a shift in body language. 'There will be a full investigation of the accident, which may reveal more information in time, but we understand that Hannah was driving down Hill Road and lost traction on the turn just before the intersection with the timber track. As you know, from there it's a sheer drop to the valley below. The ute flipped when she hit the edge of the road at speed, and while she survived impact and was able to make a call for help, she died at the scene.'

Lane glanced around the crowd, trying to gauge how the group was reacting. No-one else seemed to find the story strange, although most seemed upset. Sarah burst into tears, and Trish and the woman on the other side of her moved to wrap her in a group hug.

'Sarah, do you want to say something?' Karpathy asked.

Sarah shook her head, but Karpathy didn't move on to someone else. Instead the group sat silent for an excruciating moment, all eyes on Sarah as she wept. A few others in the crowd also began to cry.

'Jeez,' Lane said to himself under his breath. 'This is pretty brutal.'

He searched for Mina in the crowd, expecting to see her looking as bemused as he was, but she had disappeared into herself. She wasn't crying but was rubbing the palms of her hands up and down her thighs, digging the heels of her hands in as if trying to relieve a muscle ache.

He suspected that Hannah's memorial wasn't the one she was thinking of right now.

•

Lane watched Karpathy move through the crowd, hugging people, squeezing their outstretched hands and kissing cheeks. He cast his eye over those who were still seated, and when Lane saw his gaze rest on Mina, who was still hunched over, Lane stood up and strode to meet him halfway, blocking him from approaching her.

'I don't think I've ever attended a memorial quite like this,' Lane said.

'I imagine not. Funeral services are about helping the survivors process their trauma. We've just put a little more science behind it.'

'Science?'

'Yes. I came across it while in the fog after my father died. I was desperately searching for information on how to help a big group of people deal with a shared traumatic event. It's amazing what you can find when you look.'

'Is that your area of expertise? Psychology?'

Karpathy laughed. 'No, although in hindsight maybe I should have gone out for it. I studied agriculture.'

Before Lane could ask if he'd left the farm to do that, Karpathy added, 'At the local TAFE – the same course you're doing. I just went through to the diploma.'

'Perhaps you should recruit a psychologist next,' Lane joked.

Karpathy looked at him, his smile fading a smidge. 'We don't recruit people, Lane. The people who need us find us.'

'Oh? How?' Lane asked.

Before Karpathy could answer, a gunshot cracked through the silent night air.

Lane turned instinctively, frantically scanning the people milling around the bonfire. Looking for injuries. Looking for Mina.

Karpathy put a hand on his shoulder as a second gunshot rang out.

'Breathe, Lane.'

Lane forced himself to let out a breath, realising that no-one else looked more than mildly startled. 'What was that?'

Karpathy pointed out into the black. All the way down in the valley, a powerful spotlight turned on and then off, followed by another gunshot.

'Hunters,' Lane said. 'Your neighbours?'

'Yes, Russ Smith and his sons. We've talked to them about how there are people here with trauma related to guns, but they have to protect their stock. Sometimes they text me when they're gearing up, which is nice of them, but it's not always possible. If they see a fox, they're going to deal with it.'

'Gun trauma? Are you talking about me?' Lane wondered if Mina also had issues with the sound and, if so, what she had shared with Karpathy.

Karpathy squeezed his shoulder. 'I can't share other people's stories with you. But you should consider opening up to the others. You might be surprised who you find a mirror in.'

Of course. Trauma-dumping as a bonding exercise.

A fourth gunshot sounded.

'We did ask the council to set a curfew on hunting, limiting it to the daytime,' Karpathy said. 'But the words they used, if I recall correctly, were "political suicide".'

'Is it possible that might change after the council election you mentioned?'

Karpathy grinned at Lane like he was the most brilliant person he'd ever met. 'No. Even the councillors who are friendly to us on other matters – like building approvals – won't budge. It would take at least one more election cycle to get the numbers we would need.' He let his hand drop back to his side. 'You're a clever guy, Lane. I hope you don't let that go to waste.'

'I don't think that's up to me anymore.'

'You really believe that, don't you? What a shame. Maybe some employers will be small-minded, but there are places that won't waste a sharp mind for stupid reasons. We wouldn't.'

'Stupid reasons like murder and kidnapping charges?' Lane asked. He wanted Karpathy to believe that he was falling for the pitch, but he didn't want him to think he was that naive.

Karpathy shrugged. 'We know who you are … and yet here you are. Think about it.'

•

Back in his room, Lane tried to go over what he had learned as he undressed in the dark, but the long day had turned his thoughts to mush. He would try again in the morning.

Next door, in Sweeney's room, a woman giggled and then whispered an apology. Sweeney said something back in a low voice.

Lane grabbed a pillow off one of the other bunks, and then climbed into his own bed. He pulled the pillow over his head to muffle any sounds from next door, but he needn't have bothered. He was asleep within moments, and didn't know anything except his own jumbled dreams of green eyes and gunshots.

CHAPTER EIGHT

THE DINING HALL was rather less crowded on the second day. Lane had no idea how long the memorial gathering had pushed on after he went to bed, but evidently a lot of people were feeling it the next morning.

Lane met Dave at the kitchen door, and took the two covered plates out of his hands.

'Thanks, mate,' Dave said, and went to join the short breakfast line.

Lane tried not to look at Mina, who was a few spots ahead of Dave. She looked pale, and like she hadn't slept much.

The man who could possibly be Alain stood by the urn, clutching a cup of the not-coffee.

'Good morning,' Lane said.

'Well, it's definitely morning,' the man croaked, in the thickest New Jersey accent Lane had ever heard.

Which took him back to zero possibilities.

Lane sat at the same table from the previous day, and pushed Sweeney's plate over to the empty spot opposite him. He was a little surprised when Sweeney sat down a few moments later. After he'd skipped lunch and dinner, Lane had thought he might have sworn off the farm's food altogether.

Dave joined them, as did Gretel.

'Still having power trouble?' Lane asked her.

She gave him an odd smile. 'I haven't checked yet. I'm sure I'll be able to sort it today.' Once again she had no plate, but took a sip from her glass bottle. Lane wondered if she'd been going home to eat in the dark.

Would it be rude to ask if he could just switch over to eating oatmeal like everyone else? The eggs were the best he'd ever eaten, but he couldn't eat the ham steak and the bread was too weird. He poked it with his fork.

'It's made with zucchini flour,' Dave said. 'It's a little chewy, but I don't mind it. Once you get past expecting it to taste like regular white bread, it's fine.'

'At least it's gluten-free,' Sweeney said.

Lane couldn't help looking over to find Mina, who was surveying her table options. To his surprise, she sat just one table over from them, even though there were seats left in the far corner. However, it was also the only table that was completely empty, so maybe her desire to eat breakfast alone was stronger than her desire to stay clear of him.

'Gluten might not be your problem,' Gretel said. 'They put so many additives and who-knows-what in bread these days.'

'Gluten is definitely the problem,' Sweeney said, although he spoke with an unfamiliar gentleness; Lane had never heard him use a tone that wasn't either snapping or grunting. Lane wondered if Gretel might be the woman he'd heard laughing in Sweeney's room. 'I've got the stomach biopsy results to prove it.'

'Doctors always want to zoom in and refuse to look at the big picture,' Gretel said. 'People these days don't have a clue what's in their food. It's no wonder the world just gets sicker and sicker. Have you ever tried doing a cleanse?'

Mina must have been listening to their conversation, because she groaned out loud.

'I know you're a sceptic,' Gretel said, turning around in her seat to look at Mina. 'But I think if you tried it, you'd be amazed what –'

'I have tried it!' Mina snapped. 'The master cleanse, the liver-cleansing diet, the goddamn magical leek soup. You name it, my mother gave it a go and dragged me along for the ride. You know what it did for her? Fuck-all. She still got cancer. Even when she was dying she struggled with letting herself eat enough.'

'Maybe that was your mother's instincts trying to tell her what her body needed to fight it.'

Mina let her spoon clatter onto the table as she got up and walked out.

Lane put his own cutlery down, flexing his hands open and closed. He wanted to follow Mina, to see if she was alright, but he knew that was the last thing she needed. Still, Lane had yet to see any sign that Mina had friends here, anyone who might support her.

Was this what he'd reduced her to? He'd found some measure of comfort in the belief that he'd made things better for Mina. Before they'd met, she'd been stuck. Haunted by the mystery of what happened to her sister, and tormented by the speculation of others. In the brief glimpses he'd had of her life after him, she seemed to be flourishing. Travelling the country, advocating for the families of victims, connecting with other survivors. But now she'd found a new way to retreat from the world, hiding out here.

Gretel watched Mina go, and then turned back to the others with a sympathetic smile. 'Some people aren't ready to hear it yet.'

Lane didn't want to sit here and chitchat with Gretel – he wanted to jump to Mina's defence. But he was here for a reason, and that was mining for information about Matilda and Alain.

'Have you lived next door long?' he asked.

'Sort of yes, sort of no. My uncle owned the land before I did, so I was around somewhat as a kid.' She chuckled. 'I remember the day Reggie and his wife bought the land; Uncle Greg came in laughing about the nutters moving in down the hill. They were probably down here laughing about the nutter living up the hill.'

'Oh?'

'They were chalk and cheese. This is cattle country, so when the Karpathys showed up talking about goats and compost and organic vegetable gardens, no-one quite knew what to make of them.'

'Your uncle was more traditional?'

'That's the funny part: they probably had more in common than most people around here. My uncle had organic vegetable gardens too, and taught me all about how to grow and hunt my own food. But he also built a cellar almost as big as the house. You know: for when the communists came.' She shook her head, her expression affectionate. 'But I think mostly he took against the Karpathys because they offered the asking price, and he'd been hoping to buy the land cheap. It's tough to make a living farming on lots these small. It's a good size for me, because I only have myself to feed, and I make my money from my pottery business.'

How then was Karpathy making a profit – a sizeable profit, judging from the cars and equipment Lane had seen – on such a small parcel of land? Was there that much money in organic lettuce?

Mina would know, he thought ruefully.

•

By the time Lane left the dining hall, Mina was nowhere to be seen, meaning he'd missed his opportunity to watch her pick a job for the day.

The ticket board was a corkboard hung on the outside wall of the dining hall. It was set up with columns labelled 'to do', 'in progress', 'done' and 'can't progress'. Index cards with tasks written on them were pinned to the 'to do' column; presumably these were the 'tickets' a resident could pull. A little shelf at the bottom held a stack of blank cards and a black marker.

Someone had pinned a postcard to the bottom-left corner showing the familiar half-circle warning sign: *Your fire risk today is moderate – high – extreme – catastrophic*, running from green to red. The card was peppered with pinholes, suggesting that in the summer someone marked the day's fire rating every morning. Today, of course, nothing was marked. Lane had always thought it would be more efficient to use a full circle and add the flood warning level to the bottom, so the scale could run from 'catastrophic flooding' to 'catastrophic fire'.

He examined the cards left in the 'to do' category. He didn't want to risk picking the same job for the day as Mina – she would think he was following her.

Most of the tasks on the board, like weeding, harvesting or caring for various animals, had multiple tickets. There were a few with only one ticket, but they all took skills Lane didn't have, like plumbing or fencing. He was a detective; surely he could deduce which one Mina would be least likely to choose.

His first impulse was that all he had to do to avoid her was check the 'in progress' column and pick a to-do item no-one else was working on already, but there were two problems with that. One was that Mina might not be at work yet; she might be taking some time to collect herself before coming to pick a job. The second was that there were a surprising number of jobs claimed already. He'd assumed, based on the sparse breakfast attendance, that most residents were sleeping in, but maybe they'd decided to work their feelings out in the fields and gardens instead. Or they'd stopped by the board last night to claim an easy job, knowing they'd be feeling it in the morning.

Eventually, as much as he hated the idea, he realised there was only one option – return to the wash-and-pack shed. Mina wouldn't pick the job he'd been doing yesterday, and if she did, he wouldn't be to blame for any awkward encounter that ensued.

•

Working in the wash-and-pack shed had a rhythm that made it easy to think. He'd been so focused on getting to the farm, where he'd been immediately thrown for a loop by Mina's presence, that he hadn't had the chance to plan his next steps.

If he kept his eyes and ears open, then he would pick up an understanding of how the farm worked – and spot any details that might be worthy of suspicion – without putting too much effort in. Where he really needed to focus was on identifying the people who had been at the farm long enough to know something about Alain and Matilda.

Lane was actually enjoying the routine of the work when Karpathy knocked at the door.

'You've got a phone call,' he said.

Lane followed him to the office, mentally running through the reasons why someone would need him on the phone. Carver had got cold feet and pulled the plug. Sweeney had dobbed him in for something and his leave was cancelled. Something was wrong with Lynnie. Lynnie was hurt. Lynnie was dead.

Karpathy pointed at the phone lying on the desk, and Lane waited for a moment, wondering if Karpathy intended to watch him take the call. But he gave Lane a cheery nod and left the room.

'Lane, hi!' Lynnie said at the end of the line, sounding both alive and upbeat. He let himself enjoy a moment of relief. 'I wasn't sure they would actually put me through to you. I got the farm's phone number from their Facebook page and took the punt.'

Lane was tempted to warn her to stay away from the farm's social media accounts – the internet was where they dangled their hooks, and he didn't want her pulled in by them – but he didn't trust that this conversation was private. If Karpathy had handed Lane a mobile phone, he'd have ferreted out any spyware or recording apps in a matter of minutes, but he knew very little about how landlines were tapped. He looked at the handset, which was slim and black, then at the cradle. It was a simple system: a space to hang up the handset and buttons to dial out. Not even an LED screen or anything programmable. He couldn't see any bumps or extras that could be a listening device. He vaguely recalled reading that you could sometimes tell a line was tapped at the start of a call; there might be a tone, or pips, or a few seconds' delay in the connection. But he hadn't been on the line for the beginning of the call.

'Lane, can you hear me?' Lynnie asked.

'Sorry, I think the connection's bad,' he said. 'Can you hang up and call me back?'

He hated lying to her to get what he needed, but if someone was listening, he couldn't very well tell her he was worried about that.

'No worries,' she said. 'That's weird, though – it was crystal clear with the man who answered first.'

They hung up and the phone immediately trilled. He grabbed it with an anxious glance towards the door; he didn't want Karpathy to come in again at the sound.

'Can you hear me now?' Lynnie asked.

'Perfectly,' Lane said. No pips, no oddities, no third person breathing on the line. Of course, all that meant was that he hadn't proved it was an insecure line. He could never prove to his own satisfaction it was actually private.

'I'm sorry I didn't get a chance to see you before you headed down Mexico way,' she said. 'Exams, you know?'

'I'm not actually south of the border. The farm is on the New South Wales side of the river, not in Victoria.'

'Oh, duh,' she said. 'I guess you can't cross state lines, right?'

'I can. But I'd need a valid reason.' He couldn't even leave the property without a valid reason. 'I can't just pop down searching for the good coffee.'

'Why would you? The best coffee's in Canberra.'

'I'm not touching that.' He wished he hadn't brought up the subject of coffee. He was on his third day without any, and he could feel the caffeine headache coming. Right now it was a tight spot of tension in the jaw, but by lunchtime it would be a blinding pain. 'Anyway, the rules are surprisingly generous. You should ask William – I'm sure he knows them backwards and forwards.'

He was proud of how casual he'd kept his tone. His voice hadn't cracked or gone odd at all when mentioning the name of the man who was now doing double duty as Lane's lawyer and his future brother-in-law.

Not casual enough, though, because Lynnie sighed. 'I understand why you're unhappy about this.'

'I'm not unhappy.'

It was true.

He just wasn't happy, either. And in that way, he knew he had robbed himself. He had always imagined that if Lynnie got engaged, he would be overjoyed. He had thought he would have had an inkling it was coming, and be looking forward to it.

He'd never inserted himself into Lynnie's love-life, even when she was growing up in his care. The few boys she'd dated briefly had been quiet and inoffensive. Gentle, nerdy types who she could go to the movies or the beach with. He'd never felt the need to sit outside the front door polishing a handgun. Obviously he'd run background checks on them all, through every legal database his private investigator licence gave him access to and a few dubious sources for good measure. He'd always found and checked their Facebook, Instagram, even Reddit accounts for questionable interests or weird groups. But that was just basic parenting these days. Mostly, Lane had trusted Lynnie to make her own choices. But he'd been there. This time, he hadn't had the option. He wanted to trust this choice, but he had nothing to go on but details that worried him.

'And I'm sure you understand why I'm not happy about what you're doing,' she continued.

'I don't want to talk about that,' he said in a hurry.

'I'm not trying to start the argument again. I'm trying to say, can we just agree to treat each other as adults who are making our own decisions, even if we aren't super thrilled about them?'

'Sure,' he said, feeling anything but. What he wanted was for her to trust his judgement on both matters, but he knew that wasn't fair.

'Do you need anything?' she asked.

Coffee. A phone. The last five years of his life back.

'It's always nice to get a letter,' he said.

The rumble of an engine caught Lane's attention. The farm utes had sat idle in their shed since his arrival, because Dave was concerned about churning up the sodden farm roads. An outside visitor, then? The engine cut out, and two car doors slammed.

'I can do that. Anyway, I've got to get back to work. Want me to call again tomorrow?'

Someone knocked on the outside door of the admin building, hard enough to rattle the thin walls.

'Maybe at the end of the week?' It hurt not to grab the offer for her to call every day, but a daily call was a daily opportunity for Karpathy to chitchat with her before fetching Lane.

They exchanged goodbyes as a conversation drifted down the hallway. Karpathy and two voices Lane didn't recognise. He spun around in the office chair, considering his options. He was in here, with permission, and Karpathy was occupied. Lane eyed the filing cabinets on the far wall.

'Just give us her things,' a man bellowed. 'We're her parents.'

'I know you are, and I'm sorry for your loss,' Karpathy said. 'We all loved Hannah here.'

'We don't want your condolences,' a more soft-spoken woman said. 'We've got a funeral to arrange. We just want to get this done and go.'

'I understand that. But I can't release anything to you until I've been instructed by the executor of Hannah's estate to do so.'

'The executor of her estate?' Hannah's father scoffed. 'She was nineteen, she didn't have a legal will. We're her next of kin and executors.'

'Really, though,' Hannah's mother cut in (Lane wondered if this was their usual dynamic: him getting riled up and her smoothing things down again, or if they were just fracturing in a terrible situation), 'she didn't bring much. We're talking about one suitcase of clothes and her purse. We're happy to leave the wages owing until after it's all settled.'

'No we are bloody well not. You're going to give us the payslips and the money owing right now. That's why he's being such a pig, Maree. Her unpaid wages are going to disappear in a puff of flimflam accounting.'

'Jock, I understand why you are very emotional right now –' Karpathy began.

'We're Mr and Mrs Cudney to you,' Jock snapped.

'Of course. I promise you every cent owed to Hannah will be paid out to whoever she wanted it to go to. We encourage all our residents to have a legal will, and in fact I think I have Hannah's on file. I can get the name of the executor for you.'

The office door opened and Lane straightened in his chair, glad he hadn't been rifling through papers. He hoped he looked like someone stuck in an awkward situation and not an eager eavesdropper.

'Lane, mate, I forgot you were in here,' Karpathy said, looking unruffled. '

'Do you want me to stay? Things seem … heated out there.'

'It's all good. Poor things.' Karpathy wiggled the mouse to wake up his computer.

Lane tried to watch unobtrusively as Karpathy tapped in the password. The first two digits were 6 and 6 again, then Karpathy shifted and blocked his view. The movement seemed casual, and not like he was concerned about Lane behind him, but Lane decided he'd better not push his luck. As he took his leave, he did make a mental note that he'd heard the keyboard clack two more times, so it was a four-digit code, starting with 66.

Not a year then. Potentially a significant date? The sixth of June?

Or just a randomly chosen four-digit number. If that was the case, he had a one in one hundred chance of guessing the remaining two digits. As good as zero, when the computer would lock him out after a few tries.

Lane gave the Cudneys a sympathetic nod as he passed them in the short hallway. Maree Cudney had a tissue pressed to her nose, her eyes red and swollen. Jock's face was red too, but he looked ready to explode with rage, not dissolve into tears.

Lane shut the admin building door firmly behind him, and was halfway down the steps when Jock yelled, 'Who the fuck is Gretel Todd?'

'Someone Hannah trusted to respect her decisions,' Karpathy answered.

As Lane took a step back into the shadows of the verandah, he saw Mina hovering by the gate, looking at the Cudneys' mud-spattered hatchback.

The door slammed, and the Cudneys hurried down the steps, not even glancing Lane's way.

'Excuse me,' Mina said. She pulled the ring off her right hand and held it out. 'Hannah gave me this. You should have it.'

Maree looked at her, incredulous. 'She gave it to you? Are you Gretel?'

'No, I'm …' – Mina fumbled with her words for a moment – 'Deana.'

'This was my grandmother's engagement ring. Who were you to Hannah?'

'No-one.'

Maree took a long look around her, like she'd landed on another planet. 'I hope you go home soon,' she said.

•

Lane had arrived back at the wash-and-pack shed when he heard heavy footfalls behind him. He turned and saw Karpathy approaching.

'Are you going to slum it with me in the wash-and-pack line?' Lane asked, holding the door for him.

'Nobody's above any job here,' Karpathy said. But he leaned against the bench on the far wall, and left Lane to start running cut lettuce leaves under the tap alone. 'I just wanted to check you were okay after what you saw.'

'With Hannah's parents?' Lane asked. 'That sounded harder on you than anyone else.'

'I just thought it might have been distressing for you to hear Jock get so worked up. Seeing a man fly off the handle like that might have brought up some tough memories for you of your own father.'

'What do you know about my father?' Lane asked lightly.

Truthfully, it shook Lane to realise Karpathy was right. Hearing that interaction had shaken him much more than it should have. Some part of him was still that helpless kid getting bellowed at without warning.

'I haven't done a deep dive on you. But I respect you too much to pretend there isn't information out there and I haven't seen some of it.'

That burned. It had always been one of the most useful tools in Lane's belt, being able to share or hide parts of himself and his story to get others to open up. But he would never be a stranger to anyone ever again. His whole story was just a Google search away.

'If I seemed rattled it wasn't because of that,' he said. 'The person on the phone was my sister. Things have been a bit strained lately.'

He didn't want to talk about Lynnie with this man. He wanted to keep himself walled off, not make any room for Karpathy to try manipulating him. But it was impossible to do that while also persuading Karpathy that he was open and ready to be fast-tracked to the inner circle.

'That's rough,' Karpathy said. 'Family can be tricky.'

'Do you have any siblings?' Lane asked, glad for the opportunity for the question to seem natural.

Lane wasn't expecting Karpathy to say, 'Three.'

'Three?' Lane repeated. 'Four kids in a two-bedroom house must have been interesting.'

Lane had grown up in extremely close quarters too and lived in caravans for most of his life. First with his parents, then later with Lynnie. Maybe that was his in. They could commiserate, and Lane could steer the conversation toward Karpathy's childhood, his father, things he might remember.

'It wasn't like that. In fact, I only met my youngest brother when I was executor of my father's will.'

'Wow, how old was he?'

'Twenty.'

'That must have been a shock.'

'I knew he existed. My father was pretty fastidious about that, and he made sure each of my siblings received a portion of his life insurance so that they couldn't try to force the sale of the farm to get their share of the estate.'

Lane had heard of worse – people sometimes willed their descendants one dollar, or a random worthless item, to make it clear they had been denied a larger inheritance on purpose. But still it seemed cold, like Reggie Karpathy had viewed his younger children as nothing but a threat to his favourite.

It must have shown on his face, because Karpathy said, 'I think you're imagining something very different from what actually happened.'

'It's really none of my business,' Lane said, not wanting to seem too eager to dig into Karpathy's background.

'My dad wasn't perfect. He made mistakes. One of those was not realising the discord it would cause to have casual relationships with women living on the farm. Some women thought being with him, having a baby with him, gave them a special status. Then they couldn't handle when they realised it didn't.'

This time Lane worked harder to keep his thoughts off his face. So Reggie Karpathy, in a significant position of power, had been casually seeing women he employed, then treating them like the problem when they thought it meant something. That must have caused quite a bit of drama in the farm's community.

And the youngest was twenty. Which meant he'd been born around the time Matilda and Alain had disappeared. Was that significant, or a complete coincidence?

'Shouldn't they have noticed from their predecessors?'

Karpathy shrugged. 'We're talking about things that happened when I was just a kid. I was fifteen when the last relationship blew up, and she left before her child was even born. But I know they never overlapped.'

'Still, four women in fifteen years –'

'Three,' Karpathy corrected. 'I have an older sister, Naz. Our parents were together until I was nine.'

'Naz?' Lane repeated.

'That's right.'

Could Naz be short for Natalie, the friendly woman who owned the sandwich shop in Georges Bridge? She'd seemed to know Dave quite well, but also had been wary of visiting Karpathy's.

'She doesn't live here on the farm?'

'No. It was the same but different. My mother was angry when she found out my father was going to leave the property to me. She called it medieval and demanded he will it to us as joint owners.'

Lane remembered Karpathy's comments on being compared to the Amish, calling them patriarchal. And yet Karpathy senior had passed over his eldest daughter when it came time to divide his assets.

'She gave him an ultimatum, and they split up. We lived with each parent week-on week-off, until we were old enough to make up our own minds. I chose to live on the farm full-time, and Naz chose to stop coming here altogether.'

Lane thought about the photograph he had found of the two young kids at Christmas. Had Reggie Karpathy come to regret his decisions, in his last years?

'That must have been hard,' Lane said.

'Sometimes. But it wasn't some grand soap opera, either. It's hard to explain when you never met my father. Maybe Dave would do a better job of it. We were a family, but so is the whole farm. Our family wasn't some separate unit inside that whole. Dad didn't love me more than anyone else on the farm, I was just the one who was going to inherit the land. The one in charge of protecting this place.'

Lane's father hadn't loved him at all, but Lane still couldn't wrap his head around what Karpathy was trying to tell him. 'I'm sorry,' he said.

'No! It was good. I was loved deeply, but so was everyone. I guess to some being equally loved feels like being equally unloved. Our culture tells us love can only be real if it's given to one person alone. But I think if you give it time, you'll get it.'

'So you practise free love here?'

Karpathy laughed. 'Not exactly. Plenty of people here are monogamous. We even have couples who are married.'

'But no children,' Lane noted.

Despite the heavy topic, Karpathy had kept a smile on his face, but now he looked grave. 'That's a decision people have made for themselves,' he said firmly. 'But I know my father came to question whether it was ethical of him to choose to bring children into a world with an uncertain future. I feel the same way. If you already know the boat is sinking, you don't keep boarding passengers.'

Ah, Lane thought. Karpathy couldn't tell farm residents that they had to leave if they fell pregnant or decided to start a family – the law was very clear on that. But the implication was obvious.

Lane wondered when Reggie Karpathy's moment of enlightenment about not having any more children born on the farm had arrived. Around the same time as the drama when his youngest son was born? If so, could it have anything to do with Alain and Matilda?

•

When the other man had left, Lane sat, ignoring a tray of unwashed lettuce leaves that someone shunted through the produce window. He felt like he'd just gone three rounds in the ring. Karpathy had clearly felt a need to control the conversation, throwing out curve balls when Lane had been steering it for too long. He'd shared so much, but there hadn't been any real vulnerability in it. He'd been so determined to stay on message, to frame the story the way he needed Lane to understand it. Lane wondered if all new residents of the farm had this conversation with Karpathy at some point. Maybe he'd played that role for a long time, even before Reggie Karpathy died, appearing cheerful and open while subtly laying down the law about how relationships on the farm had to work.

Lane didn't feel closer to Karpathy, but suspected he was supposed to. Wasn't that how Lane tried to present himself to new people? Offering up the information he was willing to divulge in order to get the other person to divulge in turn? The question was: what was Karpathy going to want from Lane?

CHAPTER NINE

'DO YOU HAVE any idea what this welcome ceremony entails?' Lane asked Sweeney, as they walked to the bonfire pit.

'No idea,' Sweeney said. 'If it turns out to be a weird sex thing, you're not allowed to stay.'

The set-up was eerily reminiscent of the previous night, with Hannah's memorial. The only difference was that the residents seemed a little more cheerful, and many had drinks in their hands.

Karpathy greeted them cheerfully, then reached behind the urn and pulled out a silver thermos. 'It's been brought to my attention that you're struggling a bit with caffeine withdrawal,' he said.

Lane was torn between hope for what was in the thermos and concern that someone (perhaps even multiple people) had been observing him and reporting back to Karpathy.

'Green tea,' Karpathy said, untwisting the lid. 'It has caffeine, but much less than coffee does. There's enough to stop the headaches, but after a few days your body will adjust to the lower amount, and you can go down to zero with way fewer side effects.'

'I appreciate that,' Lane said.

'It's my fault entirely, usually I warn people to wean off before they arrive. We're learning so much from you already about how we can do better in the future.'

Lane kept a smile on his face, even though the words chilled him. 'So, do I need to stand somewhere in particular? Is there some kind of hat involved? A feat of skill?'

'Come stand with me by the fire,' Karpathy said.

Lane really hoped he wasn't going to ask him to walk on hot coals.

'We know that arriving at the farm can be intimidating. Some of us have lived here a long time, and it's never easy being a new person. To help ease the way, we like to give all new arrivals a buddy.'

Oh no. Lane took it back. He'd definitely rather walk over hot coals.

'Deana?' Karpathy asked. Mina stepped out of the crowd, her face stony. Karpathy took her hand, and then Lane's, and then put their hands together.

Lane couldn't help but note that this was a tactic of high control groups – pairing up new members with a buddy to supervise them.

'Of course, we have two new arrivals to celebrate tonight,' Karpathy continued. 'This is a bit out of the ordinary, but in Hannah's sad absence, Gretel has offered to stand in her place.'

Mina still hadn't pulled away from him, and so Lane didn't either.

'Gretel, have you brought a gift for Rick?'

A gift. Lane remembered Sarah mentioning giving Hannah a gift, dropping it into the conversation like it held significance. Had Sarah been Hannah's buddy, then?

Gretel took Sweeney's hand, and rolled something up onto his wrist.

'A women's bracelet?' Sweeney asked, examining it in the firelight.

In the group, someone gasped.

'The point of the gift isn't what it means to the recipient,' Karpathy explained. 'The gift is something precious to the giver.'

Lane was struck by how manipulative that was. A newcomer suddenly became the custodian of their buddy's sentimental item, forcing a bond between them. And that would make it extremely difficult for the gift-giver to leave the farm, if it meant leaving a precious item behind.

'Deana?' Karpathy asked.

Lane had a horrible vision of Mina giving him something designed to torment him. A stuffed snake. A shell casing.

She moved her hand so she was cupping his with his palm up. She lifted her other hand up, her fist closed, and placed it in his open hand. She looked him dead in the eye and opened her fist a little, dropping absolutely nothing into his hand.

In a way it was a precious gift. She was trusting him enough not to reveal to the others that she was faking. He closed his hand around it and pulled it close to his chest with a grateful nod.

•

Gretel walked with Lane and Sweeney as they made their way back to their cabin. Theirs was the last one in the row, so it made sense for her to walk that far with them if she planned to carry on up the hill and back to her home for the night.

Lane paused at the gate when he heard running feet on the gravel.

'Hey,' Sarah called out.

'Yes?' Lane asked.

'Not you.' She sniffed, and scrubbed at her nose. She pointed to Sweeney's wrist. 'You can't give my bracelet away. That's not right.'

'It's not yours,' Gretel said mildly. 'You gave it to Hannah. She trusted me to distribute her things. Hannah isn't here to give gifts to any future buddies, so I think it's right for Rick to have it.'

'My grandmother gave that to me for my eighteenth,' Sarah said. 'Hannah knew that I would need it back before I left.'

'Sarah,' Trish hissed. 'You're not supposed to talk about leaving.'

'It's really fine,' Sweeney said. 'I don't need a women's bracelet.'

'Wait, why can't you talk about leaving?' Lane asked.

'It's nothing,' Gretel said.

Sweeney went to take the bracelet off, and Gretel put a hand on his arm. 'No,' she said.

Lane expected Sweeney to shake her off. It was just a bracelet, and it clearly meant a lot to Sarah. But instead he looked at Gretel, then down at the bracelet.

'Sorry,' he said to Sarah, and then he pushed past Lane to go through the gate and into his side of the cabin.

HIS STOMACH MUSCLES *began to quiver, rattling against his already upset stomach. He paused, let his forehead rest on the floor. The rest of his body followed suit without him deciding to do so. 'That tremble is good,' the yoga instructor's voice said. He'd long forgotten her face, but whatever managed the files of his mind had decided her voice was worth holding on to forever. 'When we're anxious, our body tenses up. That tremble forces you to let go of all that trauma.'*

He'd been primed like a pump, hadn't he?

CHAPTER TEN

LANE HAD HIS pants halfway up when the door to Sweeney's side of the cabin swung open.

'Time to head to the office and juice up your leash,' Sweeney said, ignoring Lane's frantic rush to get himself properly clothed.

'Doesn't the battery last a week?'

'They're on solar here,' Sweeney said. 'Between the shitty weather and their system being cobbled together with duct tape and hope, the department thinks it's too high risk. If the power goes out and your battery runs down before it comes back on, you'll get a window of opportunity to peace out. So I get an alert as soon as you hit forty-nine per cent.' He tapped his smartwatch.

Sweeney escorted him to the admin building, grumbling under his breath about having an extra work task to do, and hooked Lane up to the charging cable. It was a little over a metre long, giving him a decent amount of freedom to move in the small office.

Lane crossed his fingers, hoping he and Sweeney weren't about to spend an hour staring at each other in silence while the ankle bracelet charged. To his relief, once Sweeney was satisfied it was charging correctly, he headed for the door, ignoring the cheerful, 'Goodbye,' Lane said to his back.

Lane counted to one hundred, just in case Sweeney changed his mind and came back, before stepping forward. Moving carefully – not wanting to accidentally tug the charger loose – he tested how far he could go. The desk, the door and the filing cabinets were all within his range.

First he needed to check for a camera. If there was one, it would capture him searching for it, but that would be easier to explain away than getting filmed tossing the room.

Someone had left one of the headlamps lying on the edge of the desk. He picked it up and then closed the window blinds. Some light still leaked in around the edges, but it was dark enough for his needs. He looked around for any small points of light that might be a camera.

No lights. He flicked on the headlamp and moved the beam slowly around the room, searching in a grid pattern. First up high in the corners of the ceiling, then across the walls, then over the floor and under the furniture. Not all cameras had a light, but even the tiniest had a lens, and it would reflect the torchlight back at him.

Nothing. Satisfied, he put the torch away and turned on the overhead light.

It occurred to him that Karpathy had showed no signs of being protective of this room. This was the second time Lane had been left alone in it, so it was unlikely there was anything sensitive within easy access. The only place Karpathy seemed protective of was the locked door leading to the shed at the other end of the building.

Lane tried the computer first. He didn't know how many guesses at the passcode it would give him before locking him out, so he decided to err on the side of caution and limit himself to three. He knew from watching Karpathy that the first two digits were 66, so he opted for the systematic approach. 6600. 6601. 6602.

With one hundred possible combinations and three attempts every four days, he would manage to unlock it before his six months here were up, but there had to be a better way.

He left it, and turned instead to the filing cabinets, tugging on the drawer marked *A–C*. It didn't budge.

He cast his eyes around the room and found a coffee cup filled with rings of keys. He sifted through and found a pair at the bottom that were the right size and shape for filing cabinets. The key fit perfectly, and he started flipping through employee files, starting from the back. He noted there wasn't one for Hannah Cudney, but he quickly came to one labelled *Carver, Matilda*.

He pulled Matilda's file out with shaking hands. He'd been starting to feel like she was a ghost, that nobody would ever admit she'd been here. But here it was: undeniable proof. Flipping through the file, he found a handwritten application for a farmhand job, listing her experience with fruit picking and livestock handling, but no contact details for references. There was a printout of her days worked, and her hourly wage. Next was a payslip, which matched the calculation of hours worked and money earned. The payslip was dated six months after she was reported missing, and seemed to cover the entire time she had worked at the farm to that date.

There was a photocopy of a cheque made out to cash, and a bank reconciliation showing it had been cashed at an Albury bank the day after it was issued. Something had been written at the bottom of the page, but it was redacted with a black marker. He turned the paper over, hoping whoever originally wrote it had pressed hard enough to still make it out, but was disappointed.

The last page in the file chilled him. It was a printout of Matilda's Missing Persons profile. So those on the farm had known that the police were looking for her but had done nothing to help.

He replaced the file in the drawer and moved down to *S–V*. Alain Serling's file was nearly identical to Matilda's. A handwritten application form. The time tracker, a cheque issued and bank reconciliation. His cheque was issued and cashed two months after Matilda's, Lane saw. There were no notes, written or redacted.

There was a copy of his Missing Persons profile.

And one more document. A printed topographical map of the farm. Someone had marked it with an *X*.

•

What possible reason could there be for a map like that in an employee file? Why file copies of Missing Persons reports?

Because they were keeping tabs on the cases? Out of concern for missing friends? Or to track whether the investigation's spotlight was drifting too close to the farm?

It was proof that the farm was hiding *something*. Otherwise they would have reached out to the police to provide updated information on Matilda's last known location. Until he'd read those files, Lane was beginning to wonder whether there was nothing to see here. The way Karpathy ran the farm was a little controlling, maybe. A little weird, definitely. But nobody seemed unhappy, or frightened. The farm threw up roadblocks when people wanted to leave, but they could and did leave all the time.

Brandon Roby had reminded him that sometimes adults wanted to disappear. For most of his career, Lane had focused on missing children, where that wasn't a realistic possibility. But for adults, disappearing by choice was much more likely than murder.

So what was the map for?

A big part of Lane wanted to leave the office and immediately sprint down the hill to see what he might find at the spot marked on the map. But he needed to be smarter than that. The hilly layout of the farm meant that it was hard to move around unobserved, and if he tried anything in broad daylight, someone might spot him and ask questions he couldn't answer. Especially with the little houses arranged high on the hill – he had no way of knowing if there was someone inside watching out their window.

Instead he forced himself to be patient, and took a few days to learn the evening routine of the farm. He took his time with his evening meals, and stayed in the dining hall afterward, reading a book from the swap shelf in the corner, or chatting to anyone who was willing.

Now that the rain had cleared up, and the spring days were lengthening, a lot of the farm residents went back to work after dinner. Others hung around, chatting or playing music. But almost all of them disappeared as the sun did, heading back to their cabins before it became too dark.

Lane walked back to his own cabin each night and leaned against the front fence. It was hard to wait – after long days washing lettuce and packing boxes, he wanted to go straight inside and collapse into bed. But he stayed awake, needing to check if the rest of the farm also settled into sleep, or if there was a nightly security patrol, or a second shift of workers with tasks that had to be done in the night.

There was no way for Lane to set an alarm, so on the night he was ready to make his expedition, he sat cross-legged on his bed to keep himself awake.

When he estimated it had been an hour since he last heard anyone make noise, he got up. Of course, it might have only been minutes – it was hard to judge time without a clock, and sitting in the dark doing nothing made it even harder.

He stepped carefully in his socked feet to avoid waking Sweeney on the other side of the thin wall. If he did wake up, he could always say he was on his way to the toilets, but it would kill any chance of walking to the marked spot tonight.

He might face questions if Sweeney checked his GPS history in the morning, but he knew he would have better luck asking for forgiveness than permission. He'd say he couldn't sleep and went for a walk. It wasn't even a lie.

Outside he fumbled to put his boots on in the dark. He couldn't remember the last time he'd been in such absolute darkness. No streetlights, no verandah lights left on by neighbours, no hallway fluorescents. Just dark. He turned in a circle, and the only light he could see was something red blinking in the sky – a satellite, or maybe a plane.

He eased the door open again and grabbed the little push light off the wall. It would light him up like a beacon, but his night vision just wasn't good enough. He'd trip in the dark and go arse over tit down the hill.

He had to work from memory – he hadn't dared steal the map from the file – but the marked spot had looked easy to find: a large, mostly flat area about halfway down the hill. He wove around the toilet block, then slipped into the little alley between the dining hall and the admin building. He paused there for a moment, looking at the shed that Karpathy had warned him not to enter. The shed had no windows, but there was a whirlybird on the roof for ventilation. Was he imagining it, or was there a faint glow, like a light was on inside?

He clicked his own light off and stepped close to the shed, putting a hand on the corrugated-iron wall to navigate by. He pressed an ear to the metal, straining to hear if anyone was moving around inside. He couldn't make out anything but caught a crackle of noise somewhere behind him. Movement on the gravel road.

He pushed himself against the wall. An animal? A person? He waited, but silence surrounded him. He resumed walking.

Even after a few days of sunshine, the grass underfoot was wet and slippery as he made his way downhill. He almost lost his footing a few times. He couldn't see any further than a foot in each direction, so he focused on listening for any hint that someone was coming to see what he was up to. A few times he thought he heard movement, clicked off the light and froze in place, but nothing came of it.

When he reached the plateau that he was sure matched the one marked on the map, he lifted the light as high as he could to scan the area. At the very edge of the glow, he saw the corner of a squat little hut, built from mudbricks. For a moment he wondered if the map had marked a claimed house site – if he knocked on the door, would he find Alain living inside? Then the overwhelming smell hit him. He shifted the light, tracing to the other corner of the building, which supported a pipe fence. The fence surrounded a patch of earth, bare of any plant life and thick with stinking mud.

His heart sank. It was the pig shed.

If his suspicion was right, and the X marked a burial site, then they had built a pig shed on top.

He'd planned to look for signs of a clandestine burial – uneven patches of soil, discolouration, unusual plant growth – but what did that even look like underneath a building?

He paced the outside, examining the walls for cracks or damage that might indicate the building had shifted as something decayed down below. Once he reached the far side, he took a deep breath, then grabbed the top bar of the fence. He examined the ground of the yard, trying not to breathe in. It was useless. The space was being actively wallowed by pigs – it was nothing but uneven patches and discolouration.

He peered inside the door, which stood open. The pigs were asleep, piled together in one corner. He was startled by the size of them. He'd been picturing something pink and the size of a dog, not these great black-and-white beasts.

He stepped inside carefully, keeping one eye on the pigs in the corner. The floor was covered in straw, damp and earthy-smelling. A pitchfork leaned against the far wall, and he grabbed it. He put his light down on the floor so he could rake the straw into a pile, revealing the floor was built from the same mudbrick as the walls. He sighed.

He stepped back into the slightly fresher air of the yard and wondered what the hell he was doing. If he did find some sign of a burial under there, what then? Was he going to call the police and have them come dig it up? He'd be laughed off the phone.

The sound of heavy breathing cut through his thoughts. He looked over to the door of the hut to see one of the pigs standing there, staring at him. It took a step forward, and the light went out, crushed under its back foot.

In absolute darkness, Lane asked himself a question he should have considered before climbing into a pigpen: were they dangerous? The only thing he knew about pigs was that they would happily eat a human body. Did the body need to be dead first?

He sprinted forward from the pen, hands out in front of him, knowing that any direction he went would bring him to the fence even if he couldn't see it. Cold water splashed up his calf as he ran through a puddle, but he kept going.

The next puddle turned out to be knee-deep; the mud at the bottom sucked at his foot, refusing to let go. Behind him he could still hear the pig breathing.

'Fuck!' he snapped, not caring anymore if anyone could hear him.

Light dazzled his eyes. He heard a sound like someone shaking a can full of marbles, and Mina's voice rang out.

'Go to bed, you little shit, you've been fed and you know it.'

In the light, Lane could see the fence within easy reach. He'd been about to run full tilt into it. He grabbed on and hauled his leg free, then he clambered over and landed on the other side in a muddy heap.

'Why do you keep trying to get yourself murdered by animals?' Mina asked. The beam of her headlamp cut across him as she stormed around to meet him. In one hand she had a noisemaker made from an old Milo tin, and in the other a long thin stick with a loop of cable on the end.

'I didn't think pigs could kill me. People make children's movies about them!'

'They make children's movies about pirates, and they killed people all the time.'

Lane climbed to his feet. He almost wiped his knees, then realised just in time that he absolutely didn't want any of that muck on his hands if he could help it. 'Thank you,' he said, stepping into her light.

She stepped back and swung the stick around so it was between them. Up close he realised it was a snare, the loop designed to slip over an animal's head and catch them by the neck. Judging by the easy way she handled it, Mina knew exactly how to use it.

Was that the plan then? Was that why she hadn't turned him in? So she could catch him one night in the dark, silence him permanently and feed him to the pigs?

He didn't believe it, but he did believe the white-knuckled grip she had on the stick.

He held his hands up, palms facing her, to show he didn't have anything hidden.

'Give it back,' she said.

'Give what back?'

She rolled her eyes. 'The letter.'

Lane was lost. The letter? The only letters he could think of were the ones the department had sent her. Why would he have them? She'd said she didn't even get them.

Or had she sent him a letter? One she thought he could blackmail her with?

'I've never received a letter from you,' he said. 'If you sent me one the governor must have confiscated it.'

He had no idea why Carver would do that, but given the number of secret schemes the governor was running, it wasn't implausible.

'Knock it off,' she said. 'You snuck into my room and went through my things. You took one of the letters.'

'I have no idea what you're talking about,' he said, bewildered. 'But I can prove that I haven't been in your room.' He pointed at the ankle bracelet. 'You can ask Sweeney to check my GPS history.'

Her expression wobbled, and she lowered the snare. 'If I do that he'll see your little jaunt tonight.'

'Going to visit the pigs in the middle of the night might be weird, but it's not really against the rules. Not like going into a cabin without permission.'

'Who else would go through my things?'

It stung a little that she thought he was a person who might do that, but he couldn't really fault her for it. 'What was the letter about?'

'It's a long story.'

'It's a long walk back up the hill.'

As they began walking, Mina said, 'Before I tell you anything, you need to level with me. I've never met anyone less suited to life as a farmer. Why are you really here?'

'I'm on a case, sort of. I'm trying to find a missing woman, Matilda Carver. She stayed here twenty years ago, and nobody has seen her since. Another man went missing within a couple of months of her: Alain Serling. I thought there was a third case, but he turned out to be hiding, not missing.'

She stopped walking and turned to face him. 'So other people have gone missing from here?'

'What do you mean, other people?'

'I'm looking for someone too. Rebecca Goncharov. She worked here for about half a year and then left, saying she was going to take the train to Melbourne. That was six years ago. She was never seen again.'

'Six years ago?' Lane's heartbeat quickened. 'I've been over the Missing Persons cases in this area back to front and upside down. Why haven't I seen Rebecca's profile?'

Mina sighed. 'Probably because she's not considered to be missing from here. She got on the train in Albury and called her family from Melbourne to say she'd arrived. That was the last communication anyone had from her. But in six years, no-one has come forward saying they actually saw her down there. Not a single frame of CCTV footage, no activity on her bank cards. The family are convinced Reggie Karpathy knew more than he admitted. A few years ago they persuaded the Melbourne police to talk to him again, but they ended up sending out a Georges Bridge officer, who reported back the same story Karpathy had told before: that Rebecca had left and they hadn't heard from her since. So we decided that if the police weren't going to push forward with the investigation, we would have to take it into our own hands.'

'Why you? Are you related to the Goncharovs?'

'The last couple of years I've been doing advocacy work for the families of Missing Persons. It started out as …' She hesitated.

'Go on, I think I know what you're going to say. It's alright.'

'It started out as looking at the cases you had notes on. The ones who could be other victims of your father.'

'The Karpathy farm is inside his travel range, but adult women and men weren't his preferred victims.' His father had killed at least one adult man, but only to help conceal another crime.

'Like I said, it's just where I started. Through that I met other families searching for their loved ones. I realised I could do more good for them than chasing your father's ghost. There's a lot that could be better – legislation, police procedures, media regulations. So I write letters, and go to meetings with politicians, and attend inquests to support the families. That's how I met Rebecca's family. They told me they'd already tried to come here themselves and ask around. They were stonewalled.'

Lane felt vindicated by that; he'd been right to caution Carver against coming here himself.

'The Goncharovs were devastated. So I asked myself: what would Lane do?'

Lane was touched, until she continued.

'You'd refuse to take no for an answer and trample every boundary between yourself and the truth. So I decided to take a more subtle approach and come here myself – not as a friend of Rebecca, but as a prospective resident. I lived on a farm for most of my life, I knew I could handle a few months here.'

'And the fake name?'

'I was worried they might have a blacklist of people linked to Rebecca. A few articles on the inquest mentioned I was there. And I didn't want to come into a situation like this knowing they could look up my name online and find out everything about me. I invented a tragic backstory about losing my father recently. Karpathy tries to use that sometimes to manipulate me. Since daddy issues are about the only trauma I don't suffer from, it doesn't work.'

'Careful. Thinking they can't manipulate you is a dangerous assumption. Whatever's going on here, they've been sharpening their axe for twenty years.'

They reached the top of the hill, and Mina pointed to a small outbuilding behind the admin building. 'You should stop and wash those clothes. Has anyone showed you the laundry?'

'We'll wake up Karpathy if we do that. Isn't his bedroom in the admin building?'

'It's all the way at the front, and the machines are pretty quiet,' she said. She headed that way and he had to follow, as she had the only light.

'If there's someone in there, they'll hear it,' he said, pointing to the locked shed.

'Why would someone be in there at two in the morning?'

'There's a light on,' he said. 'Do you know what they use it for?'

She shook her head, making the light bob about. 'It must be above my clearance level. But someone probably just left a lamp on.'

He wavered for a moment, then nodded. It might cause trouble if someone in that shed heard them, but it would definitely cause trouble if he went back to his cabin covered in pig muck.

There was an awkward moment when they entered the laundry. There was no overhead light, so Mina needed to stay while he stripped off his muddy clothes and bundled them into the wash. For once he was grateful for the farm's interchangeable uniform, as he was able to quickly find and pull on a slightly too small shirt and a slightly too large pair of pants from a pile of clean clothes waiting to be folded.

'Tell me about Alain and Matilda,' Mina said once the machine was humming beside them.

He told her the little he knew. Her eyes widened when he mentioned the files he'd found, and the map.

'How did you connect Alain and Matilda to the farm? The inquest didn't pick up their cases.'

'Social media. Old photographs. The electoral rolls.'

Her eyes widened. 'The electoral rolls. That's genius.'

He shrugged. 'I do have some idea what I'm doing as an investigator, even if I am a little rusty.'

And with that he'd made it awkward again. Mina's smile froze, and Lane figured, since he'd already brought up the elephant in the room, the mood couldn't be ruined any further.

'We could help each other,' he said. 'The two cases have to be connected; this many missing people in two decades can't be a coincidence.'

And, much as he hated to put Matilda and Alain on the backburner, he had a much better chance of cracking Rebecca's case. Six years was so much easier than twenty. So many more of the people he'd met so far had been around then. Like Dave.

Mina stared at him, and for a moment he really thought she was going to go for it. Then she sighed. 'Lane, you and me … I think we're like bleach and ammonia. Toxic enough on our own, but mix us together and there'll be no survivors.'

He wanted to fight for her help, but if he did, he'd just be proving her point. 'Can you at least tell me what you've found out about this place so far?'

Mina leaned in and dropped her voice. 'Nothing.'

'Nothing?'

'As best I can tell. I arrived a few months ago, expecting to bust open, I don't know … a serial-killing cult. A human organ trafficking ring. Suicide pacts. Something.' She shrugged. 'But they're just people living on a farm. Being a pack of weirdos isn't a crime, and god help us all if it was.'

'Then where's Rebecca?'

She sighed. 'That's the tricky part. I can't just go up to people and ask. I remember watching you question people about my sister's case, but that was different. Everyone knew who she was, and knew that you were in town to look for her. Any question I ask about Rebecca here risks blowing my cover.'

Lane had encountered the same problem, so he sympathised. 'We need some kind of icebreaker,' he mused. 'To create a situation where her name would come up naturally.'

Mentally he wrote that down on an index card and pinned it to a noticeboard, hoping some part of his subconscious would pull the ticket and work out a solution.

'We?'

'Sorry. We, as in you and me, separately, not bothering each other,' he said.

'That's not going to work. We can't go around poking into the same case separately. The right hand won't know what the left is doing, and we'll both end up with maps in our employee files.' She sighed. 'I'm being ridiculous. I should go home.'

He couldn't argue with her logic.

She did it for him. 'You're not going to be able to do this on your own, though.'

'Why not?'

'Because there are people here who won't ever be comfortable talking to you.'

'Because I'm a criminal.'

'Not just a criminal. A man. They might talk to me, but I don't have the skills to investigate. You have the skills, but they won't talk to you.' She ran her hands through her hair.

She wanted to agree to work together, he could feel it, but if he pushed, she'd just go back to arguing against the idea.

'What about the letter that was taken?' he asked instead. 'What was in it?'

'I'm not sure. I have a stack of letters that Rebecca sent to her family while she was staying here. I kept them in my bag, and someone has taken one. I'm not sure which one, but I counted them and it's definitely one short.'

'When was this?'

'I think today, while I was helping to move the goats. It's not like I count the letters every day, but when I came back into my room, I was immediately sure someone had been messing with my bag. It felt off.'

'Are there other people in your room? I'm alone in a room set up for six.'

'Yeah. There're four cabins that sleep twelve each, but none of them are full. Karpathy likes to have room for new arrivals. There are four of us in my room.' She made a face. 'Three. I'm still not used to it.'

'You were sharing with the girl who had the accident? Hannah?'

She nodded. 'She arrived a few weeks before I did. It was me, Hannah, Sarah and Trish.'

'Do you think Sarah or Trish might have gone through your things?'

'Why would they take a letter?'

'Why would anyone?'

'That's what's bothering me. Why just one? Why take any at

all? If there's something important in that letter, I've already read it, and I can always get another copy.'

'They're not the originals?'

'The ones I have are photocopies. Rebecca's mother still has them all.'

'Are they actual letters, or emails?'

'Actual letters,' Mina said. 'She was very into scrapbooking, and illustration. They're beautiful. They're full of little botanical sketches and self-portraits.'

'And you can get another copy?'

'I'd need a few days. I can call Rebecca's parents, see if they'll mail them. Then I can compare and see what's missing.'

'That might not be safe,' Lane said. 'You said you don't have your own phone, and I don't know how secure the phone in the office is.'

'That's a bit paranoid, isn't it?'

'Someone went through your things,' Lane pointed out. 'Someone knows you have those letters. Someone knows why you're really here, and we don't know who. I think a little paranoia is rational.' Which reminded him. 'Has Karpathy ever said or done anything to make you suspect he knows who you really are?'

She shook her head.

'It's just …' He didn't want to admit he might have outed her, but he had to. 'If he's read articles about me, surely he's seen pictures of you.'

'Not necessarily,' she said. 'Most of the articles had pictures of you, your father or Evelyn. Technically your kidnapping victim was never named. Anyone with half a brain cell knows it was me, but I've never formally agreed to be identified. Running a picture of me alongside an article about you and 'an unidentified woman' would have been sailing pretty close to the wind. If Karpathy went one jump further and looked up Evelyn, he would have seen plenty of pictures of me, but it's no sure thing.'

'Maybe.' Lane wasn't convinced. 'Just be careful around him.'

Lane checked the timer on the washing machine. Twenty minutes left. An awkwardly long time for them to hang around together, and yet desperately short.

'You mentioned you were sharing with Hannah,' he said. 'What was she like?'

Something about Hannah's accident still didn't sit right with him. She wasn't supposed to be out on the road, in that ute.

'Nice, I guess. We didn't really click. She hung around with Gretel a lot.'

'Gretel's the neighbour, right?' What Lane wouldn't do for a notebook so he could keep this stuff straight.

'Yep.'

'The one who won't eat food grown here?'

Mina sighed. 'If you think there's a hot lead there, I'm sorry to disappoint. She's even weirder than the people who live here.'

'You really don't like her, huh?'

'My mother had a pretty twisted relationship with food. Carbs were the enemy – no, wait, fat was the enemy – whoops, back to carbs. She was obsessed with every superfood fad the magazines latched onto, because if goji berries were a nutritional powerhouse you could eat a handful and skip dinner. When

Gretel gets into that territory, it's like nails on a chalkboard to me.'

'I'm sorry.' Lane's mother had been of the belief that teenage boys could eat anything they wanted. The closest thing Lane had ever got to nutritional advice was: 'The Pluto Pups in the hot food van are past their sell-by date – if you call them out on it, they'll give one to you for free.' He couldn't empathise with Mina, but he could sympathise.

'Did Hannah tell you where she was going, the night she died?'

Mina tilted her head. 'What's this about?'

'I don't know. Don't you think it's a little suspicious? Three missing people, and then an accidental death?'

Mina looked like she was going to argue with him, then relented. 'She didn't tell me where she was going, no. I noticed she didn't come to bed, but that wasn't unusual.'

'Was she seeing someone?'

'No-one specific. She was young – maybe twenty-two? There're a lot of young people here; if a bed is empty one night, it doesn't raise any eyebrows. I did notice when she wasn't at breakfast that day, but I never imagined something like this. I thought maybe she'd just left.'

'Would she have said goodbye to you, if she was leaving?'

'No,' she said, with a finality that surprised him. 'She never skirted the rules.'

'The rules?'

'When people leave here, they don't say goodbye,' she explained. 'If you're going, you need to just go. No parties, no hugs, no weepy farewells. People leaving can cause a domino effect, and Karpathy doesn't want to deal with losing a huge chunk of his workforce all at once.'

That made a twisted sort of sense. But it also made it more difficult to decide this place wasn't for you: leaving the farm meant leaving everyone on the farm and, for those who'd come searching for connections, being abruptly alone again.

It also made it much easier to cover up deaths, if residents thought it was normal for people to simply disappear.

But if Hannah had decided to leave, she would have told Karpathy, and she wouldn't have taken one of the farm utes. So the question remained: why was she on the road that night?

When the washing cycle had finally finished, they hung up Lane's clean clothes on the drying racks. As he stepped out into the early morning dark, he realised his mistake.

'Crap,' he said. 'I dropped my light in the pigpen.'

'I've got a light,' she said. 'I'll walk you back to your cabin.'

'Is it safe for us to go get the light back? Will the pigs leave me alone if you're with me?'

'You can get a replacement light from the storeroom.'

'I'm more worried about someone finding it.'

'No chance,' she said, clicking on her headlamp. 'You saw how boggy the pen is. That light will be buried under half a metre of mud by morning. Besides, as long as you replace yours without anyone noticing, if they somehow find it they'll have no way of knowing it was yours. Every cabin has the same lights.'

The same lights. Just like they all wore the same clothes and ate the same foods.

Lane glanced at the dark windows of the other cabins as they passed. 'We should probably get our stories straight in case anyone saw us wandering around out here.'

'Lane' – amusement coloured her voice – 'if anyone saw a man and a woman sneak out in the middle of the night to do a load of laundry, they're not going to ask why, they'll draw their own conclusions.'

CHAPTER ELEVEN

LANE WAS PICKING at his breakfast, struggling to keep his eyes open, when Mina dropped heavily onto the bench opposite him.

'Good morning?' he said, a little uncertain. 'It's Deana, right?' he added, worried it would look odd if he was suddenly very familiar with her when she'd been avoiding him until now.

She smirked. 'And you're Lane, yeah?' She poked at her oatmeal. 'I hear it's going to be a busy day today. It's cheese day tomorrow, so there'll be a bit of a scramble to finish any jobs that can't wait for the day after. Are you going to man the wash-and-pack shed again?'

'I suppose.' Lane had been sticking with that job to avoid stepping on Mina's toes, but he'd hoped to branch out a bit now that they'd reached a new understanding. The wash-and-pack shed was a great place to think, but he'd really like to sign up for a job with more opportunities to talk to people, like weeding and harvesting in the gardens, or a kitchen shift.

'It might need another set of hands today,' she said. 'They're harvesting extra, trying to get the lettuce out before it bolts.'

Lane gave her a quick nod. 'Do you want my ham steak?'

'God, yes.' She stabbed it with her fork with a speed that startled him. 'I'm starving.'

•

They were halfway to the shed when Karpathy called out his name from the admin building verandah. 'Phone call,' he shouted.

Mina looked at Lane, anxiety etched on her face.

'My sister,' he explained. The days had started to blur together so much that he had forgotten he'd arranged to talk to Lynnie again today.

'Tell her I said hi,' Mina said. 'In spirit, I mean. Please don't actually tell her I'm here.'

'Never,' he said, and hustled back to the admin building.

•

'How's farm life?' Lynnie asked. She was calling from somewhere outside – he could hear the faint murmur of voices in the background, and a light wind. He pictured her sitting at an outdoor table of a cute little cafe, or maybe in the quad before her first lecture of the day.

'It's an adjustment,' he admitted. He glanced over at the closed office door, then switched the call over to speaker. 'Apparently we're making cheese tomorrow, which everyone is very excited about.'

Making small talk felt like lying, even if everything he was saying was true. There was so much about life here, what he was really doing with his time, that he had to leave out.

'Cheesemaking sounds fun,' she said.

'I guess.' He fished the filing cabinet key out of the coffee cup and opened the drawer marked *G–J*. There was no file labelled *Goncharov, Rebecca*, even though Rebecca had definitely been at the farm. Had the file been destroyed when her family pushed too hard? Or was her file somewhere else?

'It could be a really useful skill,' Lynnie said. 'You never know. Maybe you'll find out you love it. You could start a cheesemaking business. Be your own boss.'

He flipped through a few more files and came across *Harrington, David*, a file that would have been established ten years ago. He noted that there was no *Holland, Lane*. He checked the R's, confirming there was no *Roby, Brandon*.

When Hannah's parents came, Karpathy hadn't gone to the filing cabinet; he'd unlocked the computer. So at some point more than six years ago but less than ten, they'd stopped keeping paper employee files.

'Lane? Are you still there?'

'Yes, sorry. I was caught up in imagining myself as a professional cheesemaker.' He sat down at the computer desk and wiggled the mouse to wake the screen up, then had another go at guessing the last two digits of the passcode. 6604. 6605. 6606.

No luck today.

'You think you'd be into it?'

'No, the only way I could see it happening is if I had a magical talking rat piloting me like in that Pixar movie.'

'I don't think that rat could talk.'

'Hey, did you send me that letter yet?' he asked. He went back to the filing cabinet and found the *K*'s. He wasn't sure if they would have employee files for the family members, but to his relief they were all there: *Karpathy, Reginald*; *Karpathy, Samuel*; *Karpathy, Tatiana*. It was a stretch, but could 'Naz' be a nickname for Tatiana? Or could Tatiana be Sam's mother?

'I'm still working on it,' she said. 'I want to send you something, and I'm waiting for it to arrive.'

'It's not, like, a cummerbund, is it?' He pulled out Tatiana's file and checked her birthdate, looking for clues to what the computer passcode might be. Based on the year, she definitely wasn't Naz, and her birthday wasn't the sixth of June.

'No. Ew. No-one in my bridal party will be wearing a cummerbund.'

He checked the two other files. No June birthdates.

'Well, if you haven't sent it yet,' he said, 'this might sound weird, but bear with me.'

It was a risk, asking her over the phone when he still wasn't completely sure no-one was eavesdropping on the line, but he was beginning to feel that had been a silly idea.

'Have you ever done any botanical sketching?'

Lynnie had never been interested in more than dabbling with art, but she'd made extra money as a teenager doing face painting at children's parties, so she was pretty skilled at simple flower illustrations.

'Yeah. I took one of those online courses once. I can do a pretty good sketch of billy buttons, since they're really just little yellow balls.'

'Could you send me one? In your letter?'

He hoped she wouldn't ask any questions. Even if he could tell her why he was asking – which he couldn't – the plan he was forming was still half baked.

'Sure,' she said. 'And Lane? Please try to stay open-minded. Maybe it seems ridiculous to you that you might find something out there that you're passionate about, but you could. You deserve to.'

They said their goodbyes. He sat for a long moment, staring at the silent phone. Maybe Lynnie was right. Maybe she did care more about his future than he did.

Somehow she still loved him enough to really believe he had one. That he could do something else. Be someone else.

•

When Lane returned to the wash-and-pack shed, Mina was sitting at the break table, looking down at a series of pages spread out in front of her. 'I've brought the letters for you to see.'

Lane stepped over to look at them. They were only colour photocopies, but despite the flattened colours and fuzziness, there was an obvious charm to them. Rebecca wrote with a looping, open hand, and punctuated each paragraph with little sketches or designs – flowers, cartoonish portraits, even a little map of the farm.

'Are these in the order she sent them?' Lane asked.

'She didn't date them, but her family are pretty confident they've kept them in the right sequence.'

Lane ran a finger under the map. It was in the top-right corner of the second letter, so sent nearly seven years ago. He recognised the driveway, the Karpathy house and the orchards, but the four housing blocks mustn't have been built yet.

The pig shed had.

'I've figured out which one is missing,' Mina said. 'I've re-read them a couple of times, and there should be one where she mentions going to see a doctor. It caused some friction with her family, so it stood out.'

'Friction? Why?'

'She was a childhood cancer survivor. Hodgkin lymphoma. She'd been five years cancer-free, but was due for a check. She'd originally planned to go home and see her regular doctor, but found a doctor here instead.'

'Can you think of any reason why someone would take that letter?'

Mina shook her head. 'The only thing I can think of is that maybe they didn't mean to take it? Maybe someone interrupted them and they took it by accident.'

'Was there anything else missing? Cash, jewellery, your phone?' Coincidences did happen. Could it have been an interrupted robbery, a crime of opportunity that looked like a conspiracy?

'No. But I didn't have any cash or valuables in my bag. And I still don't own a phone. That's one thing I like about this place: no-one thinks that's weird.'

Lane understood that – the internet had been a cruel place for Mina, home to people who lived to speculate about her family and invade her privacy. But at the same time, a phone he could access unsupervised would have been a huge help.

'Where would that letter have fit in the sequence?'

She tapped a space about midway through, and shifted the letters on either side to make a noticeable gap.

'What do you notice, seeing them laid out together?'

She considered the letters for a moment. 'They get a lot shorter,' she said.

The first two letters were three and four pages respectively, while the last letter was a few bare sentences.

'Definitely. But that might be nothing. It's easy to write multi-page letters when it's new and exciting; she might have just lost enthusiasm over time.'

'Know from experience, do you?' Mina joked. 'Do you get those lonely heart letters from women?'

Lane had been thinking of Lynnie, actually, and himself. Like the visits, the letters they'd exchanged when he first went to prison had dwindled to the occasional succinct check-in.

'Not anymore,' he said. 'The early ones lost interest when I didn't reply, and I haven't had any in years. I think I'm too close to possible parole to feel like a safe option anymore. They want a distant fantasy who can never hurt them.'

'Oh.' Mina frowned, and Lane couldn't read her expression. Perhaps she'd expected him to deny getting any at all. Maybe the mention of his parole chances had spooked her. Maybe he'd just killed the joke by being too earnest.

Lane picked up Rebecca's last note. It read:

Dear Mum and Dad,
I've decided to extend my stay, but I want to see you soon.
Maybe you could come here. I have some amazing news.
Love, Rebecca

There were no sketches, but she'd signed off with an oversized, lopsided heart.

'Do you have any idea what news she was referring to?' he asked.

'No, and neither do her parents. She might have got the all clear from the doctor?'

'How often did she write?'

'Every two or three weeks.'

'So from medical testing to the last letter ...' He counted the letters between. 'About four months? That would be a long time for routine test results.'

He studied the letters some more. 'Huh.' He ran a finger along the edge of the bench, sweeping past the pages laid out there. 'What do you notice about her handwriting?'

'It's ... pretty?'

'It is.' He took the last note, and laid it next to the first note. 'How about now?'

Mina stared at one, then the other. 'It's bigger. The letter shapes are all the same, but something feels different.'

Lane nodded. In his opinion, handwriting analysis was closer to a party trick than a forensic science, but even he could see that something had changed. There was an easy flow to the first letter, while the last letter had marks of hesitation: letters drawn and then gone over again, a sense of carefulness.

Like someone trying to match the shape of the letters against a reference?

'When does it change?' Mina muttered, looking along the row of letters. 'Here.' She tapped a letter about halfway along. Three on from the letter about seeing the doctor.

'Are you sure?' That letter did look off, but it also looked quite similar to the one before it. If someone was faking Rebecca's handwriting, why would they have got worse at it over time?

'Maybe this is just her real handwriting, and the early ones were her trying to be neater,' Mina mused. 'Whenever I get a new diary I start out writing like I'm calligraphing my wedding invitations.'

'Perhaps.' There were obvious signs she'd put more effort into the earlier letters. There were very few drawings in the later ones, and those were perfunctory and rough. But couldn't that also be evidence they were the work of someone other than Rebecca? 'You said there was friction. Was that over the phone?' Phone calls were a lot harder to fake than letters. Even harder six years ago, before voice-changing technology got really creepy.

'No. In the letters back to her, her parents got upset with her for not coming home. They told her it was stupid not to see her regular doctor who had all the history. She just ignored it.'

'But she had a phone, right? She called her parents to say she arrived in Melbourne.'

Mina nodded. 'She had one, but phone reception here is absolutely pants, and I doubt it was better six years ago.

They only communicated by letter.'

'For the sake of argument, let's assume someone else started writing to Rebecca's family a few months before she was reported missing, pretending to be her. Why?'

'To put them off? It would stop them looking for her.' Mina rubbed her chin. 'But then, why just go silent at the end? You've gone to all this effort, why not write that she's leaving the farm to go mine opals in Lightning Ridge? Become a jazz singer on a Carnival cruise ship?'

'A specific lie can be disproven, which would bring the full beam of suspicion back on this farm. Silence might have felt safer.' Lane rolled his neck, hoping that releasing the tension might knock some thought loose. 'But what would delaying an investigation by a few months achieve? Maybe they needed that time to be confident police wouldn't find the body?'

Mina made a face. 'There are a bunch of ways they could have made a body disappear immediately. If they buried her, a few months wouldn't change much.'

For a fraction of a second, Lane could feel the weight of a shovel handle, the way the edge of the blade pushed back against his foot as he forced it into the earth. He pushed himself to keep breathing. In two three. Out two three.

'I think you've jumped to murder really fast,' Mina said, seeming oblivious to his funny turn. 'Maybe she really did just leave. Heck, maybe she left a stack of letters behind and asked a friend to drop them in the mail at regular intervals. Maybe the handwriting is shitty because she dashed them all off in one go, trying to get them finished before she lost the light.'

'Do you think she might have had a reason to want to disappear on her family?' He thought of Brandon Roby, the 'missing' person who was happily cleaning windows in the greenhouse.

'If she did, I wouldn't have heard it from them,' Mina said with a sigh. 'The thing is, the families of missing people – especially young people – feel like they have to present a perfect picture. They worry that if they reveal any hint of discord in the family, the police will shrug it off as an obvious runaway.'

Lane knew that well enough. Half his job was untangling the innocuous lies people told, thinking they couldn't possibly hurt the investigation.

Which reminded him. 'The ring that you gave the Cudneys. Was that Hannah's gift to you, at your welcome?'

'Yes.'

'A family heirloom is a pretty serious gift. Did you feel pressured to give up something really precious?'

'Well, Karpathy did make sure I knew the ceremony would be held in front of everyone,' Mina said. 'I'm pretty inured to peer pressure, but I could see someone feeling like they had to show they were taking it seriously. But it's complicated. Hannah said she hated that ring. Her mother used to pull it out when she was little, make her try it on, go on and on about how she would wear it when she got married one day.'

'It was kind of you to give it back.'

She shrugged. 'It was three sizes too big, so I always felt like it was about to slip off. But it obviously meant a lot to Mrs Cudney. She should have it.'

Lane wondered if Karpathy had seen that interaction and, if so, what he would think of it.

'Did Hannah seem different to you in the days before her death?'

'Different how?'

He shrugged. There were a lot of ways a person's behaviour might change that could be telling. 'In any way. Sad. Worried. Happier?'

Sometimes people who had decided to end their life perked up in their final days. Having made the decision left them with no more worries, and distributing their belongings, putting their affairs in order and writing their goodbyes gave them a final sense of purpose.

'Worried, maybe. She was worried a lot in general.'

'What about?'

'Life. She mentioned early on that she always struggled with an anxiety disorder, but it had got much better since she moved to the farm. Maybe it was giving up caffeine.'

'But she was worried about something?'

Mina shook her head. 'I wasn't someone she confided in. But she seemed spooked, withdrawn. She stopped coming to meals.'

Lane chewed that over. There was a simple, sad explanation for what had happened to Hannah. After a period of changed behaviour, she'd taken a ute without permission, slipped away and killed herself in a single vehicle accident. Her choosing to end her own life explained every oddity except one: why Karpathy was clearly lying about why she had left the farm.

CHAPTER TWELVE

CHEESE DAY MEANT that they were all herded into the kitchens after breakfast. Lane had imagined the kitchen as old-fashioned and rudimentary, in line with the farm's overall 'school camp' vibe, so he was surprised to find huge stainless-steel benches, a commercial dishwasher and two six-burner cooktops, one on either side of the room.

'One electric and one woodstove,' a woman said, seeing him look. 'Depending on whether sunshine or trash wood is the more abundant resource at the time.'

The farm seemed to have no shortage of cash to pay for equipment and fittings. But then, was that odd? The farm had been in the Karpathy family for years. They generated their own power, grew their own food, collected their own water. Aside from the little bit of food they bought in, their only major expense would be wages.

Which would be huge, Lane conceded, counting the people as they filed in.

The woman who'd explained the set-up had long black hair, salted with grey, and green eyes. She was one of the two potential Matildas he'd identified. He stuck close to her, hoping they would get a chance to chat further.

Fortunately, she didn't seem put off by his presence, holding out her hand for him to shake. 'I'm Alessandra.'

'The lawyer.' Lane immediately crossed her off his list. Matilda hadn't even started university, while Alessandra had completed a law degree before coming to the farm.

She pulled a face. 'Just Alessandra is fine. We're paired up today.'

She showed him how to scrub up and where to find the aprons and hairnets, then they got to work filling a large stockpot with goat milk.

'I always thought goat milk had a strong odour,' he said as he stared into the pot, where tiny bubbles had started to form in the warming milk. There was a hint of a scent there, but it was mild and creamy.

'That smell and taste develops over time,' Alessandra explained, dipping a thermometer probe into the liquid. 'Anything off the shelf in a supermarket is at least a few days old. And the pasteurisation process really brings out the funk. This milk is raw, and the goats were milked this morning.'

'Raw milk?' he asked. That was one of those topics – like edible insects and biosecurity laws – that seemed innocuous on the surface but could also mean Alessandra was about to drag him down a rabbit hole. A surprising number of people believed that raw milk was some kind of wellness cure-all that Big Pharma didn't want them to know about.

'It's best for cheesemaking,' she explained. 'Supermarket milk has been heated and cooled already, and pushed through a fine sieve to break up the fats so it's all nice and uniform. We would need to add an enzyme to reverse that process, so starting with raw milk means fewer steps. It's perfectly safe once it's been processed into cheese. The milk itself, well . . . legally I have to tell you not to drink it.' She winked.

A jar with a white powder inside was making its way from station to station. Alessandra measured out a spoonful and showed him. 'Here's one of the great treasures of the Karpathy farm. We've been breeding this cheese culture since shortly after I arrived. Some people say the age of a culture doesn't really make a difference in the taste, but they haven't had ours.'

'How long have you been here?' he asked.

'It'll be twenty-five years next February. My silver jubilee.'

'Wow,' Lane said. 'So you've been here the longest of anybody I've met.'

'Except young Sam,' she said. Then she caught herself. 'Karpathy, I mean.'

He was beginning to piece together an understanding of the farm's history. It seemed like it had become what it was today through a slow accretion, not a planned foundation. There were obvious turning points – the breakdown of the relationship between Karpathy's parents, then his father's period of wild flings and unplanned children, and the decision to make the farm child-free. This would have resulted in an exodus of members, and a cultural shift as they were replaced by people more comfortable with the group's new normal.

Assuming for a moment that Matilda, Alain and Rebecca had all been murdered, what had precipitated that? Alessandra was the first person he'd met who might be able to answer that question.

It would have happened around the same time Karpathy senior decreed the farm would be child-free – could Matilda have been pregnant? It seemed an unlikely escalation, when Karpathy had been merely uninterested in his younger children, not hostile towards them. Why would a man make provisions in his will for his first four children, but turn to murder over the fifth?

Lane cautioned himself against getting too attached to a false friend – just because two things happened at the same time didn't mean one caused the other.

'But Karpathy would have been, what, ten when you arrived?'

And fifteen when Matilda disappeared, Lane thought. Young, but serial killers had started younger. Could that have been what changed: Samuel Karpathy coming of age?

'Oh, don't make me feel old.' Alessandra laughed. 'He was a teeny thing when I arrived, still missing teeth. It's so strange to think of that.'

'You and I can't be that far apart in age, so don't go calling us old,' Lane joked.

Again, he shouldn't focus too much on one theory. Who else might have arrived around that time and started using the farm as a hunting ground? He glanced around the kitchen, counting the men who could be the right age for it.

'Now that the culture is in the milk, we have to keep it at

the right temperature for about an hour,' Alessandra explained. 'It's fiddly but not hard. Then the magic happens.'

Lane leaned against the counter. 'You must have a lot of stories, having been here so long.'

'I suppose.'

Lane suspected he'd overstepped; Alessandra was frowning down at the thermometer now, looking sad. Giving up a law career to spend twenty-five years making cheese and growing lettuce was a big change. Maybe he'd touched a sore point. 'I'm happy to watch the pot, if you want to take a break?'

'How about I watch the pot and you go start the washing-up?' Alessandra countered.

Right. There was no time for idle hands here. He made his way to the sinks at the far end of the room, where an intimidating cluster of pots, utensils and cups had formed.

He had filled the dishwasher and barely made a dent in the pile when Mina joined him.

She put the plug in the sink and turned the tap on full blast, creating enough noise that they could speak in hushed tones without worrying about the people working on the other side of the room.

'It's back,' she said. 'The letter about the doctor visit.'

Lane nearly dropped the cup he was holding. 'They came in again and put it back? Are you sure?'

'I went through those letters a thousand times,' Mina said. 'It was gone and now it's back.'

'Back with the others? Or did you find it somewhere else?'

It was still possible that Mina had just mislaid it, although Lane doubted it.

'Back with the others. Exactly where it was before it went missing. I bet I was right that they didn't mean to take it in the first place. Then they panicked and put it back, hoping I hadn't noticed yet.'

'The timing makes sense. They took it the day before yesterday, then had to wait until you were busy to put it back.'

'So it could have been anyone.' The water had nearly filled the sink, so she moved the tap to start filling up the next one rather than lose their noise cover. 'I asked Sarah and Trish if they'd noticed anyone in our room lately, and apparently it's been Central Station. They've both had people come hang out, and others have been in to help sort through Hannah's things or reclaim things they loaned to her.'

Mina started washing cups and handing them to Lane to dry. He turned so he could survey the room as he worked.

'Do you know the lady in the far corner?' he asked.

She glanced over. 'Moira?'

'She's about the right age to be Matilda, and has the right eye colour.'

'She isn't,' Mina said with complete confidence.

He waited, and she sighed and elaborated. 'I know something about Moira that you would have mentioned already if it was also true of Matilda.'

It took him a moment to parse that, then he nodded. Whatever it was, clearly Mina thought it was none of Lane's business. That killed his list of possibilities. Unless he had missed someone, Matilda was not just living a secret life here on the farm. Which brought him back to his other theory: murder.

ALRIGHT. IT WAS okay to go to the mat when you needed to, but then you had to get up again. On the count of three.

One.

Two.

Three.

The motion pushed all of the air out of his lungs, along with a groan that didn't sound like his own voice. He paused, listening for the sound of someone stirring. Silence.

Elbow. Knee. Halfway there. All he needed to do was get to the door. He couldn't think about the hallway, about the stairs, everything beyond. Just get to the door.

His fingertips brushed the smooth painted wood. Something fizzed in him. He was doing it.

CHAPTER THIRTEEN

IT TOOK A few more days for Lynnie's letter – actually a package – to arrive.

He didn't need to open the package, as it had already been slit open. Sweeney, he presumed. At least the guard wouldn't think anything of the contents. Sweeney still kept mostly to his room outside of meals, although Lane had spotted him out walking the picturesque hills a couple of times.

Inside the package was a letter, in an envelope that had been unsealed, along with a book titled *I Could Do Anything If I Only Knew What It Was* and a cheerful sketch of a bouquet of billy buttons. Lynnie had coloured in the little round heads of the flowers with bright yellow pencil.

He worried for a moment that the work was too new, too fresh, but he doubted anyone could tell it had been drawn only a few days previously. He grabbed a pen he'd scrounged from the dining hall and wrote the initials *RG* on the back, along with a date that would have been a few weeks after Rebecca's arrival.

He pulled Lynnie's letter out of the envelope and put the sketch inside before slipping it into his pocket.

Lynnie's letter spoke of her upcoming exams and of having toured a few wedding venues in Sydney. She'd been shocked to find out how far ahead the most popular options had to be booked. She hoped he was staying safe, watching out for spiders and wearing sunscreen.

Lynnie's letters were always a moment of Zen for him, and this one was no different. He read it twice, then tucked it away inside the book. He wasn't super thrilled about that gift; it was a book about choosing a vocation, which felt like a rather heavy-handed hint on Lynnie's part.

He checked his pocket for the sketch, before heading out to find Dave. On his way, he noticed Mina squatting under a tree, looking at something.

'Check this out,' she said, pushing aside a low shrub to show him a ring of red mushrooms. They looked like the sort of mushrooms that mice in little acorn hats danced under in fairy books: red with white spots and stout white stems.

'What are they?' he asked.

'Fly agaric,' she said. 'They're out of season, but with the bizarre weather we're having lately, they popped up anyway. You know some people think they grow in a ring like that where there's a body buried?'

'I've never heard that.'

'Probably because it's just a myth. I have heard a theory that they grow in rings in spots where there was once a tree. The wood has decomposed all the way back to soil, but there're still enough nutrients left that mushrooms make a ghost of the tree's shape.'

'Are they edible?'

'Hell no. Don't ever eat one. But they're cool-looking.' She let the shrub spring back into place. 'I had to stop Echo from chowing down on them.'

At the sound of his name, Echo came trotting around from the other side of the tree. Once he saw there wasn't any work for him to do, he found a sunny patch of decaying leaves to roll in.

'Do we need to tell someone? So they can get rid of them?'

She shook her head. 'Eradicating mushrooms is close to impossible. They won't do any harm if we leave them where they are. Even if something could be done, Karpathy would never spray them. He doesn't even use the pesticides that are permitted on organic farms.'

'What does he do about the weeds?'

'Depends what they are.' She stood up and stretched her back out. 'A lot of things we consider weeds are actually edible. Purslane, chickweed, goosefoot. Those get pulled up and put in the soup.'

Lane nodded like those plant names meant anything to him.

'Some things the goats can eat. With blackberry, they put an electric fence around and set the pigs on it, because they'll dig it up at the roots. But for the most part, they rely on good old human labour.'

'That must get expensive.'

She shrugged. 'I think it helps when you can pay people in enlightenment.'

'Don't people here get paid?' Brandon had said something about needing to talk to Karpathy to get money. Didn't anyone here have money of their own?

'Oh, they do.'

'How did you get around that? Doesn't Karpathy need your real details for your taxes and the like?'

She reached over to Echo and started combing leaves out of his golden fur with her fingers. 'I just asked him to pay me in cash and let me sort it out myself.'

'So he is willing to be a bit dodgy?'

'Most small businesses are.'

'Brandon mentioned there's something weird about how people are paid here, then clammed up. Do you know what he meant?'

'Oh yeah,' she said, crumpling a leaf up and tossing it away. 'Since technically life here is all inclusive – you don't need to worry about food, clothing, rent, anything – Karpathy offers to hold on to your pay and give it to you as a lump sum when you leave, or when you want to make a big purchase.'

'He just offers? Or does he apply a lot of pressure?'

'I agreed pretty quickly, because I didn't want to make waves,' she said. 'He did frame it like he was doing me a favour. Freeing me from the temptation to fritter it away. "Imagine how it would feel to leave here with a huge cheque to start your new life." But you can see how there's an upside for him, too.'

Definitely. He filed that away for future consideration. 'It must be tricky at the end, to figure out if you've been paid correctly,' he mused.

'True. And have you seen anyone fill out a timesheet, or punch a clock? I think it would be really easy for Karpathy to pay everyone for eight hours a day when actually they're doing ten, twelve or even more, because we're all in this together and their hands are free.'

Lane could see it. 'What if someone tried to work less than eight hours? Or couldn't work? Have you seen anyone get kicked out, or fired?'

'No,' she said. 'But I don't think anyone who wasn't pulling their weight would get a very friendly reception from the others. I think it would take a lot of guts to try. If he's got people willing to put in the work, I can see why Karpathy would avoid pesticides. I've read some concerning things about groundwater leaching and toxic substances building up in the soil, bioaccumulating.' She shook her head. 'I'm sounding like Gretel now. But that's how they get you. Nine times out of ten, it's a barrage of nonsense, but then they'll hit you with an excellent point. If you're not careful, you'll end up thinking she's onto something with the crystals and the tisanes and the perineum tanning.'

'Do I want to know what that is?' Lane asked.

'No, and it's exactly what it sounds like,' Mina replied. 'If you ever have to run an errand to her house, start calling out "hello" when you get within a hundred metres of the gate. Otherwise there's a solid chance you'll stumble upon her doing her "sun salutation" on the front lawn.'

•

Lane found Dave in the vehicle garage, elbow-deep in the engine of a khaki-green ute.

'Is that the one that was damaged in the accident?' Lane asked.

'Nah,' Dave said. 'That was one of the newer ones; I wouldn't try to fix a hybrid. It's gone to the mechanics in Georges Bridge. Actually, I wanted to talk to you about that. Someone needs to pick it up tomorrow, which means two drivers need to go to town – one to drive in, and one to drive the other ute back. Interested?'

Lane was desperate to go into town; it would give him an opportunity to talk to Natalie again. It hurt him to say, 'I can't. I don't have a valid driver's licence. It's on my list to sort out before my parole hearing.'

Lane's disappointment must have been obvious, because Dave said, 'Come anyway then. You can do the boring jobs while I go to the pub. We'll find someone else to help with the driving.'

'Sounds like a plan.' Lane pulled the envelope out of his pocket. He knew he was taking a risk by bringing up Rebecca's name when someone here knew that Mina had some connection to her, and he and Mina had been spending a lot of time together. But if he didn't take any risks at all, he might as well just go home.

'Hey, I found something and thought you might be the best person to ask. You've been here a while, and know everyone.'

'Oh yeah? Gimme a sec.' Dave grabbed a squirt of soap from a nearby dispenser, then rinsed his hands at the sink.

'It was being used as a bookmark in a book I took from the swap shelf,' Lane said. He'd put some thought into the story. He couldn't say that he'd found it in the cabins, which hadn't been built at the time Rebecca was on the farm. In any other building, it didn't seem plausible that a piece of paper could lie undisturbed for years. But a particularly nice bookmark could easily have been shuffled from book to book. 'It looks like something that whoever left it there might want back.'

Dave examined it, frowning.

Of course, even if Dave did remember well enough to connect the dots and think the artwork was one of Rebecca's, he wouldn't say her name. Lane's plan was to give it a few days, and then claim that some other person had identified the artist and use that to gently question Dave about her.

So Lane was floored when Dave's face softened. 'RG. That would be Rebecca – well before your time. She was always sketching away.'

'Oh. So it probably belongs to someone else now? Did Rebecca have close friends on the farm?'

Dave's smile was sad. 'A few. I think she and Alessandra got on well. But most of the people she was close to have left.'

'Okay, I'll speak to Alessandra.' Lane reached for the sketch, but Dave didn't let go.

'You know who would really appreciate this?' he said. 'Her family. It's a bit of a sad story, Rebecca. After she left here, she went missing. They were devastated, and I'm sure they'd love to have another piece of her art.'

'She went missing?' Lane repeated. Again, he hadn't expected Dave to just come out and acknowledge that.

'Yeah. It was a real shock. I …' His jaw tightened, as he stared at the fake sketch. 'I can't help but wonder if there was something I could have done to prevent it.'

'What do you mean? You said it happened after she left?'

'Exactly. If I could have persuaded her to stay, she'd be here, safe with us. Or if I'd at least tried to talk her out of taking the train to Melbourne alone.'

'She took the train? Did you see her get on?' Lane asked.

Dave looked at him, his eyebrows pulling together.

'Sorry,' Lane said, forcing out a self-deprecating laugh. 'Old instincts.'

'Fair enough. Look, I wouldn't mention this to Karpathy, okay? There's some tension with Rebecca's family. But I have their address and can mail this to them.'

'No!' Lane said, a little too quickly. He didn't know exactly how much the Goncharovs knew about what he and Mina were up to, but that could get messy. 'I mean, mail can be complicated if I'm involved. If the family gets upset, then the media could make a meal out of a convicted murderer sending unsolicited mail to a missing woman's family. I would hate for you to get in trouble for aiding and abetting me.'

'I don't think they'd be upset,' Dave said, handing it back. 'But I get you.'

•

Lane didn't let himself get too enthusiastic about a trip down to Georges Bridge, because he assumed Sweeney would spike the idea immediately.

'Dave's going to take responsibility for you?' Sweeney asked, blinking like the mid-morning light was bothering him. Lane assumed Sweeney had overslept, he hadn't seen the guard at breakfast.

'Yes.' That was probably a generous interpretation of what Dave had said, but it wasn't like Lane planned to escape.

'Fine,' Sweeney said.

Lane hesitated. Sweeney had been adamant about not letting Lane go to town when they first arrived, now he didn't care. His demeanour seemed off, like maybe he was feeling unwell again.

But Lane wasn't going to argue against his own good fortune.

The other driver Dave managed to rustle up turned out to be Gretel.

'I need to go to town too,' she said. She had an enormous box in her arms, which she placed gently on the seat beside her and belted in. 'So it works out nicely. A lot of the markets I usually do were cancelled because of the weather, so I've listed some things for sale online and need to go to the post office.'

Lane didn't really understand the connection Gretel had with the farm. She wasn't a resident, she was a neighbour. She didn't seem to do any of the farm work, but she was clearly deeply integrated into the community.

'Hey, Gretel,' he asked, 'did you live on the Karpathy farm before moving to your own?'

Gretel chuckled. 'No, no, I was always on the outside looking in,' she said with a smile. 'Sammy and I grew up together, though. We've always been good friends. He tolerates me.'

'You grew up together?' he said. He'd pegged Gretel as years older than Karpathy – too much of an age gap for them to have been childhood friends.

'I babysat him,' she explained. 'I never lived on the farm, although I might have wanted to if things were different. I was very focused on getting my own land, so my teens and early twenties were all work, all the time. I didn't have the luxury of taking my foot off the accelerator to live in a commune.'

'It's not a commune,' Dave interjected. 'It's –'

'An intentional community. It's just us three, Dave, you're not on the six o'clock news. We can relax about the terminology.'

'Why the hurry?' Lane asked.

'My uncle always made it very clear the farm was going on the auction block the day he qualified for the pension. He was cashing out and buying a houseboat. He did it, too; fished for Murray cod until the day he toppled over.'

'You would have been paid on the farm, though, wouldn't you?' Lane said. 'Karpathy pays the residents for their work.'

'Of course he does. But only for eight hours a day, and between my job at the servo and the babysitting, I was able to earn a lot more'

He remembered something else he'd wanted to ask. 'You mentioned on the day we met that you don't eat the food grown on Karpathy's farm. Is there a reason for that?'

Dave made a warning noise from the driver's seat, but Gretel lit up like she'd been hoping he'd ask.

'It's not really that I don't eat Karpathy's produce. It's that I don't eat anything not grown on my own farm.'

'You're entirely self-sufficient?' Lane asked. 'That's impressive.'

He glanced at Dave, wondering if he would interject again, but he seemed focused on navigating the road's tight turns safely. The ute was barely crawling along, and Lane felt for him, retracing the route where Hannah had lost her life.

'I have to be,' Gretel said. She fidgeted with a beaded bracelet on her wrist. 'I was sick a lot as a kid.'

'I'm sorry to hear that,' Lane said.

'Thank you. Have you heard of cyclic vomiting syndrome?'

'No. But it sounds awful.'

'It's basically the label they give someone who throws up all the time and doctors can't figure out why. But it always cleared up within a few days of going to stay with my uncle on his farm. He grew his own food, hunted, fished. Eventually I went to live with him full-time.' She looked out the window. Clearly it was a painful topic. 'I was never sick again after that.'

'Wow. Did you ever figure out what caused your intolerance?'

He wondered if that was why she and Sweeney had hit it off; navigating life with a gluten intolerance or allergy had to be hard.

She laughed. 'Everything! Food these days, people have no idea what they're putting in their bodies. It was no better back then. There were days I ate boxed macaroni and cheese for all three meals. God knows what kind of additives and weird extracts I was scoffing down, wreaking havoc on my health.'

Lane smiled and nodded, although he could guess at a few better explanations than mysterious food additives. Macaroni and cheese was the sort of meal a precocious child could prepare themselves – Lane had mastered it by five. Cooking for herself three times a day, and then later being placed in the custody of her survivalist uncle? He understood now why Gretel might feel at home at the Karpathy farm, among people like Brandon Roby, even if she wasn't a resident.

'That makes sense,' he said. 'But we make our own cheese at the farm. I saw every ingredient going in; there was nothing mysterious.'

'I'm sure,' she said. 'But my farm is clean.'

'Karpathy's farm seems pretty clean.'

'Compared to what I'm sure you pictured farming to be like before you arrived, no doubt it seems downright fastidious.'

Lane nodded, thinking about the borrowed cotton clothes he was wearing.

'Did you know that when a human being takes a medication, only about twenty per cent of the active ingredients are absorbed?' she asked.

'No,' Lane admitted, baffled by the non sequitur.

'Where do you think the other eighty per cent goes?'

'I guess they pass straight through?'

'Exactly! And then what happens to them?'

'How graphic an answer are you hoping for here?'

She cackled. 'That's right: it ends up in the sewage. Then what happens?'

'I honestly don't know. It's sewage, it's gone.'

'No it isn't. That's the problem with people these days. They think the things they get rid of disappear. Whether you flush it down a toilet or throw it in a bin, neither of those things are portals into the void. Everything you've ever thrown away still exists, you know. It's just in a landfill somewhere.'

'Unless it's broken down,' Lane said.

'Yes. Human waste breaks down. But what if that waste contains medications? The human body is an exceptionally harsh environment. To survive long enough to be effective, medications are purposely made to break down slowly. They don't break down in sewage. They end up in the water. They end up in the soil. Then they're taken up by plants, and you get an extra dose of antibiotics with your steamed carrots.'

'How are they getting from the sewage to the soil?' Lane asked. He looked at Dave. 'Are the composting toilets being emptied onto the gardens?'

'No!' Dave said. 'After two years of composting, it's perfectly safe. And we empty them clear across the other side of the property from the food gardens. They fertilise the wattle trees.'

Gretel shook her head. 'Even if you were on town sewerage, it wouldn't be safe. I keep telling Sam, like I told his father, he shouldn't be so lax about letting people take medications while they're living on the farm. Just say no.'

'Even medications they need?'

'There's no such thing,' she said lightly.

'Riiight,' he said, remembering the privet berry syrup she'd offered him. He was tempted to ask if she had a syrup that could replace insulin or antidepressants or antiretrovirals, but he really didn't want to know the answer.

'Sam is doing better than most, of course,' she said.

'Like how he's avoiding microplastics?'

'Yes, and pesticides and artificial fertilisers. And most farms aren't being nearly vigilant enough about PFAS.'

Lane didn't even want to ask, but she continued regardless. 'Forever chemicals. They're in just about everything, from non-stick pans to shiny cardboard. Did you know that when they get into the body, we can't process them? At least medications have the decency to pass on through. There's only one way to get PFAS out. If you give blood, some of the PFAS will go with it and your body can make new, clean blood.'

'I think you're overwhelming the poor boy, Grets,' Dave said.

Lane knew Dave was barely a year older than him, but he couldn't exactly point that out without revealing he'd seen the birthdate on his employee file. He'd noticed that Dave liked to emphasise that he was older than Sam Karpathy, too. Perhaps an ingrained habit from ten years of knowing him as the boss's son.

They arrived in Georges Bridge a moment later, and he and Dave got out of the car, leaving Gretel to slide into the driver's seat.

'Is that true?' Lane asked Dave, as they watched the ute drive away. Gretel wound down her window and gave them a cheerful backward wave.

'It's complicated,' Dave said. 'Nothing she said is wrong, exactly. But the food we grow is safe. She's a smart lady, but sometimes being smart means worrying about things other people don't even notice.' He punched Lane lightly on the arm. 'Take any medication you want. Just don't wee in the damn gardens. Anyway, like I said, I'm off to the pub. Let me know when the ute is ready.'

'Don't you need to drive us back?'

'I'll have one. Maybe two, if you do me a favour and don't rush through everything, eh?'

'I reckon I can do that.'

Lane had every intention of rushing, but he certainly wasn't going to hurry back to Dave. He was going to make the most of every second he got here.

CHAPTER FOURTEEN

IT WAS A novelty being totally unsupervised. Well, not totally. He had the ankle bracelet on, and it would trigger a statewide manhunt if he didn't come find Dave in a reasonable amount of time.

Dave walked off towards the pub. Lane walked in the direction of the service station on the corner, where the mechanic had his workshop. He stopped before reaching it and waited until he saw the pub door swing shut behind Dave, then he hooked a left and went into Natalie's sandwich shop.

Natalie was standing behind the counter, slicing tomatoes, and her eyes widened when she saw who had made the bell above the door jingle.

'Wow, hello,' she said.

'It's alright, I'm allowed to be in here,' he said, putting his hands up in a placating gesture.

'Oh, I'm sure,' she said. 'It's just, when people go to Karpathy's, we don't usually see them again for a few months.'

'When they leave?'

'Mmm. Or if they stay. Karpathy likes to keep new arrivals all to himself for a while before they rub elbows with us townies.' She said it like she was joking, but there was a hard edge to it.

That was odd. It wasn't that far to Georges Bridge, and surely people had errands they needed to run. What if they needed to get a script filled at the pharmacy, or had something to mail, or just wanted a change of scenery? But now that Lane thought about it, he hadn't seen anyone other than Dave leave the farm at any point.

Surely it took more effort to arrange for everything to be done by Dave than to just let people borrow a vehicle and run to town themselves?

Could it be deliberate? Indoctrination was a lot easier when people were isolated from the outside world.

So why had Dave gone to such lengths to bring Lane into town so soon after his arrival?

It took a moment before it twigged. Precisely because of the novelty he'd felt. To any other new arrival, running errands was just a chore. But to Lane, it was a tantalising brush with the world he'd been excluded from for years. And this level of freedom was only available to him as long as he stuck out the leave program.

'What can I get you?' Natalie asked.

'Uh, I don't actually have any cash on me,' he said. 'I was just hoping I could have a chat with you?'

'Hey, I didn't ask, "What can I sell you?"' she said, her smile genuinely warm now. 'I could use a break. How does coffee and a lamington sound?'

A coffee. Lane could cry. 'Thank you so much. It's black, no sugar.'

While she made two coffees, Lane looked around the store. It was a small place, designed only to fit the display case, drinks fridge and a queue of people, but there was a tiny table with two chairs tucked in a corner. Over the table was a noticeboard, overflowing with colourful flyers for school fetes and small businesses. On the far wall, Natalie had framed certificates of appreciation for her donations to fundraisers, sports teams and community groups.

'Things must be really starting to dry out for you guys on the farm,' Natalie said, stirring cream into her coffee.

'We've had a nice run of sunny days,' Lane said.

'There's more to come.' Natalie tipped two spoonfuls of sugar in. 'I think we all prayed a little too hard for the rain to stop. There's nothing on the ten-day forecast, and she'll be over thirty degrees by the end of the week.'

She came out from behind the counter carrying both mugs.

'Can I ask you a weird question to start?' he said, once they were seated with their drinks. 'Are you related to the Karpathy family?'

'Not a weird question. A very sensible question. In a place like Georges Bridge, it's a great idea to check who someone is related to before you start talking shit.'

He laughed. 'I'm not planning to talk shit.'

'Either way, no, I'm not a Karpathy.'

'Oh. Samuel Karpathy mentioned a sister, Naz. I thought that could be short for Natalie.'

'It's short for Nadya. Dr Nadya Higgs, if you want to get fancy. She's still here in town, over at the GP clinic.'

Karpathy's sister was the town general practitioner. In Rebecca's letter to her family, she mentioned going to see a doctor. Was that why the thief briefly tried to take the letter, and put it back when they realised its absence would only draw more attention to it? They didn't want Mina to make a connection between Rebecca and Dr Nadya Higgs nee Karpathy?

He wanted to ask Natalie how long Nadya had worked as a doctor, how many doctors the town had, but neither question would sound natural.

'Do you know the Karpathy family well?' he asked instead.

'I know Nadya well.'

He took a sip of his coffee, and had to close his eyes. After so long, she probably could have made it with ditch water and he'd have had the same reaction, but even if he hadn't been desperate, this was good coffee.

'What about Dave?' he asked. 'You two seem to know each other well.'

'Dave runs a lot of the farm's errands here in town,' she explained. 'We're friendly. He's a friendly guy.'

'Do you know many of the others?'

'Not a lot. I don't go up there, and like I said, only a few of the residents come to town. I'm sure you've noticed that they like to keep to themselves.'

Before he could answer that, she said, 'What about you, Lane? What brought you to Karpathy's farm?'

The question threw him for a moment – she'd already asked him that, the day they drove up Hill Road together. But then, Dave and Sweeney had been in the ute with them. Was she checking to see if he had a different answer when they were alone? Why?

'I'm on study release from Albury Correctional Centre. Karpathy has agreed to teach me how to be a farmer.'

'And that's what you want? To be a farmer?'

She was looking at him like she was trying to see through to the back of his skull. He wondered if this sandwich shop had been one of the businesses Carver cold-canvassed, trying to secure a spot for Lane close to Karpathy's farm.

'I don't know,' he said. Full honesty was not the way to go, but ninety-five per cent honesty could look a lot like it. 'I just wanted to be out of prison for a while.'

'Do you think if another opportunity arose that would still let you out on study leave, you'd be interested in that? Something that suits you better than farming?'

He frowned. There was an intensity to this conversation he hadn't prepared for. 'Why do you ask?'

'I just know that prison can be a tough place. And feeling like you have no options, that's an even tougher place.'

'I don't think I'd be good at selling sandwiches,' he said. It was a kind offer, but his spot at the farm was a best-case scenario. He didn't want to leave.

'I didn't mean here. I'm sorry, I can't help you that way.' She took a sip of her coffee. 'What do you think you *would* be good at?'

'The only thing I'm good at isn't an option,' he admitted. 'My qualifications are all in criminology and private investigation. Turns out there aren't a lot of careers in that field once you've served time. And my life of crime wasn't even long enough to spin it into some kind of Frank Abagnale consulting criminal schtick.'

'What did you like about your work as an investigator?' she probed.

Lane fidgeted with his coffee cup, spinning it slowly on the table. 'It makes me feel useful. I'm good at chasing down information, figuring out when to latch on and refuse to let go. I want to help people when no-one else can.'

'Have you considered looking at jobs in search and rescue?'

Lane wasn't sure that he followed her logic. 'The SES is a volunteer organisation; finding a paid position will be a condition of my parole.'

'There are ways to do it for a living. I can ask around my network, find you some leads, if you want.'

'That's very generous.'

'The skills you have could make you excellent at it. That's worth the effort, to me. With search and rescue, time is of the essence and resources are thin. You need to read the clues, ferret out the information that witnesses don't realise is important, and figure out where to prioritise the search before it's too late. And unfortunately, sometimes it is too late. Handling that is a skill too, and one that I bet you have.'

Her smile faded a little.

'Are you doing okay?' he asked. 'After Hannah's accident, I mean?'

'It's tough sometimes. But I'm fine.'

'Can you clear something up for me? Hannah was on the way into Georges Bridge to pick up some sandbags when –'

'No, that can't be right,' Natalie interrupted. 'We were run off our feet trying to get enough sandbags to people whose houses were about to go under. We couldn't have spared any for a property so high up in the hills. They weren't at risk of flooding. But then, I suppose she wasn't to know that. Oh.' She looked stricken. 'If I hadn't missed her call, I'd have told her not to come. She wouldn't have been out on the road at all.'

'You had a missed call from Hannah?'

Natalie nodded. 'It's an eerie thing. When I got home and listened to the message, I thought she'd called me for help after the accident. But then I checked the time stamp and it was about half an hour earlier. I honestly think it was just a pocket dial. Listen …'

She pulled out her phone and navigated to her saved messages.

The sound was tinny through the speakers, but still distinct. For thirty seconds, before it cut off, the voicemail captured the drumming of rain on a roof and someone gasping for breath, like they'd been running.

'Were you and Hannah close?' he asked.

'We'd met. I don't recall giving her my number, but it's easy enough to find.'

He drained the last of his coffee. He considered asking for a refill, but the green tea had been working so far to stave off the headaches, and he didn't want to reset all his progress with too big an indulgence.

'What about past residents?' he asked. He was tipping his hand now, but subtlety wasn't getting him anywhere. 'Have you ever met a Rebecca Goncharov? Alain Serling? Matilda Carver?'

Natalie made a startled noise, and her shoulders straightened. Lane worried that he had tipped his hand even further than he'd planned. Did Natalie recognise the name Carver from the prisoner governor's request for a study release position? Had she just put his whole scheme together?

'I met Rebecca a few times,' she said. 'She was really sweet. The others ...' She shrugged. 'Sorry.'

'It would have been a long time ago,' Lane said. 'We're talking twenty years.'

She frowned. 'That's before my time. What are you playing at, Lane Holland?'

'What do you think? What about the farm worries you so much that you're willing to work so hard to get me out of there?'

'I think for some people it's a wonderful place,' she said. 'I just don't ever want someone to feel like they're trapped up there because there's nowhere else for them to go.'

•

Lane needed to find a phone. He'd considered asking Natalie, but she'd already done him enough favours and it felt wrong to use her phone when she was going to be a subject of the call.

There was an old payphone along the footpath from her shop, but when Lane got close he discovered the phone itself was gone, and it had been converted into a free wi-fi hotspot. A great resource, if only he'd had something that could connect to the internet.

A few doors up from there he found the library. He entered, and breathed in the smell of books. Even though Georges Bridge was just a small country town, its library was far more well stocked and welcoming than the library he'd become used to in the Special Purpose Centre.

'Morning. Are you one of Karpathy's people?' a young man behind the counter asked. He gave Lane a once-over, his expression flickering briefly when he clocked the tracker on Lane's ankle, but he recovered quickly and smiled. His name tag read: *Aaron, he/him.*

'I suppose. You know the farm well?'

Aaron shrugged. 'My uncle runs the burning workshops there.' He didn't sound particularly impressed. 'He doesn't let the younger cousins go, but I've helped out a time or two.'

'What do you reckon?' He wondered if Aaron would try to warn him away, as Natalie had appeared to.

Aaron made a face. 'They're a bit weird, hey? Nice enough, I guess. But, you know …'

Lane waited.

'Karpathy says all the right things, and it's cool of him to host the workshops. It's more than most do. But if he really wants to save the world, he could try giving those forty acres back.'

Lane bit back a startled laugh. 'Fair,' he said. 'I don't suppose there's a phone I could use here?'

'Next to the community pantry,' Aaron said. 'No international calls.'

The community pantry was in the corner. Lane examined the shelves while waiting for his call to be answered, and wasn't surprised to see a rack of jams and pickles with the Karpathy farm label on them.

'Holland.' Carver's voice, on learning the identity of the caller, was cool. 'I hope you're not calling me from Samuel Karpathy's phone.'

'No, he doesn't have access to this phone.'

'You'd better not have a second contraband smartphone. I don't have the budget to get Sweeney to drop it a second time if you get caught.'

'I'm in the Georges Bridge library.'

'And you're calling me why?'

'I need to check something, because I think I just put my foot in it with a local shopkeeper. When you were trying to find a position for me here in Georges Bridge, did you sign the letters with your own name? Or make any calls?'

'Glad to know you think I'm an idiot. No, I delegated all the paperwork to Sweeney. Part of his promotion to the lead of this so-called pilot program. As you pointed out, my name would cause those on the farm to clam up. Why would I send you along already branded with a connection to me?'

Okay then. So it was the mention of Rebecca's name that had startled Natalie. There was something she wasn't telling him, he was sure. He needed to talk to the doctor, Nadya Higgs – Karpathy's sister.

'There's one more thing I wanted to discuss.' Lane took a deep breath; this was probably going to go down like a lead balloon. 'It would really help me if I could talk to your wife. Matilda's mother.'

'Why?'

Because the employee files proved that Matilda dropping out of contact with her parents and her going missing were actually two separate events, occurring months apart. Because Brandon Roby had also chosen to go no contact with his family, and he thought it was possible Rebecca Goncharov had too.

Because Lane should have pressed Carver on that possibility when he first discovered her connection to the farm, but he'd been afraid to, when he needed Carver's help to avoid trouble over the contraband phone and to secure approval for this little jaunt into the world.

'I've heard your recollection of Matilda's last weeks of contact with you; I'd like to hear hers.'

'You think her version is going to be different?'

'I think there are very few people who can give me information about that time, and I'd like to squeeze out every single drop.'

Carver sighed. 'If you upset my wife I'm going to lay you flat, you know.'

That sounded a lot like a yes.

'The only problem is I haven't really thought this through,' Lane confessed. 'I'm grabbing opportunities as they come up. If you give me your wife's number, I can call her now.'

'Absolutely the fuck not. I need to talk to her first. She can't just get a random call from one of my inmates on a Monday afternoon.'

'Well, I don't know when I'm next going to have access to a phone I trust. What if I tried to call her at, say, seven pm the day after tomorrow? If I don't call, assume I wasn't able to find a way. And if she doesn't want to talk to me, she can just not answer.'

Seven pm would be after the dinner service, so Lane might be able to slip away somewhere ... Where? The Smiths, the neighbours they'd heard out hunting? Another neighbour? It would be early enough that an unexpected knock on the door wouldn't be too upsetting.

He would need to come up with some excuse for Sweeney to explain why he needed to cross the geofence, though. Otherwise the guard would get the alert and come drag him back by the ear.

'Alright. But I'm not giving you my wife's number. Call this phone again, and I'll redirect it to my mobile before I leave work on Wednesday.'

That meant Carver would almost certainly be hovering over the call, but Lane had expected that anyway.

•

The mechanic's workshop smelled like melted plastic and roast chicken. The latter turned out to be because Lane was interrupting his lunch.

'G'day,' the man said, putting his knife and fork down and standing up.

'Sorry to interrupt. Dave Harrington sent me to collect Karpathy's ute; he said you'd have it ready.'

'Ah.' The man's face turned grave. 'His lot aren't much for showing up at a specific time. They just turn up whenever they need something and expect that to work out. I'm Bob Greene.' The man held out his hand.

'Lane Holland,' Lane said, shaking it once.

If his name stirred any recognition for Bob, the mechanic didn't show it.

'You've really turned this job around fast – I'm impressed.'

'There wasn't that much to it. Your chassis is fine. I was able to knock out the dent in the roof, and we replaced the windshield. The rest was just checking to make sure all the systems are working and it's safe to drive.'

'That doesn't seem like much damage for such a serious accident.'

Bob shrugged. 'You'd have to read the accident report, but I don't think the poor lass hit anything. Most damage was from the roof coming to rest against a rocky outcrop.'

'There wasn't any damage from the jaws of life?'

'Mate, if they'd had to use the hydraulic rescue tools, you wouldn't get the car back at all. You don't fuck around with trapped drivers; they would have peeled the top off like a tin can.'

'You're in the SES?'

'Nah, I'm with the Rural Fire Service, so we work pretty closely together. I'm familiar with their procedures.'

'Right. So they didn't need to open it up because' – he lowered his voice, trying to show respect – 'she'd already passed?'

Bob gave him an odd look.

'Natalie and I were actually just talking about me signing up with the SES,' Lane explained. 'I'm really interested in how they do things.'

'Right. Well, you could always ask Natalie, but if the girl was inside the car, dead or alive, they'd have opened it up. You get the victim out. She must have been outside the car when she passed.'

So Hannah had crashed the car, called emergency services to say she was trapped, managed to get out of the ute and then died.

'Did you have to clean the interior, or do the police do that?' Lane asked. He was resigned to Bob thinking he was a ghoul.

'Detailing is part of the service, but it didn't need a lot of cleaning,' Bob said.

Lane knew that the police wouldn't have cleaned any blood out of the interior either. So Hannah had had what seemed like a fairly minor accident and wasn't suffering from serious blood loss.

Then why did she die? That wasn't Bob's question to answer, Lane supposed. He might never know, unless he could finagle some way to get the medical examiner's report.

'There is one thing you might want to keep an eye on,' Bob remarked. 'When the tow truck brought the ute here, there was no petrol left in the tank. I called the cops to check, and they said they didn't drain it as part of their inspection.'

'It's a hybrid,' Lane says. 'I don't know much about how they work.'

'They still need petrol to run.'

'You said it hit rock – could that put a hole in the fuel tank?' Or could someone have drained the tank on purpose?

'Nobody at the scene smelled or saw petrol leaking, and I've gone over the thing millimetre by millimetre and can't find any fault. But I won't bullshit you – I've worked with plenty of hybrids and plenty of utes, but hybrid utes? I'm no expert. This model only hit the Australian market at the beginning of this year.'

'Really? Are they expensive?' Lane wondered how Karpathy could afford to buy at least two of these utes, if they were so cutting edge. Was running such a small farm really that lucrative?

Bob shot him a sideways look, and Lane realised that probably wasn't the most appropriate question.

'Damn right they are. Anyway, keep an eye on it. If it seems to be going through petrol too fast, or you smell anything, pull over immediately and call me. I'll tow it out to Albury and someone with more expertise can take a crack at it.'

'I'll let Dave know.'

'I've put the charge on Karpathy's account, so she's good to go,' Bob said.

'Insurance isn't paying for it?'

Bob shrugged. 'Not my business.'

Maybe Karpathy didn't want his premiums going up. Or maybe he didn't want an insurance claim putting another set of eyes on the circumstances of the accident.

'I'll park it in the bay out front for you,' Bob said. 'One more thing. I found this ... I assume it belonged to the girl?'

He went to the counter and, after a few minutes of shuffling around invoice books and empty mugs, pulled out a rose-gold mobile phone still connected to a short charging cable.

Lane's heart stopped. A mobile phone. Not just any mobile phone, either – Hannah's. The holy grail for any investigation. And Bob was just going to give it to him.

'Shouldn't the police have collected her personal effects?' he asked, taking it with a thankfully steady hand.

'I don't think they found it. It was an odd thing; she'd tucked it inside the cover of the driver's seat.'

She'd called for help and then hid the phone? Perhaps she'd been disorientated.

Or maybe hiding the phone was such an ingrained habit she'd done it automatically before getting out of the car.

'Anyway, I let the cops know and they said they'd already signed her other bits and pieces over to Karpathy. Said I should just give it back to you guys when you came to collect the ute.'

That probably wasn't the correct protocol – not that Lane was an expert in procedure anymore – but it was clear the local police hadn't placed much importance on this accident. They saw it as open and shut, job done.

Lane tucked the phone into his back pocket and tried to ignore it. It wasn't like he could use it. He needed to hand it over to Karpathy.

But then, Karpathy might not even know it existed. Bob had spoken like this was the first time he was mentioning it, not like it was something he'd already spoken about to Karpathy or Dave.

It wasn't like it mattered. It was probably locked, and so would be useless to Lane.

While Bob left to sort out the ute, Lane pulled the phone back out of his pocket and examined it. The battery was dead, after nearly a week lying dormant in the ute. But he did have the charging cable.

Surreptitiously, Lane found an outlet in the waiting area with a USB port, and plugged the phone in, just to see if he could switch it on. He kept an ear out for the rumble of the ute moving slowly through the workshop.

When the battery was at one per cent, Lane held down the power button. Immediately he was presented with a square array of dots, and a prompt to draw the correct pattern to unlock the screen.

He held the phone gingerly by the edges and tilted the screen under the workshop's fluorescent light. There.

On the screen, a shape smeared by Hannah's fingertip. Perhaps she hadn't been diligent about cleaning her screen. Or maybe she'd unlocked it in a hurry, her hands still grimy from working in the gardens.

There were only a few unlock patterns that would leave that shape smeared on the screen. He tried one, and the phone vibrated in his hand and flashed an error message.

On the second attempt, the lock screen dissolved and was replaced by Hannah's home screen. She had no background photo, only a black space filled with app icons. Internet. Email. Messaging.

There were no notifications – no missed calls, no unread messages.

The sound of the ute's engine cut off, and Lane yanked the charger from the wall and tucked everything back into his pocket. The phone buzzed, probably to complain of a low battery.

'Here you are,' Bob said as he re-entered the workshop. He held out the keys. 'She's all yours.'

•

Outside, Lane unlocked the ute and slid into the passenger seat. He tried not to imagine the ghost of Hannah in the driver's seat.

The ute had a USB charger port, but it was no good to Lane while the engine was switched off. Turning on the engine without a licence probably wasn't illegal, but he wasn't willing to take any additional chances.

He opened the glove box, which was bare of anything except the manual and logbook. He tried the centre console next, and hit pay dirt. There was a second USB charging port at the bottom. He plugged the charger in – still useless until the ute was switched on – and then tucked the phone into the bottom of the console and closed the lid. The phone would charge while he and Dave drove back to the farm, and if Dave found it, Lane could pretend he'd had no idea it was there. If Bob ever mentioned the phone to someone else, he could pretend that in the excitement of going to town, he'd forgotten all about it.

Technically he wouldn't be stealing the phone. He would just be failing to bring its existence to anyone else's attention.

REACHING THE KNOB *presented the next challenge. He took a deep breath. He dug his toes into the floor and pushed so that he could slide one knee forward underneath him, then the other. He sat back on his heels, hands on his thighs, and closed his eyes. Thunderbolt pose, he thought, trying to believe it was funny. He swore one day he would tell this story like it was funny. Somewhere else, with a beer in his hands and sun on his face, he'd tell this story and they would all laugh.*

CHAPTER FIFTEEN

DAVE WAS IN the front bar, nursing a half-full pint glass and chatting to an older man in a dark blue police uniform. His face fell when he saw Lane standing in the doorway.

'Argh, that was quick,' he said, looking forlornly at what was left of his beer.

'Sorry,' Lane said, even though he couldn't possibly be early, after the extra time he'd taken to speak to Natalie. 'Actually, if you're not ready to go yet, I was wondering if there's a doctor in town?'

The cop glanced over at him but didn't say anything. He made Lane anxious anyway, even though he'd done nothing wrong.

'If you're not well, you can chat to Deirdre back home,' Dave said. 'She's a nurse.'

The bartender, a young woman with dyed black hair pulled into a ponytail, called out, 'The Georges Bridge Medical Centre is on the corner. They don't take walk-ins, but sometimes they'll squeeze you in if someone hasn't turned up for their appointment.'

Lane held up the ute keys, and Dave held out a hand for them. Lane took that as an agreement they'd stay in town a while longer.

•

'We don't have any appointments left today,' the medical centre's receptionist said. 'But you can fill out the new patient form and we'll find you a time later in the week.'

She slid a clipboard across the counter, but the form stymied Lane immediately.

'I'm sorry, I don't carry my Medicare card with me,' he said. 'I can give you the details when I come back. For my phone number, do you think you could look something up for me? I live on Samuel Karpathy's farm; I think you can get the phone number from his Facebook page?'

She stared at him.

'I'm sorry to be a pain,' he said.

'Take a seat,' she told him. 'Dr Higgs will call your name when she's ready.'

'You said there were no appointments?'

'Take a seat,' she repeated.

He perched on one of the too-firm tub chairs and picked up an old copy of *Gardening Australia*. He flipped to a random page, and after he'd spent a few minutes staring at a picture of a drooping lemon tree, a woman's voice called. 'Lane?'

Lane would not have picked Sam Karpathy and Dr Higgs as siblings. She was petite, and her face was tanned a deep brown, although he knew from the photo he'd found that she'd been quite pale as a child. She had sharp brown eyes, and her blonde hair – dyed, he assumed – was pulled up into a neat twist.

Dr Higgs showed him to a small examination room off the waiting area, and Lane tried to take in as many details as he could. She had a corkboard over her desk with the usual collection of thankyou cards and public service posters. She'd also pinned up a church roster that showed she was due to bring the biscuits for the coming Sunday service, and a card wishing her a happy birthday.

Next to her computer were two framed photographs. A wedding picture of her and a man Lane didn't recognise, and a copy of the same Christmas photo Lane had found.

Perhaps, then, Dr Higgs was the source of the photo. Had she found the picture and sent a copy to her father or brother? Maybe it had turned up, as old pictures sometimes did, when they were putting together the funeral service booklet.

'What can I help you with today?' Dr Higgs asked, taking a seat at her desk.

Lane wasn't sure what to make of the fact that he'd been offered special treatment because he'd mentioned Karpathy's farm. What did that mean? Clearly she'd pushed other patients back in order to see him. Did residents get fast-tracked, and if so, did that mean she was closer to the people there than Karpathy had implied?

'I was hoping to ask you some questions,' he said. 'I understand that where I live – Karpathy's farm – is where you were born.'

Dr Higgs leaned back in her chair. 'Where did you learn that?'

'From Natalie, in the sandwich shop.'

'And why were you and Natalie talking about me?'

He pointed to the framed photo. 'I found a copy of that picture. I felt like there was more to the story.'

Dr Higgs didn't have a very good poker face. He could see she was trying to stay impassive, but something sad broke through. 'There isn't. Is there something medical I can help you with?'

Lane glanced at the framed degrees on the wall. She'd graduated from medical school in just enough time to have completed her residency and started work as a GP before Rebecca disappeared.

'Do you treat many residents of the farm?'

'No,' she said. 'But I'm always happy to, if they need help. I can try to help you too, if you need it. But I have a lot of patients waiting and can't waste time playing games.'

'Did you see Rebecca Goncharov? This would have been six years ago.'

She looked at him, her face as clear a 'yes' as if she'd shouted it. 'That's confidential.'

'Did her tests come back negative? Was she healthy?'

Again, a look of utter sadness crossed Dr Higgs's face.

Rebecca's cancer had returned. And she'd known it.

But she hadn't told her family. And not only had she kept it from them, she'd claimed to have some mysterious good news to share.

'Was she getting treatment?'

'Stop it,' she said, not unkindly. 'Are you asking me this because you're afraid, Lane?' Dr Higgs opened a drawer, and then laid something on the desk. A pamphlet for a local men's homeless shelter. 'Natalie and I can help you.'

'Did you help Rebecca?'

'I'm not going to answer that.'

'Did you know that Rebecca wasn't the first person to disappear after going to live at your father's farm? Did you ever meet Matilda Carver or Alain Serling? Or any others that you know of?'

Dr Higgs had so far proved very bad at keeping her thoughts off her face, which meant that Lane believed she really was as shocked as she looked. She composed herself. 'My brother means well, and our father did before him. But the farm attracts vulnerable people like moths to a light. I would be more surprised if no-one had ever died or gone missing shortly after a stay with them.'

Lane frowned. He hadn't said anything about people dying. 'Are you saying there are people who died shortly after leaving your brother's farm?'

She stood up and opened the exam room door. 'Thank you for coming, Mr Holland. If there's anything medical I can help you with, speak to my receptionist. For any other matters, it would be best if you dealt with Natalie from now on.'

Once he and Dave were in the repaired ute, headed up Hill Road back to the farm, Lane struggled to focus on anything other than the phone hidden inside the console between them.

'What happens when someone on the farm gets sick?' he asked Dave.

'Like I said, Deirdre's a nurse. Or if you prefer to stick to natural remedies, Gretel's a walking encyclopedia. I know there's a lot of work to be done, but nobody will blink if you need a few days to rest and recuperate.'

'Thanks,' said Lane. 'That's good to know. But I mean really sick. With something that would take a long time to recover from. Or something they might not recover from at all.'

Dave shot him a concerned look. 'You okay, mate?'

'Yeah. I'm just curious.'

'Well, I don't know. It hasn't come up.'

Lane side-eyed him. 'It hasn't come up even once in the ten years you've lived here?'

Dave shrugged. 'We live well. The food we eat is clean and nutritious. We get plenty of exercise, we breathe clean air. We don't need drugs to get ourselves going in the morning or help us unwind at night. Is it so hard to believe that no-one gets sick?'

'Right.'

Yes, Lane thought, it *was* hard to believe. Maybe lifestyle could move the needle a bit, but vegetables and fresh air weren't magic. At the same time, he couldn't make the dots connect.

Rebecca had found out her cancer was back, and a few months later she disappeared. What did it mean?

A thought occurred. Alain's Missing Persons profile had mentioned that he needed daily medication for asthma. A chronic illness. It was hard to imagine a connection, but Lane found it difficult to dismiss. Surely the farm wasn't so committed to maintaining the fiction of their perfect lifestyle that they were killing people who fell sick.

CHAPTER SIXTEEN

LANE BROUGHT THE book Lynnie had sent him to dinner – not because he wanted to read it, but because for once he didn't want to get drawn into the table conversation. Too many things were swirling around in his head, and he ate his soup with one hand while staring down at the first page.

Dr Nadya Higgs knew something, but she didn't trust him enough to reveal it. Rebecca Goncharov had almost certainly been sick. Natalie was running some kind of outreach service through her sandwich shop to help people leave the farm, and Hannah had tried to contact her.

And nothing about Hannah's accident added up.

He stayed on in the dining hall, blindly turning the pages, while the other residents finished their meals and drifted out.

He felt more than saw Mina sit down next to him. It was comforting, to have come back to a place of such familiarity that he recognised the way the dining hall benches shifted under her weight.

'*I Could Do Anything If I Only Knew What It Was,*' Mina read from the top of the open page. 'I did not peg you for a self-help guy.'

'Who else is going to help me?' Lane asked, and then immediately felt bad about the joke. A lot of people were trying.

He glanced around the room. They were the only ones left, but he couldn't share the new information before he'd had a chance to sweep for eavesdroppers. He'd be putting Natalie at risk.

'I need to figure out what to do with my life,' he said lightly. 'I'm beginning to suspect farming isn't my calling.'

Mina laughed. 'You're not going back to crime-fighting?'

He explained about the licence issue, and her face fell. 'I didn't even know investigators needed a licence. Shit, do you think I should have one?'

'If it's something you want to pursue seriously, then yeah. If you're worried about getting in trouble, I think you're fine. Our circumstances are very different.'

'You could always write a book,' Mina suggested.

'That would probably fall under the proceeds of a crime,' Lane said. 'Plus I think there's a certain amount of skill and talent involved.'

'You could use a ghostwriter.' Mina kicked at the floor with her toe. 'Mum's publisher circles back to me every now and then to see if I'm interested in writing a memoir. There'd be an audience for one, still. But I couldn't even if I wanted to. They'd have to shelve it in fiction.'

Lane could picture her in front of an audience in a Melbourne bookstore, reading aloud from the only chapter anyone really cared about. Spinning the story they'd agreed to in the dark, while they waited for the police to arrive.

That it was Lane who had fired the gun, not Mina.

He groped for the right words. Surely there was something he could say that might bridge the gap between them.

I've never told anyone, and I never will.

I'd do it again.

I wish it had been me.

Before he could find them, Mina continued. 'Maybe you could be a ghost detective. Have a front person with a licence, and you do the actual investigating.'

Was she kidding, or making an offer?

'That would have to be someone I was very close to,' he said. 'Someone who really trusted me. Historically I'm not good at relationships like that.'

'Yeah, me neither,' Mina said with a sigh. 'What I've been through is tough for people to understand. And it's still hard not to be suspicious of the ones who want to.'

'Do you get bothered much these days? Or have the trolls lost interest?'

She shrugged. 'For the most part they have. The true obsessives never will. For some of them, there's no level of evidence that will convince them they're wrong; they just reformulate their conspiracy theories and go back to banging the drum.'

'That's a very unfortunate thing people do,' Lane said. 'You see it in doomsday cults. When the leader's prophecies are wrong, when the end of the world doesn't arrive on schedule, you'd expect people to pack up and leave. But they cling even tighter to their leader and their beliefs.'

'Human beings are so weird.' She clicked her fingers. 'I've got it. Reality TV.' She was smiling, but Lane suspected it was a deliberate pivot to a less serious topic.

He could almost picture it, some kind of gritty docutainment series about him trying to reintegrate into society. 'I can't imagine anyone actually tuning in.'

'I got an offer once to be a "celebrity" on one of those dance competitions. It was about six months after ... you know, everything, so my profile was pretty high, but I still thought it was ridiculous. It made more sense once I saw the actual celebrities they managed to cast that season.'

'I'm pretty sure the only thing I'm worse at than writing would be dancing,' Lane said.

'There's lots of options. Maybe that one where they parachute celebrities into the jungle and commit war crimes against them. I bet that pays well.'

Lane laughed. 'I think I'd rather wait tables.'

They left the dining hall and started walking in the general direction of the cabins, but without any real purpose.

'I did get an interesting suggestion from Natalie, in the sandwich shop in Georges Bridge. Have you met her?'

Mina shook her head.

'She suggested going into search and rescue.'

Mina looked thoughtful. 'I could see that. You know, search and rescue is one of the roles Echo could have ended up in, if he'd passed muster.'

'I thought he was training to be a cadaver dog?'

'Those crews aren't always looking for people who are alive.'

'Has Echo ever alerted here on the farm?'

'No. But Echo walked past my sister's burial site a hundred times and never alerted.'

They walked in silence for a moment, then Mina asked, 'Why were you discussing your career plans with a woman in a sandwich shop?'

The sun was almost gone for the night, but there was enough visibility that Lane could subtly check no-one was in earshot. When he was confident they couldn't be overheard, he gave Mina the general gist of his conversation with Natalie.

'Weird,' she said.

'Have you met her?' Lane asked.

She thought about it for a moment, then nodded. 'When we passed through Georges Bridge the day I arrived, Dave had to pick a few things up. I was tired so I waited in the car, and she came over to the window and introduced herself. She offered me a biscuit.'

The biscuit tin, Lane remembered. It had been covered in stickers with information on services in the area. A subtle thing, but enough to make Natalie stick in your mind as a person who might be willing and able to help.

'You drove in with Dave?' he asked. 'You didn't come in your own car?'

She shook her head. 'I offered to drive myself in, but Karpathy said that if he allowed people to bring cars, he'd end up losing half his growing space to park them. Dave picked me up from the train station in Albury.'

'So if you wanted to leave the farm, what would that involve?'

'I guess I'd need to ask for a ride back to the station.'

'Dave said he drove Rebecca to the station,' Lane remembered. It was a small thing, but just one more roadblock to leaving. A resident couldn't sneak out if they were done; they needed Karpathy and Dave's cooperation. Not to mention they would only have the ticket money on hand if they'd brought it with them – they needed to talk to Karpathy to get their wages paid out. Another block, another opportunity for Karpathy to talk them out of it.

'Gretel has her own car,' Mina said, 'although I'd hate to ask her for a favour. You could hitch a ride on one of the trucks taking harvests to town or the markets, or I suppose in a real pinch you could flag down the postie van. I don't know how you'd get from Georges Bridge to Albury, though – there's no public transport out here.'

'The postie only passes once a day, though,' Lane said. 'If someone needed to leave urgently, and didn't feel comfortable asking Karpathy or Dave, they wouldn't have a lot of options. They could ask a neighbour for help, but Gretel's pretty intertwined with the farm, and the Smiths …' The gun-toting Smiths wouldn't seem welcoming to anyone. He wondered if that impression of the Smiths was deliberate on Karpathy's part. If they were notifying him of their plans to go hunting, it would be easy to schedule outdoor events to coincide. That would give all the residents a strong impression of the neighbours as a possible threat, not an option if they needed to seek help.

'It would be tricky,' Mina agreed. 'But there are ways.'

Unless, Lane thought, the person hoping to leave knew that the region was flooding, and that if they didn't leave immediately they could be trapped here for weeks. If that was the case, might they be motivated enough to take a ute without permission?

'I think I found out something else,' he said, and told her about his rush appointment with Nadya and what he'd discerned. 'It's not completely confirmed, but I'm confident.'

'Wow,' Mina said. 'So you think Rebecca knew for months that her cancer was back, but she never said anything to her family? Why keep it a secret?'

'I was hoping you would have some idea.'

Mina shook her head. 'I need to tell Rebecca's mother,' she said. 'That's huge.'

They parted ways in front of Mina's cabin, and Lane kept walking. He looped around the back of the accommodation huts, then went past the dining hall and the admin building to the garage where the farm vehicles were kept. He stayed alert to his surroundings as he walked, looking for any sign that anyone else was still out after dark.

He retrieved the phone from the ute and turned it on, checking for a signal. There was none. So when Hannah had called Natalie before leaving the farm, she hadn't been doing it from here.

He slipped the phone into his pocket, well aware that this meant he could kiss goodbye any plausible chance to deny he'd stolen it.

He tried to walk casually, while still glancing left and right to make sure no-one could see him as he stopped behind each building to check for signal. There was none at the admin building, which surprised him because he'd seen Karpathy take calls while standing out on the verandah. He assumed the farm's business phones were on a different network from Hannah's. He worried that he was going to find a signal at the locked shed, which would be another dead end unless he was ready to risk breaking in to find out what was inside. But the bars remained as resolutely flat there as they had everywhere else.

The dining hall was also a wash, as were the four accommodation buildings.

The thought occurred to Lane that maybe he was wasting his time. Maybe Hannah had called from somewhere along the road, and the sound of rain was from the ute's roof. But she had called Natalie half an hour before she crashed, and that timeline didn't work when the accident was so close to the farm. He was sure that the sequence of events began with her running to or from somewhere, making the call to seek help, then deciding to take matters into her own hands and drive to town.

Then, outside the greenhouse, the phone buzzed in his sleeve. He stepped into a shadowed spot and had a look. It was a prompt to download a system update. For a moment he assumed it was just a coincidence, then he realised that the wi-fi signal had lit up in the corner of the screen.

The phone had automatically connected to a network, one that Hannah had the password for.

He opened the wi-fi panel. The currently connected network was named 'Chalice Well', which didn't mean anything to Lane. He didn't think it was the name of anyone he'd met.

He scrolled through the settings, and confirmed that Wi-fi Calling was switched on. So Hannah definitely could have made the call from here.

He opened up the browser, and the tabs she'd had open reloaded. He thumbed from one to the next, but didn't find much. The Facebook homepage, a clothes shopping site and a bunch of pages for something called 'Archive of Our Own'. The last tab was the Facebook page for Natalie's sandwich shop, open to her contact details.

He opened the web history. Going back months, there were occasional single-day bursts of activity on social media and the archive site. It looked like she came into range of the network once a week, with the frequency increasing in the weeks before her death. Then, a few days before, there was no activity at all until she searched for Natalie's shop. He found no other sign she'd been looking for resources to help her escape, or trying to reach out to people on the outside, unless she'd been selectively deleting her history.

He tucked the phone up his sleeve, buttoning the cuff to stop it falling out, and looked around. The greenhouse was quite close to the northern edge of the property, so for Hannah to have got properly out of breath before she made the call, she must have run from one of the other three directions. Unfortunately, that meant almost anywhere on the farm.

He felt like he was on the edge of figuring something out, but it just kept slipping through his fingers.

CHAPTER SEVENTEEN

AT LEAST HE'D solved the problem of how to phone Carver on the day they'd agreed. On Wednesday evening he took Hannah's phone up to the greenhouse, where he could be sure he wasn't overseen.

'You actually called,' Carver said by way of greeting.

'I'm resourceful. Look, I need to ask you a favour.'

Movement down the hill caught his eye: the door of the locked shed opening. Karpathy and Dave emerged, deep in conversation. Worried that he might be spotted, Lane slipped inside the greenhouse. Leaving the door propped open – heeding the warning sign about the carbon dioxide risk, even though the weather had still been too damp to run the biochar kiln in recent days – he retreated into the shadows at the rear.

'This is already me doing you a favour,' Carver said.

'No, it's me doing you a favour. I need to talk to your wife so I can find your daughter. Don't try to bullshit me.'

Sweat prickled on his forehead, and he wiped it away with his sleeve. It had been a warm day, so the inside of the greenhouse was uncomfortably hot.

'Fine. What do you want?'

'I need documents. A medical examiner's report for a recent accident: Hannah Cudney. You must have friends in the police force who could get you a copy, right?'

'Holland, I spent years trying to get access to the coroner's documents about the Rainier Ripper Jane Doe. Why would I have done that if I could just ask a friend to slip them to me under the table?'

'Because you didn't want the documents themselves. You wanted the police to admit that the body might be Matilda and investigate the possibility properly.'

Carver sighed. 'I'll see what I can do.'

'Thank you. Is Mrs Carver with us?'

'I'll get her.'

The governor's wife came on the phone moments later. 'Hello, Mr Holland,' Mrs Carver said. 'Patton's told me a lot about you.'

'I can imagine.' She hadn't said anything about Carver still being with them on speaker, but Lane assumed it was the case.

'What can I help you with?'

'I'm hoping to ask you some questions about Matilda.'

'Of course,' she said. 'Have you found anything?'

She sounded so hopeful.

'Maybe,' he said. 'She definitely came here.'

'Oh!'

'Matilda was travelling with a boyfriend at the time she dropped out of contact with you, right?'

'Hmm, sort of. They were together at school, and they both knew it wasn't going to last past the gap year. He was going into the navy, she was going overseas. I think they both took it as a break-up when he went home.'

'Do you still have his contact details?'

'No, I heard he works overseas now.' Her voice dropped, even though she was presumably talking to him from the privacy of her own home. 'I think he's in military intelligence.'

Damn. Lane had hoped he could talk to the boyfriend, maybe get more insight into the days when Matilda would have come into contact with Karpathy, what might have made her decide to come to the farm.

'Mrs Carver, do you have any idea why Matilda might have come here without telling you where she was going?'

She was quiet for a long moment, then said, 'We loved Matilda very much.'

'Of course.'

'We still do.'

'That's very clear.'

'Twenty-one is a hard age,' she said. 'All my friends warned me.'

'Did you fight?'

'Not so often that I thought much of it at the time. The usual things that parents and their adult kids fight about. She didn't call enough. She forgot Patton's birthday. She thought we were trying to control her and we thought she was on a bad path.

The longer she was away, the angrier she seemed to get. So I started suggesting she come home, that maybe she wasn't ready to go overseas.'

'Was that the only reason you thought she might not be ready to go away?'

'I don't know what you mean.'

'Would you say she was in good health? Had she said anything to you about being worried about any symptoms?'

'No, Matilda was always a healthy kid. She barely took any days off school, all the way through.'

'Was she on any medications?'

Mrs Carver was quiet for a long time. 'No. She – she had been on a – you know – but she'd gone off it before she left. She said the side effects were worse than what they were supposed to treat, especially when she kept forgetting to take it.'

Lane's heartbeat sped up. 'What was it supposed to treat?'

Mrs Carver cleared her throat. 'Depression. She was on an antidepressant. But she just had low moods sometimes, she was never suicidal.'

She sniffled quietly, and Lane wasn't surprised when Carver came on the line. 'I told you not to upset my wife.'

'It's fine,' Mrs Carver said.

'I understand,' Lane said. 'It would be hard to get people to take the case seriously if you admitted to any conflict, or that she might have struggled with her mental health. But I promise you, I'm taking this seriously.'

Behind him, the greenhouse door slammed closed. He jumped halfway out of his skin, then pressed a hand to his beating heart. It must have been the wind. This place had him more skittish than a racehorse.

Moving forward, he pushed the door, but it didn't budge. It was locked.

No, that couldn't be right. He'd seen the lock when he talked to Brandon in the greenhouse. It was the kind that someone needed to slide closed, it couldn't just lock by accident.

'I need to go,' he said to the Carvers, and ended the call before they could reply.

With a click, the roof vent closest to him shut.

'Hey!' he yelled. 'I'm in here, let me out!'

The second roof vent shut. Then the third.

He strode over to the last vent and stood underneath. Cupping his hands around his mouth he yelled with every ounce of volume he could muster up. 'I'm in here! Open the door!'

He could see a human shape moving outside, but the windows were still so streaky with old smoke that he had no idea if anyone could see him or not. Brandon and the others had cleaned it the other day, but they'd been focused on the ceiling, to let sunlight through. When he looked up, he could see endless sky through the pristine glass, going grey now the sun had almost fully set, but that was no help at all.

He continued to yell until his throat ached, and then he realised he could smell smoke.

No.

No.

No.

He ran around the greenhouse until he found the metal pipe that vented from the kiln. A curl of white smoke rose from it, confirming he wasn't imagining the smell.

'Stop!' he shouted into the pipe. 'Help!'

His answer was a larger billow of smoke.

He dropped to his knees. That was what they taught you as a kid, right? Get down low and go, go, go. The smoke would rise, leaving him with breathable air at the bottom. For a few minutes, maybe.

He had the phone, but who could he call that would be able to send help in time? Frantic, he looked up the phone number for the Karpathy farm, and wasn't surprised when it diverted to the message bank. There was no-one in the admin building at this time of night.

He rummaged around the lower shelves, looking for something heavy enough to break the glass. He pushed aside terracotta pots, metal sieves, empty watering cans. Finally his hand closed on the head of a rubber mallet.

He stood up, ready to swing, when the bolt rattled and the door swung open.

'Hey,' Gretel said, the greeting absurd in the face of him standing there on the verge of tears, death-gripping a mallet. 'I heard shouting?'

'The biochar kiln is running, don't come in,' Lane said. He dropped the mallet on the ground and rushed to the door.

'No it isn't,' Gretel said, her tone soothing.

'I could see the smoke,' Lane said. 'I could smell it.'

'I'm sure you could. Our bodies are slaves to our minds, if we let them be.' She patted him on the arm. 'You've had a fright. Do you want to come up to my place for a cup of tea?'

'No.' Lane looked down the hill, still agitated, trying to see where Karpathy and Dave had gone.

'Are you sure? You're not going to get into any trouble with Sweeney; I'm sure he trusts me.'

'Thank you, but no.' Lane looked at the ground. Any footprints in the mud around the door had been wiped out by his and Gretel's, and there was no sign of any disturbance in the gravel that surrounded the biochar kiln. Someone had locked him in on purpose. Why?

Once he'd managed to shake Gretel off, he went to the kiln and pulled aside the corrugated iron that served as a lid. Someone couldn't just light a fire and leave no trace.

The inside was a brick-lined pit, and aside from a light layer of ash inside, it was empty. There were no footprints or handprints in the ash, only striations left by a shovel, probably from the last time the kiln was cleaned out.

Lane kneeled by the top, where the metal pipe that lead to the greenhouse was installed. And there he found it, tucked into the mouth of the pipe: a handful of fresh, green eucalyptus leaves smooshed into a ball. Breaking it apart, he found that a lit match had been jammed into the middle, scorching the leaves black.

Nothing produced smoke like trying to burn still-green leaves. So clearly smoke had been the goal.

But had they been trying to scare him, or kill him?

HE PRESSED ONE *palm against the door, then the other. He leaned his weight on them, let his head hang between his arms for a moment. So close.*

A week ago this would have been so simple. Get out of bed. Walk to the door. Turn the knob. Now every step was a battle.

He didn't have the core strength to just reach for the knob. Instead he had to press his palms against the wood and pull himself up, hand over hand.

Then it was in his grip, cold and round. He took a deep breath and twisted.

Nothing happened.

The door was locked.

CHAPTER EIGHTEEN

LANE BARELY SLEPT that night. He dozed off occasionally, but every time an animal called out or a settling building creaked, he woke up again, sure it was a person trying to get into his cabin. When the dark started to turn grey ahead of the sunrise, he gave up and decided to take advantage of the early wake-up to sneak back into the garage and return the phone to the ute console. He hated to give it up, when there was so much he could do with it, but he couldn't risk Sweeney deciding he was overdue for a random search of his cabin.

He skipped breakfast, because someone had tried to hurt him and he didn't want them to see him looking exhausted and jumpy. He went straight to the wash-and-pack shed, keeping the door open so he could watch for anyone approaching the shed and try to keep track of where Dave and Karpathy were. Dave disappeared into the garage and pulled the roller door shut behind him. It was loud enough that Lane was confident he would know if the man came out again, so he switched his focus to tracking Karpathy as he meandered around the farm, checking in with his flock.

After a while, he saw Karpathy coming down the gravel road with Alessandra. He had an arm wrapped around her shoulders, pulling her close to him, and their heads were bowed together, talking. They went into the admin building and Lane went in search of Mina, confident that Karpathy would be distracted there for a while.

He found Mina working on repairs to a star-picket fence that had washed away in the flood.

Lane wished he'd grabbed a hat. It was still technically spring, but the days had grown warmer, and the muggy weather that had followed the rain was behind them. The soil beneath his feet felt firmer, even if still far from the baked clay of farms out west.

She looked at him. 'Shouldn't you be in the wash-and-pack shed?'

'I might fall a little behind,' he admitted. 'But I'm also really bad at this, so I don't think anyone will notice.'

He could smell smoke. 'Is something burning?' he asked, wondering if he was having some kind of olfactory flashback.

'There's a grassfire in the Smiths' back paddock. The Rural Fire Service will have it out soon enough. We're lucky there's no wind today.'

She lifted the slide hammer – a large steel tube with handles on either side – like it weighed nothing.

'Can I help?' he asked. He expected her to hand him the hammer, but instead she pointed at the ground in front of her.

'Can you hold the picket steady for me?' she asked. 'The hardest part is getting the hammer on without the bloody thing falling over.'

She pointed to the pile of star pickets. He grabbed one and held it upright, pushing the sharp end into the ground.

'That's great,' she said. 'Except, see how the other pickets all have the side with the holes facing the same way?'

'Sorry,' he said, twisting it around. 'I could never get the hang of flat-pack furniture, either.'

'I still can't believe you convinced anyone you wanted to learn to farm. No, not there, unless you want an elbow to the eyeball. Actually, just squat down and hold it here.' She tapped a foot near the base.

He crouched as instructed and looked up at her. She gave him a short nod of approval, fitted the slide hammer over the top and slammed it home. The blow rang through the picket, but Lane held on until she told him to let go.

'Have you ever seen the biochar kiln in use?'

'A bunch of times, yeah,' she said, swinging the hammer again. 'They ran it nearly every day before the rain set in, trying to get rid of the dead wood before the fire season starts.'

'I'm surprised you can do that and chat at the same time.'

'Gravity does most of the work,' she explained. 'Look.' She hefted the hammer then let go, throwing her arms into the air like she was doing the YMCA. The hammer fell, driving the picket in further.

'Can I have a go?'

'Knock yourself out. When this one hits the ground,' she pointed to a hole in the picket a few inches above the ground, 'it's in deep enough.'

To his surprise the slide hammer was easy to use, although he quickly found himself out of breath.

'So if I wanted to run the kiln, what would I do?'

She frowned. 'Karpathy is really particular about the kiln. You can't just use it for a lark. If you do it wrong, you can make bad char that damages the gardens, or waste a bunch of fuel for nothing.'

'Meaning only a few people are allowed to do it?'

She nodded. That made it more likely that it had been Karpathy or Dave who had lit it – anyone else hanging around the kiln would have raised suspicions.

He swept his gaze left and right, grateful that the hilly layout of the farm made it easy to ensure that no-one was looking their way, then showed her the bundle of scorched leaves he'd taken from the kiln the night before. 'Is something like this used to start it?'

She examined the burnt tips of the leaves. 'You found this in the biochar kiln?'

'Yes.'

She shook her head. 'The biochar kiln needs to be filled with very dry wood, then lit from the top and covered. The point is to keep the oxygen low, so you make carbon, not carbon dioxide. This would do the opposite, creating as much smoke as possible.'

That's what Lane had thought. 'Then someone tried to kill me.'

She listened to his story with a thoughtful frown. When he was done, he expected her to offer a reasonable explanation, to assuage his paranoia. Instead she asked, 'Do you think they overheard the whole conversation?'

'Maybe. Or maybe I've just gone too far, prodding in corners and asking uncomfortable questions.'

'Do you think it's time to leave?'

'I barely know more than I did when I got here. I've confirmed Alain and Matilda worked here, but that's it.'

'That confirmation could be enough to get the police involved. The families could ask for an inquest.'

'All they'd have is my word I saw it in the files. And I'd have to explain how I got access to them.'

'I'll tell them I found them,' she said.

He wanted to pull his own hair out. 'We only get one shot at doing this undercover. If I leave, and the police brush it off, or the files get dismissed because, I don't know, you could have planted them, we're not going to be able to come back and try again.'

She met his eyes, her expression so intense he had to fight the impulse to look away. 'Is this about finding Matilda?' she asked. 'Or is this about *you* finding Matilda?'

•

Lane stewed on that as he walked back to the wash-and-pack shed. It wasn't about his ego. He just didn't trust that anyone else could actually find the answers. If they could, it wouldn't have become a cold case. He was the only one willing to do what it might take to get there.

He could actually hear Lynnie's voice: *Isn't that the same attitude that landed you in prison?*

He wasn't surprised when Karpathy fell into step beside him. Lane stopped and turned to look at him. He wasn't going to let Karpathy follow him all the way back to the shed. He didn't want to be alone in there with him.

'I've noticed you two are spending quite a lot of time together,' Karpathy said, nodding up the hill to where Mina had returned to her fencing.

'I suppose,' Lane said, although he didn't think it was a lot, on balance. He spent most of his time working his assigned tasks, or at meals, or sneaking around. The farm seemed dedicated to filling every moment of the day with some kind of activity, preferably in a group. He snatched brief moments with Mina to exchange information. If that was excessive, just what did Karpathy expect?

'My worry is that you're turning a little too far inward, and missing out on opportunities to connect with other people here.'

'It's really not like that,' Lane said. 'I'd like to get to know everyone better.'

'Great. Hey, are you free on Saturday night?'

'Yes.' What plans could Lane possibly have that Karpathy wouldn't know about?

'Every year we have a little party to mark the beginning of the fire danger period. In a week the restrictions will come in, so we won't be able to light the bonfire anymore. Saturday night will be the last one of the year.'

Lane hesitated. After his experience in the greenhouse, a bonfire party didn't sound like his idea of a relaxing time.

'We don't usually invite people if it's their first year on the farm,' Karpathy continued. 'I think you need to experience the bushfire season firsthand to understand why it's an important tradition for us. But you should come along. Meet people. You know, Alessandra really likes you.'

'Alessandra?' Lane repeated. He could remember exchanging about four sentences with Alessandra on cheese day. But not wanting to arouse Karpathy's suspicions further, he simply said, 'Sure. Sounds like fun.'

•

Lane had an hour to go before quitting time, and no hope of clearing the backlog that had built up while he was helping Mina fix the fence in time, when Mina knocked on the shed door.

'I thought you might need some help,' she said, surveying the stack of unwashed and unsorted baskets with a sigh. 'I'd ask who trained you, but it was me.'

'Careful,' he said. 'Karpathy is already suspicious of us spending so much time together. I think he might have set me up on a blind date with Alessandra.' He frowned. 'Is it still a blind date if you've met the other person before?'

'Weird thing for him to do, if he was trying to murder you just a few hours ago,' she said, picking up a basket of lettuce and rinsing it under the tap.

'It is weird. But that's not proof he wasn't the one who did it.'

'Is your date at the bonfire on Saturday?'

'Did he invite you too?'

She nodded. 'He didn't try to matchmake me with anyone, though.'

'Maybe he wants you to go with him,' Lane said. 'Maybe that's it – he tried to kill me to get me out of the way because he wants you for himself.'

'No,' she said, and the swiftness of it carried certainty.

'Is he not interested in women?'

'I've never seen him show any sign of interest in anyone, of any gender, the whole time I've been here. There's never anyone sneaking out of his room with last night's shoes in their hand.'

'It's not unheard of for leaders of high control groups to claim to be celibate as a cover, when they're actually having secret, exploitative relationships with their underlings.'

She turned around and leaned against the bench. 'Would it bother you? If he was interested in me?'

'I think Karpathy is manipulative, and probably dangerous. It would be odd if I was comfortable with the idea of the two of you together.'

For some reason she found that funny.

'What?'

'Nothing,' she said, shaking her head. 'It's just, when I first met him, he reminded me a lot of you.'

'How so?'

'He was very obviously working to make me like him. He wanted me on his side, to open up.'

Lane had noticed the similarities himself, but it still stung. He turned the tap off, dried his hands on a towel, then leaned on the bench beside her. 'I was working an angle. That wasn't the real me.'

She made a noncommittal noise. 'Then I don't think I've ever met the real you.'

'That's not true. I think you and Lynnie are the only people who actually know me. No,' he corrected himself, 'not even Lynnie. You're the only person in the whole world I'm not lying to in some way.'

Mina laughed. 'That's really fucked up.'

He couldn't disagree.

'Hey,' he said, 'I found a wi-fi signal near the greenhouse. Do you have any idea where that might be coming from?'

It was a pretty ham-fisted way to get off an uncomfortable subject, but she didn't call him on it. 'I don't know much about that stuff. Maybe it's Brandon's? He loves the greenhouse, and he's into tech.'

'It was named "Chalice Well" – does that mean anything to you?'

'Nothing useful. Chalice Well is a spring in England, one of those spots that supposedly have healing waters.'

She looked sad, and Lane decided not to press it any further, assuming that she had learned about it during her mother's cancer treatment.

'I think we need to avoid each other for a while,' he said. 'Let Karpathy think he's still pulling the strings. This bonfire will be a good opportunity to talk to the inner circle, the people who were here when shit went down with Matilda, Alain and Rebecca.'

'Sure,' she said, although she sounded sad. She pushed away from the bench and went as if to leave, then paused in the doorway. 'What are you lying to Lynnie about?'

'What I'm doing here. The fact that you're here.' He took a deep breath. 'And she still thinks I killed our father.'

'Why not just tell her the truth?'

'If I tell her, she'd need to decide what to do with that information. Even doing nothing is still making a choice. What gives me the right to burden her with that?'

'What gives you the right to choose for her?' Mina asked, and let the door close behind her without waiting for an answer.

CHAPTER NINETEEN

LANE'S ANXIETY EASED when he saw Alessandra standing next to the food table on Saturday evening. She looked like she'd come to the bonfire directly from a day working in the garden. Her hair was still scraped back in the low ponytail she wore under her sunhat, and there were damp grass stains on the knees of her pants.

It was clearly not the ensemble of someone invested in being set up with him.

He wondered idly whether Alessandra really had told Karpathy that she liked him. For all he knew Karpathy was playing the same game on the other side, asking Alessandra to make nice with Lane.

Over at the bonfire, Dave sat on a tree stump with a guitar in his lap. 'Play "Khe San",' Lane called to him, getting a few weak chuckles from some of the older residents and blank looks from the younger ones.

To his surprise, Dave did strum the opening bars of the old song, followed by a brief section of 'Wonderwall', and then a melody that it took Lane a few seconds to recognise as Rick Astley's 'Never Gonna Give You Up'.

Then, satisfied with his joke, Dave launched into an old campfire song that most people present seemed to know, as voices scattered around the group joined in.

'Hi,' Alessandra said, when he reached her. 'You want to grab some dinner?'

A snaking queue had formed for people to serve themselves from the modest buffet. There was a pot of soup, a platter of the almost-bread and a plate of biscuits.

To his surprise, Sweeney, whom he had barely seen in recent days, was standing on the other side of the table, chatting to Gretel. Having a date night of his own, Lane supposed.

'I had a late lunch,' Lane said, not keen to get dragged into conversation with them. 'Maybe later.'

'Yeah, me too. It's getting so busy now that the weather is really heating up.' Alessandra toyed with the end of her ponytail. 'How are you finding life on the farm?'

Terrifying. Confusing. Frustrating. 'Everyone has been really welcoming,' he said. 'You mentioned on cheese day that you've lived here for a really long time. What was this place like when you first arrived?'

'Smaller but bigger,' she said. 'Every year there's something new, more growth. When I first came here, there was a lot more open space, but now there's more to see and do each day.'

'And the people?'

'Well.' She sounded sad. 'Most of the early people are gone. Sometimes this place feels like a river you can't swim in twice. People come and go all the time.'

'Are you still in contact with any of them?'

'No. When people leave, we respect that decision. They're always welcome to come back, but we don't chase after them.'

That sounded like a pretty way of saying that they were ostracised, which was a common control tactic for cults. It prevented people from leaving, under threat of being cut off themselves, and also stopped ex-members from telling those still entangled how much happier they could be on the outside.

He noticed Mina at the edge of the firelight, talking to a man around Lane's own age, tall and blond. Mina seemed fascinated by what he was saying, her eyes wide and mouth quirked in a smile.

Alessandra must have followed his gaze, because she said softly, 'That's just John. He's a really good guy.'

'Have you known him a long time?'

Alessandra laughed. 'You could say that. We dated for ten years. So I know how you're feeling.'

'Oh. No!' Lane shook his head vehemently. 'She and I aren't ... that's not a thing. No.'

'Are you sure?' she asked. 'Because I'm getting a strong vibe that I'm wasting my time here. Or is that sad puppy look because you'd rather be talking to John?'

'No! I want to be talking to you. But – and it's nothing personal; you seem really lovely – I'm really not looking for ...' He gestured between the two of them. God he was bad at this.

'Breathe, Lane. It's alright.' She drained the last of her beer. 'I'm sorry, I probably seem completely desperate here.'

'No way.' He raised an eyebrow. 'After all, I'm an amazing catch. Us unemployed violent felons have to beat them off with a stick.'

That made her crack a smile, at least. 'For the sake of my ego, can I add some context?'

'I love context.'

'Because John and I were together so long, I never had to worry about where I fit in. I had friends here who I'd known and worked alongside for years. Decades, in some cases.'

Lane wanted to ask about those decades-long friendships, but he let her continue uninterrupted.

'Most people who arrive at the farm are young. In their twenties, sometimes even their late teens. I was the same; I was twenty-five when I came.'

'You were a lawyer, right?'

'Yep. I was going to be the best. I was clocking eighty billable hours a week, with eyes on an office that faced Hyde Park. I –' She broke off with a rueful grimace. 'I'd rather not talk about how I crashed and burned, if it's okay.'

'Of course.'

'Long story short, I found the farm. But the thing is, over the years, you get older and the new arrivals stay the same age. The group of people my age got smaller and smaller. So when John and I split up …' She shrugged. 'I've been really happy here, but recently I've started to wonder if it's still the right fit.'

If Karpathy knew she was feeling this way, that might be

why he would try to matchmake her with Lane. Alessandra seemed like a real asset to the farm.

'That must be a tough position to be in,' Lane said. 'After twenty-five years. I mean, I've been in the same place for six years and I'm nervous about having to relearn how the world works.'

'Hey, we're not on the moon here,' Alessandra said with a laugh. 'I've been on the internet. We watch TV. But people out there are so weird.'

'Weird?' Lane echoed, although he suspected he knew what she meant. He'd found life on the farm so jarring, it made sense that she would experience the same thing in reverse.

'Yeah. They just … walk around like everything's normal. Going to restaurants. Taking holidays. Buying junk. It's surreal. Like, they know. Everyone knows. And they just walk around ignoring it.'

Apparently he didn't know what she meant. 'Everyone knows?'

Alessandra bit her lip. 'I … we're not supposed to talk to new people about this stuff. I shouldn't.'

Lane's heartbeat sped up. 'You're not allowed?'

'Of course it's allowed. It's more like, if someone hasn't figured it out on their own, it's not right to try to convince them. Why burden them with that?' She let out a heavy sigh. 'Ugh, you're probably over there worried you've stumbled into a doomsday cult.'

The thought had occurred to Lane. 'Of course not,' he said.

'We're not up here stockpiling canned goods because we think the nukes are going to drop,' she explained. 'But the world is burning through its finite resources as fast as it can. Sooner or later it has to all come crashing down.'

'But not here,' Lane said, realisation dawning.

He was surprised to hear Alessandra, who seemed so level-headed and rational, talking like this. But she wasn't wrong, was she?

Did everyone here feel this way?

'Exactly,' she said, her smile sad. 'If the supply chain suddenly collapsed, Karpathy farm would carry on as normal. There's a security in that. But it's lonely. Part of me thinks I'm better off going back out into the world, enjoying the last days of Rome. Another part of me is scared. So when two single forty-something guys moved in …'

'That explains why Gretel grabbed Sweeney so fast,' Lane said, nodding in their direction.

'I can't shade Gretel for that,' she said. 'Widow's privilege.'

That was news to Lane. 'I didn't know she lost a husband.'

'Oh, well, I mean they weren't actually married, but it was still devastating for her. Gretel was with Reggie Karpathy right up until he died.'

'Huh.'

'It was a little weird, you know,' she said, dropping her voice. 'Because she's not that much older than Sammy. Karpathy had hoped to buy next door himself, but Gretel's uncle sold it to her without putting it on the open market.' She laughed. 'Karpathy tried to nudge Sammy in her direction, hoping they'd get married and merge the properties. So we all questioned it a bit when, a few years after he'd given up on the idea, he started seeing her himself.' She shook her head. 'But she was good for him. It was nice to see him happy.'

'Would that have been messy?' he asked, as casually as he could. 'If Karpathy senior had married Gretel and then died, wouldn't she have had a claim on this property?'

'That could be why they never did,' Alessandra mused. 'Karpathy was a great guy, but he could be brutally pragmatic. I think if he and Gretel had had a kid, he might have willed everything to them to avoid the issue.'

Convenient for Sam Karpathy, Lane thought, that his father had died suddenly before any of that could become an issue.

'Alright, when I'm getting this catty, it's a sign to turn in,' Alessandra said.

'Let me walk you back,' Lane said. He didn't want to give her the wrong impression, but there was so much more he wanted to know.

Alessandra offered Lane her arm, and together they cautiously made their way up the dark path towards the little houses.

Something moved in the grass ahead of them and Lane paused, thinking of foxes and snakes. Then a woman laughed, a little too loud, and a man's voice said, 'Whoa, steady on.'

'Is everything alright?' Lane called.

The spotlight of a torch swung around, dazzling him for a second before the man apologised and shifted it lower.

'All good here,' he said. 'She stumbled a bit. It's dark.'

'It's okay,' Mina said, from somewhere in the black ahead. 'I can see in the dark. I can't usually, but the dark is different today.'

'What?' Lane said, in unison with the other man, who he realised must be John.

'It's easier if I close my eyes,' she explained.

John swung the torch light around, and after a moment it alighted on Mina, standing a few feet off the path, running her hands back and forth over the seed heads of a patch of tall grass.

'Okay,' Lane said firmly. Alessandra dropped his arm, and he stepped toward Mina. 'I don't think you should keep going in the direction of John's house. Let's go back to the bonfire.'

'I wasn't taking her anywhere,' John said. 'She wandered off – I was just trying to stop her falling down the hillside.'

'Sure,' Lane said. He reached out a hand towards Mina. She grabbed it with both of hers.

'You have very warm hands,' she said.

'Now, I'm not going to judge you,' he said, 'but have you taken something?'

'Yes,' she said, her tone confessional. 'After I finished my bowl of soup, I got back in the queue and had a second one. I'm always so fucking hungry.'

'I saw you with a beer before. Did you open it yourself?'

She nodded.

'Did you put it down at any point? Leave it unattended?'

'Hey, man, what are you implying?' John asked. He must have moved the torch, because suddenly they were in the dark and Lane couldn't make out Mina's face properly.

'No,' Mina said. 'I've never left a drink unattended in my life.'

'I think everyone needs to calm down,' Alessandra said. 'Lane, nobody here would have done what you're implying, least of all John. She's probably just dehydrated, or coming down with something.'

'No,' Mina said. 'I think Lane's right. This doesn't feel good.'

'Come on,' Lane said, pulling on Mina's hand.

Instantly the light was back on them. 'Hey, no,' John snapped. 'You're not taking her anywhere. How do we know it wasn't you who drugged her?'

'Chaperone me then,' Lane said. 'But I'm taking her to get medical attention, right now.'

•

The music cut off when Dave saw them storm back into the bonfire area, Lane with his arm around an unsteady Mina and John and Alessandra trailing behind them.

'She needs to go to a hospital,' Lane said.

Dave scanned the group. 'Deirdre?' he called.

'A hospital,' Lane repeated. He pointed to the woman closest to him. 'Go to the admin building and call an ambulance.'

'There's no ambulance station in Georges Bridge,' Dave said. 'If she's safe to be moved, it's faster if we drive her.'

Fuck. Lane didn't want to put her in a car with Dave. He knew he was breaking character, treating everyone like the threat they actually were instead of pretending to trust them, but the time for schemes was over. He needed to get Mina somewhere safe, as quickly as possible.

'Where's Sweeney?' he asked.

'I think he went to Gretel's house,' Dave said. 'We could take her up there. Gretel will –'

'Hospital,' Lane snapped. He pointed to the woman again. 'Please go and tell Sweeney I'm going to the hospital with Dave and –' He stumbled over his words, coming dangerously close to blurting out Mina's real name in his panic. 'I'm going to the hospital. If he doesn't approve, he can come after me.'

'What has she taken?' Dave asked, when they were walking as quickly down the road to the garage as Mina could manage. He looked genuinely unnerved by her spacey demeanour, which soothed Lane's distrust a little.

'Nothing by choice,' Lane said. 'The hospital will be able to identify it.'

'Honey, you can tell us,' Dave said to Mina. 'You're not going to get into any trouble.'

'Leave her alone,' Lane said.

Dave hit the key fob, and the ute that lit up as it unlocked was the same one Hannah had died in. Lane almost asked if they could take the other one, then realised that if Sweeney did actually follow them, there was a risk he'd discover the phone Lane still had stashed in the centre console.

Lane helped Mina climb into the back seat. 'Are you right with the belt?' he asked.

'Ha, you're kidnapping me again,' she said, ignoring his question. She also ignored the seatbelt, so he reached over and clicked it in for her.

'What does that mean?' Dave asked.

'It means she's fucking high, Dave,' Lane said, getting in the back seat beside her.

'I'm not high,' she said. 'I feel … Terry Pratchett made up a word for the opposite of drunk. I've gone past sober. What's the word?'

'No idea,' Lane said, and at the same time Dave said, 'Knurd.'

'You're a nerd,' she said, and they were away.

•

The ute's headlights swept slowly over the curves of the hill road as they traced that first dark trip in reverse. Dave slowed the ute to a crawl whenever they came to a corner, and when Lane peeked between the front seats, he noticed Dave didn't have his foot on the accelerator at all. They were coasting down.

'There's no point trying to go slow on purpose,' Lane said. 'Even if she sobers up by the time we get there, the hospital tests will be able to identify the drug for hours. You could take until tomorrow to drive us and not achieve anything except pissing me off.'

'I'm not trying to stall,' Dave said, although Lane noticed he did speed up. 'It's just force of habit.'

'I suppose it must be nerve-racking, driving this road in the dark after what happened to Hannah.'

'Yes, but I mean we always take this road slowly. This is a hybrid. When the ute is rolling downhill, not using the engine to accelerate, it can harvest that power and feed it into the battery.

Because it's all downhill from the farm to Georges Bridge, if you're patient you can just …' He made a hand gesture, imitating a car rolling down a hill.

'So, hypothetically, could you drive all the way with an empty petrol tank?'

Dave considered this. 'I wouldn't risk it just to test the theory. You'd need at least enough petrol to start the engine and get it out the gate. But in a pinch, I reckon it could be done.'

Suddenly, Lane had a completely different vision of Hannah's final journey down this hill. Perhaps, in her hurry to leave, she hadn't noticed the empty fuel light. Then, when she realised, she would have had a choice. She could turn back and refill at the farm's petrol tank – which was risky when she didn't have permission to take the ute – or she could trust that it was possible to make it to town.

But that would require extreme care when braking. If she slowed down too much on the curves, she could lose the momentum she needed to make it through the flat sections of the road to the next decline.

Easy, then, to imagine her headed down a dangerous road, an inexperienced driver in wild weather and an unfamiliar vehicle, perhaps worried that someone was in pursuit to bring her back. Easy to imagine her taking a curve too fast and losing traction, sailing into the void.

There was no reason, then, to think that the empty fuel tank was evidence someone had tampered with the ute. No reason to think anyone even knew she was gone.

All that was left was the question of why she was so desperate to get away in the first place.

'How are you feeling, Mina?' Lane asked. Then he gritted his teeth, realising that he'd used her real name. He glanced at Dave, but he was preoccupied with safely navigating the twisting road.

'I think I could … rip the Earth's crust from its mantle and throw it into space.' She paused, considering her next words carefully. 'Like a frisbee.'

'Yeah, sure,' Lane said. 'Would you say that's better or worse than you felt five minutes ago?'

'I don't think it would be a good idea.'

'So, worse? Any nausea?'

'I just … I don't think you're ever going to get it.'

Rolling out of Georges Bridge and turning onto the Murray Valley Highway towards Albury felt like a fever dream. After so many weeks on the farm, it took a minute to adjust to the reminder that the rest of the world existed. Lane glanced at Dave, wondering if he felt the same, but the other man was focused on the road ahead.

•

When they pulled into the hospital car park, Lane felt like a sprinter on the blocks. He would get one tiny sliver of opportunity to grab the hidden phone without Dave noticing. Was it worth the risk? Between Mina's drugging, his dubious authorisation to leave the farm, and the snarl of lies and half-truths they'd built together, he was heading into one hell of a dangerous situation. He didn't want to be left with no way of seeking help.

Lane waited until Dave had climbed out of the car and shut the driver's door behind him. Then, trusting the deep tint of the ute windows, Lane leaned forward and turned his head towards Mina, hoping that from the outside it would just look like he was checking on her. Without looking down he flipped the centre console open, stuck his hand inside and slid the phone up his sleeve.

Dave opened Mina's door just as Lane had snapped the console shut again.

'You need help getting out?' Dave asked.

'I'm feeling fine,' she said. 'Every now and then I get this wave of ick, but I can walk by myself.'

As they explained the situation to the triage nurse, her eyes swept constantly from Dave to Lane and back again. Lane wasn't surprised when Mina was taken straight back to wait inside the ward, while he and Dave were directed to chairs in the main waiting area.

'I'm going to go call Karpathy,' Dave said, and Lane was left to his own devices.

He went into the men's room and leaned against the sink. He pulled out the phone and keyed in Lynnie's number, the only phone number he had memorised.

She sounded sleepy when she said, 'Hello?' and he realised guiltily that it was nearly midnight.

'Lynnie, it's me. Lane.'

'Lane?' She sounded instantly alert. 'What number is this?'

'Don't worry about it,' he said. 'Is William with you?'

'No, I'm at home. He's in Sydney.' She yawned. 'Probably still at work, though. Is this a future brother-in-law call or a lawyer call?'

'Lawyer call.'

'Shit. What have you done?'

'It's too complicated to go into here. Can you just send him a message and ask him to be on standby? Give him this number, but let him know I might not answer his calls right away. I have to keep it on silent.'

'What the fuck? Cut the bullshit and tell me what's going on.'

Lane hesitated. 'I stole this phone.'

'Oh god.'

'That was the easy one. I've been in contact with Mina McCreery, and I think that's about to come out. Also, I'm probably going to be interrogated on suspicion of drugging her.'

'Did you?'

'No! But someone did, and if you were a cop investigating that, who would you talk to first?'

'Lane Holland. Right. I don't know where to start. Why? Where? I thought you were on a farm.'

'I have been. So has she.'

'Lane' – her voice had reached a very concerning pitch – 'this whole time you've been there, you've been hanging out with Mina McCreery? The Mina McCreery you're in prison for kidnapping?'

'Yes.'

'You have a no-contact order.'

'I am aware of that.'

'This isn't just going to murder your parole chances, Lane. You'll get more time.'

'I am also aware of that.'

She sighed. 'I don't ever want to hear another fucking word about me marrying William.'

'I know. I'll walk you down the aisle.'

'You were going to do that anyway.'

'I was. But I will. I'll make it happen, I promise you. I'm not going to make you put your life on hold anymore.' He was making promises he couldn't keep and he knew it. 'While we're having honesty hour, can I tell you one more thing?'

He didn't know why, exactly, it felt like the right moment, but it did.

'I didn't kill our father. Mina did.'

'Yeah, I know.'

'What do you mean?'

'I always know when you're bullshitting me, Lane. And you know what I think? Good for her.'

CHAPTER TWENTY

AN HOUR TICKED past, with Lane distracting himself with the trash TV playing in the waiting room. The phone buzzed in his sleeve, and Lane was about to excuse himself to go back to the bathroom, when a female doctor approached them.

'The patient has authorised me to speak to a Lane Holland,' she said, looking between him and Dave.

'That's me,' Lane said. *The patient*, he noted as he followed the doctor from the room. So the hospital had been apprised of Mina's name issue.

Mina was sitting on a bed in a curtained bay inside the ward, still wearing her farm clothes. She looked much more clear-eyed, if slightly nauseous.

'The tox screen came back negative for the drugs we commonly test for,' the doctor told him.

Mina didn't look surprised by this, so Lane assumed it had already been explained to her.

'That's not possible,' Lane said. 'I know Mina, and she definitely wasn't in her normal state of mind.'

'Yes, well, when we were going through everything Mina consumed today, she mentioned that the farm often uses foraged ingredients. That gave us a hint about what to look for, and she tested positive for muscimol. It's a hallucinogen found in some mushrooms.'

'You mean like psilocybin? Magic mushrooms?'

'Similar, but no. It's a different compound. I'm a bit of a mushroom enthusiast myself.' The doctor appeared to hear what she'd just said, and rushed to add, 'Edible mushrooms, I mean. I hunt for saffron milk caps, not for the little blue kind. In this region, muscimol is most commonly found in amanita muscaria.'

'Amanita?' he repeated. 'Isn't that the dangerous sort?'

'Hmm, you're probably thinking of the death cap. Amanita muscaria isn't quite as dangerous, but it shouldn't be messed with. You might also have heard it called fly agaric?'

'Fly agaric ... Is that a little red mushroom with white dots? Like out of a storybook?' Lane recalled the mushrooms Mina had found a few weeks previously.

'That's the one. Fun fact, some people believe the fly agaric is where the story of Santa's flying reindeer comes from. Reindeer can safely eat them, but they're still affected by the hallucinogen. Their odd behaviour led to stories that they could fly. Laplanders used to deliberately feed them the mushrooms, because their digestive systems would filter out the dangerous compounds but leave enough muscimol in their urine for humans to use recreationally.'

'Recreational reindeer urine,' Lane repeated. 'That *is* a fun fact.'

'Moving on!' the doctor said, looking embarrassed. 'The nurse has taken your other friend to be tested too, and I'd like you to give a sample if you don't mind.' She held out a plastic sample jar.

'Nobody else showed any symptoms of mushroom poisoning.'

'I had twice as much of the soup as everyone else,' Mina said.

'That could be it. Also, fly agaric is notoriously unpredictable. One might do nothing but give you an excellent night's sleep, try the next and you'll see God. It's possible that Mina's bowl had a particularly strong mushroom in it.'

'Right.' Lane thought about Alessandra, how she'd seemed perturbed by her own loose-lipped behaviour. Had she received a microdose of the hallucinogen, enough to relax her boundaries?

But she hadn't eaten the soup, had she?

'I do recommend that everyone present at the event comes in for testing and observation. But most likely the worst they'll experience is an upset tummy.'

Like Sweeney had experienced after the first meal they ate on the farm?

'How long after exposure will it show up on a test?' Lane asked.

'The body processes it very quickly. A few hours at the most.'

He would never know, then. 'Is this going to be a police matter?'

'No,' Mina interjected. 'I don't want to talk to the police.'

'Are you obligated to report this?' he asked the doctor.

She shook her head. 'At this stage it looks like no harm, no foul. Foraging errors happen. Have you ever seen that screenshot of an AI program identifying an angel of death mushroom as a common white button mushroom? There's a lot of misinformation about what is and isn't safe.'

'It seems like a difficult mistake to make. It's a distinctive mushroom.'

'And there are sites that insist the amanita muscaria is edible. Some people even go on foraging forums and identify pictures of hallucinogenic mushrooms as safe because they think it's funny.'

'We don't need the police,' Mina interjected firmly.

'Then that's that. I'm going to admit you for observation, just overnight, but I'm not overly concerned.'

'Can I stay?' Lane asked. 'If that's okay with you, Mina.'

Mina nodded.

'Well, visiting hours are over. But it's two in the morning. I think people will have more important things to do than kick you out.'

•

Lane sat in the chair next to Mina's bed and was uncomfortably reminded of being in the reverse position years ago. Him in hospital and her visiting, overflowing with contempt for him.

'So,' he said. 'How was God?'

'Oh, I only met a small one,' she said, smiling. 'But she was really nice. You probably need to eat the whole mushroom to meet Capital G.'

'Do you think it was deliberate?'

'Abso-fucking-lutely. My only question is, do the others know they're rolling at these bonfire parties, or is someone taking it upon themselves to expand everyone's mind?'

'Alessandra and John seemed genuinely surprised by how you were acting,' Lane said. 'I think if they knew, they'd have done more to defuse the situation. Dave, though – I think it's plausible he knew. Who collects the farm's mushrooms?'

'John. But that doesn't mean he's the one who laced the soup.'

'Maybe it was slipped directly into your bowl,' he mused. 'Maybe that's how it works. The first time a new recruit attends the bonfire, they get fed something to put them in a suggestible state. A bonfire, music, a bit of dancing. Lots of happy-clappy hugging. It's not unheard of for cults to use mind-altering substances as step one in the brainwashing process.'

'You think this is a cult?'

'I think it's entirely possible.'

'Then what are they trying to brainwash us into?' Mina asked. 'The cult of sustainable farming?'

'It's not the beliefs that make something a cult,' Lane said. 'Hell, basing your group on something genuinely positive can help. A loving religion, a social movement, national pride. Control is what makes something a cult. The underlying beliefs are just a way to get it.' He sighed. 'I think this is too dangerous. You shouldn't go back to the farm.'

'Why not?'

'Because we've disrupted the script. This was supposed to be our way deeper in, and instead I've shown them I don't trust them. If we go back, they're going to watch us like hawks.'

'So you're giving up?'

'No. I'll go back. But you need to be safe.'

'And you don't?'

It was a silly question, and he let it hang unanswered.

The phone buzzed against his arm, and he stood up. 'That'll be my lawyer,' he said.

•

'There isn't a Sydney to Albury red-eye, so I'm on the six am flight,' William said, instead of 'hello'. 'Evelyn too.'

'I thought Lynnie was in Canberra?'

'There is a Canberra to Sydney red-eye.'

'You don't need to come,' Lane said. 'There isn't going to be a police investigation. I've smoothed it over.'

'I am absolutely coming,' William said.

'Please,' Lane said. 'It's under control.'

'You don't get it, do you?' William asked. 'Because you're not the one who has to be there for her when she gets back from visiting you. You don't see how much it devastates her, because she won't let you.'

'I know that,' Lane said. 'But this is important. There are people who've gone missing, and a girl who's dead, and it's just going to keep happening if I don't –'

'This leave was supposed to offer you a future, Lane, not drag you deeper into the past. You don't get to be that person anymore.'

'I'm not trying to play the hero,' Lane said. 'But if you come down here and blow it up, you're going to affect more people than just me. Like I said, I've smoothed it over. Give me time to extract myself with some grace. Corrective Services doesn't have to know about any of this.'

'I'm not your fixer. I'm not here to pull you out of the fire when your schemes blow up in your face. How I fix this is by yanking your head out of your goddamn rear.'

'A week,' Lane said.

William was quiet for a long time, then said, 'A week. But we're still coming down there.'

'Great, have a holiday. The Riverina is lovely at this time of year.'

'What, smoke everywhere and the fire danger rating ticking up by the minute? Real relaxing.' He sighed. 'Maybe we'll rent a canoe.'

'Thank you,' Lane said.

'Don't thank me, it makes me feel grimy. Oh, I do have some good news, though.'

That was music to Lane's ears. 'What is it?'

'You're not in violation of your no-contact order. Mina McCreery made an application to have it withdrawn. Which makes a lot of sense, now. I actually tried to call you about it. I left a message with a Samuel Karpathy, but you never called back.'

Mina hadn't said anything about it to him, which was very like her.

'Karpathy never gave me your message.'

'I thought so. I called twice. I even thought about asking Evelyn to mention it during one of your calls, but I try not to cross the streams. I guess that's unavoidable, though.' He gave a wry laugh. 'Can I be completely honest with you?'

'Please.'

'I really hope Evelyn and I only have daughters.'

CHAPTER TWENTY-ONE

ABOUT AN HOUR later, a nurse poked her head through the curtain. 'Are you Lane?' she asked. 'Dave wanted me to give you a message. He's gone home, but he'll come back and collect you tomorrow, if you call him when you're ready.'

'He wasn't admitted?' Lane asked. 'Did he test negative?'

'I can't give you that information,' she said. 'But good news: you did.'

Mina had fallen asleep, and it seemed that the fly agaric was doing a stellar job as a sleep aid. She didn't even stir as he and the nurse conversed at normal volume.

Lane wished that he could sleep that easily. The chair was uncomfortable, but he suspected that even in a feather bed, he'd have sat bolt upright for the rest of the night. His mind was trying to churn too many things over, too fast, to fall asleep.

Shortly after six, an angel in green scrubs showed him the way to a family lounge, where he made a cup of black coffee.

By the time he returned to the ward, cradling his second cup, Mina was awake and sitting up.

'How are you feeling?' he asked.

'Hungover,' she said.

'Do you want me to get you a cup too?'

'Blergh. I think I'll keep my stomach empty for a while longer, just in case.'

He settled back in his chair. 'I'd really like to ask you something. I'm hoping for an honest answer, but I don't want to accidentally coerce one, so I need to check: do you think you're completely sober now? Or are you still communing with your small god?'

'No, she's left the building.' Mina picked up a jug of water from beside her bed and poured herself a cup. 'What's your question?'

'When did you file to have my no-contact order lifted?'

'The day after you tried to get yourself eaten by pigs.'

So not before he ever came to the farm. He felt strangely disappointed.

'Did you know I was going to be coming to the farm when you decided to go there?'

'Haven't we been through this already? No. I didn't know I would see you there. Surely you know that if I wanted to contact you, I had that power the whole time. All I had to do was ask to be put on your visitor list.'

'It just seems an improbable coincidence for us both to be looking at the same farm at the same time.'

'Let's just say I had known that you were coming to the farm, and I engineered a meeting. What would it mean for you, if I wanted to see you?'

'I think I would interpret that as' – he hoped she would read his pause as him thinking deeply about it and not realise he was just afraid to say it aloud – 'forgiveness.'

'Do you want me to forgive you, Lane?'

'Yes.'

'For what?'

'Is that a trick question?'

'Yes. But probably not in the way you think. Are you sorry?'

'Desperately.'

'For what?'

'For putting you in danger. For frightening you. For putting you in the position where you –'

'Ah.' She looked sad. 'I don't care about that. I mean, I struggled with nightmares for a while, but it turns out therapy works if, instead of treating the counsellor like a fae trickster you need to outwit, you just let them help you.'

'You don't care?'

'I couldn't give less of a shit. You know what I *would* like to forgive you for but haven't?'

'What?'

'You acted like you cared about me, but I was just a tool to you. A puzzle box you needed to solve to get the information you needed.'

'I did care about you. I still do.'

'You know, I believe you? I just think that's worse.' She scrubbed a hand over her eyes. 'You're ruthless, and you're manipulative. And I think it would be easier if that's just who you were. But the worst thing about you, Lane Holland, is that you believe your own bullshit.'

'I'm sorry,' he said, his voice choked.

She held out her hand and let him take it. She squeezed his fingers once, tight.

'I know.'

CHAPTER TWENTY-TWO

SOMEONE CLEARED THEIR throat outside the curtain, and Lane pulled it aside, expecting to see Dave. He had no idea how he was going to explain away anything he might have overheard. Even if it was possible Lane was too tired to try.

Dr Nadya Higgs stood there, looking as surprised to see him as he was to see her.

'Dr Higgs,' he said. 'I didn't realise you worked in the hospital.'

'I'm visiting a patient in the pulmonary unit,' she said. 'When I heard a patient had been admitted after eating poisonous mushrooms outside Georges Bridge, well …'

Lane nodded. It was a safe bet that there was a link to her brother's farm.

He left the curtain open so that they would see Dave when he arrived; Lane didn't want to give him the opportunity to eavesdrop on their conversation.

'Dr Nadya Higgs,' he said. 'This is ...' He paused, letting Mina take the lead on what name to use.

'Mina McCreery,' Mina said. 'You might have heard me mentioned by Rebecca Goncharov's mother, Irena?'

Lane shot Mina a surprised look, which she met with a little shrug. He did recall that she'd told him she was going to contact Rebecca's mother, to share their suspicion that her daughter had been sick at the time of her disappearance, but she hadn't told him Irena planned to set this in motion.

'Yes,' Nadya said, and the word was loaded. 'She and I had a very long conversation.'

Lane gestured for her to take the chair and went to stand on the other side of Mina's bed.

'You didn't mention, during our first encounter, that you were a private investigator,' Nadya said. 'I might have been a little more forthcoming if I'd understood you were working with the approval of Rebecca's family.'

Technically Lane hadn't been, but he didn't need to point that out. 'That can be a dangerous move to make,' Lane said. 'Sometimes it opens a door, but it can do the opposite.'

He didn't say that Nadya was a member of the Karpathy family, estranged or not. In that appointment, he had no way of knowing if showing his cards like that would be dangerous.

'I've been hoping you would make contact again, with me or with Natalie,' Nadya said to Lane. 'I didn't want to call you through my brother; I didn't know if that would be safe for you.'

'I haven't had an opportunity to come back to town, and even if one had come up, I would have respected your request not to contact you again.'

He probably wouldn't have, actually, but she didn't need to know that.

'Irena, as Rebecca's next of kin, has signed off on me sharing some information with you about Rebecca's condition.'

'Had the cancer come back?' Mina asked.

Nadya nodded. 'When I gave Rebecca her results, I talked her through all her options and gave her a referral for a specialist. Then she just didn't show up to her next appointment. I called my father and asked to speak to her, but she didn't want to come to the phone.'

'Did you hear them talking, or was this all relayed by him?'

'I heard them talking. So she was still at the farm at that time, but I never saw her again. A few months later, her family was up in arms looking for her, and my father was resolute that she'd left of her own accord and was in Melbourne somewhere.'

'Do you think that was realistic, in her condition?'

'I didn't know her condition. If she was in treatment, absolutely not. If she wasn't, then in an absolute best-case scenario, she might have been well enough to travel alone, but it's unlikely.'

'Why didn't you tell her family before now?' Mina asked.

'The rules around confidentiality are tricky. If I told them and then she turned up, as missing persons so often do, unhappy that they knew – oof. When it became an official police matter, I did make a visit to the police station.'

'How did that go?'

'They'd already formed a strong opinion that she was a young woman who had left of her own volition. My information just reinforced their view. Obviously she'd taken off on some bucket list final adventure, or had decided to end things on her own terms. One way or another she would turn up soon, and then their effort of sorting through all the confidentiality issues would have been wasted. Our local police are not big fans of wasting their efforts.'

Lane recalled Dave's chummy demeanour with the officer in the pub the day they'd gone to town. 'Is there some kind of understanding between the police and the farm?'

'Only the kind that springs up organically in a small town. The police don't go out of their way to bother those living there, but I also don't think they would help them cover something up if there was real evidence of wrongdoing.' She sighed. 'I know I should have pushed harder at the time. Like I said, I was wet behind the ears and out of my depth. The more established doctors at the clinic told me to drop it, so I did. The local police blew me off. I could have gone over their heads, but there's a lot a local cop can do to make your life difficult if you piss them off.'

'Is that why you didn't tell the inquest what you're telling us now?'

'What inquest?'

'There was an inquest into Rebecca's case late last year,' Mina said.

'We buried my father last year. They could have held the hearings out in my waiting room and I still wouldn't have noticed it was happening.'

'Do you know what happened to her?' Mina asked gently.

'No.' Nadya's eyes welled with tears, and she held up a hand, asking for them to give her a moment. She took a deep breath, and blinked rapidly. 'I was so new to this when it happened. I would do so many things differently now.'

Lane hesitated before asking the next question, especially in the face of her evident grief, but it was important. 'How did your father seem, after she disappeared?'

'Worried. He'd obviously liked Rebecca.'

'Do you think there was something going on between them?'

'No. I know that my father had something of a crisis after he and Mum split, and made some impressively bad decisions, but that was all ancient history. He wasn't a perfect guy, but dating someone a decade younger than me? He was better than that.' She dabbed at her eyes with a tissue. 'I'm sorry. I really should get going. I wish there was more I could do to help find Rebecca.'

HE SLID HIS *thumb over the lock. There had been a key in there, he was sure, but now there was nothing. Had it fallen? He dropped back down, yielding his hard-won ground, and patted at the floor, pressing his fingertips up against the baseboards and into every gap in the wood.*

When he tried to scream, the only thing that came out was a strangled gasp, but it hurt his throat all the same.

He tried to catch his breath, because his lungs were burning. Maybe he was just exhausted and confused. Maybe if he rested here for a while, he would figure out how to open the door.

Then he froze.

Footsteps.

CHAPTER TWENTY-THREE

IT WAS HARD for Lane to keep a smile on his face as Dave steered the ute through the gates to the Karpathy property.

Something was making men and women disappear from this farm. Someone had locked him in the greenhouse and tried to suffocate him. Someone had doctored their food with poisonous, hallucinogenic mushrooms. He had one week to figure out who, and why, before William forced him out.

If he survived that long.

Karpathy met them in the driveway, and pulled Mina into a bear hug without asking.

'What a drama,' he said. 'I've put a blanket ban on any mushroom foraging until everyone has done a refresher course. Do you want me to put your name down?'

'I'll pass,' Mina said meekly.

So that was that, then. No investigation, no explanation. It was a foraging error, everybody move on. Lane couldn't help but notice that Dave hadn't needed to give anyone else a lift back – no-one else from the party had presented to the hospital for their own testing.

•

Sweeney was standing out the front of their cabin, his hands jammed into the front pockets of a faded black hoodie. It struck Lane as odd, on such a hot day, but Sweeney was an odd guy.

'Holland,' he said. 'I distinctly remember telling you not to make extra work for me.'

'It was an emergency,' Lane said.

'You've put me in a real awkward position. If I say in my report that you took off without permission, we lose this gig that, quite frankly, I like. If I lie for you and say you had permission, I'm gonna get asked why I didn't go with you.'

'I know I can't ask you to lie for me,' Lane said.

'It's just fucking lucky for you I can honestly say I didn't go because I was feeling unwell last night. Don't do it again.'

'Did you have the soup?'

'Piss off.'

He pulled a folded envelope from his pocket. As he held it out, the cuff of his sleeve pulled back, and the edge of an elastic bandage peeked out.

Lane almost asked about it – he didn't remember Sweeney getting injured, not that they were spending much time in each other's presence lately. But he decided to mind his own business. He'd irritated Sweeney enough.

'This came for you. Carver told me he's screened it already.'

•

Lane took the envelope to the wash-and-pack shed. Inside was a second envelope, addressed to Carver at the Special Purpose Centre. As Sweeney had said, Carver had scrawled a clearance on the outside, even though the envelope was still sealed and he could not have checked the contents.

Inside were the autopsy results for Hannah Cudney.

He turned to the toxicology report. He was sure, based on the night they'd just had, that the medical examiner would have found evidence of muscimol in her system. Poisoning and hallucinations would explain almost everything.

But there was nothing. The screening was completely clear. No mushrooms, no pot, no alcohol. Not even traces of anti-anxiety medications she might have been taking.

He turned back to the general description of Hannah's body. With a sad twinge, he read where the examiner had noted possible evidence of self-harm, cuts to her arms and legs at varying stages of healing.

Stomach contents, empty. He remembered several people mentioning that Hannah had skipped breakfast. No chance then that she had thrown up after the wreck and choked.

Mystified, he flipped to the medical examiner's final conclusion.

Then he went to find Mina.

•

He found her at the western fence line, raking up grass left behind by Dave, who was mowing a firebreak with the farm's old Massey Ferguson tractor. Or that's what she was ostensibly doing. In reality she was holding a rake while staring across the valley to a spire of smoke on the horizon.

'Where's that?' he asked, following her gaze.

'The national park. The wind's blowing in a favourable direction for us, and the Rural Fire Service have it in hand, but the smoke is putting everyone on edge.' She gave him a wan smile. 'What's up?'

'Did Hannah have a heart condition?'

'No. She said once that it freaked her out how Karpathy had died out of the blue with no history of heart problems, that she had none either but you can't ever be sure you're safe. Like I said, she was a worrier.'

'Her cause of death was heart failure.'

He held out the report. He'd folded it over to show only the concluding paragraph, so she wouldn't accidentally read anything graphic.

'Where did you get this?'

'Friends in high places. According to this, the stress on her body from being suspended upside down after flipping the ute lead to her death.'

'Is that normal? For a healthy person not to be able to cope with that? How long was she trapped?'

He'd heard of trapped cavers dying that way, their hearts and other organs unable to handle the pressure of being upside down, but that had taken hours, not minutes.

'It's hard to be sure.' He had the precise time of Hannah's call for help from her call history, but he didn't remember the precise time Natalie had received the notification that she had died. 'It couldn't have been more than half an hour.'

'Maybe it was because she got out of the ute herself? She's upside down, all the blood rushes to her brain, her organs …' She made a gesture like she was pulling her stomach up toward her shoulders with her cupped hands. 'Maybe the sudden reversal of that process was catastrophic. Maybe she'd have been better off with a more careful extraction by the rescue crew.'

'Maybe.' Lane just couldn't figure it. He was sure that if he hung upside down for half an hour he could stand up again on his own without having a heart attack.

Mina handed back the page and said, 'Can I be brutally honest for a second?'

'When are you ever anything but?'

'You've been obsessed with including Hannah's death in your investigation. But at every turn, there's been a reasonable explanation.'

She was right. The empty petrol tank was nothing. Now there was no possibility someone had engineered her death through poisons or drugs.

'Everything except why Karpathy lied,' he reminded her. 'Why did he tell me she'd gone to town on a farm errand when the night before he was so freaked out about the ute being gone without his permission?'

Mina rolled her eyes. 'I can explain that, easy. Ego.'

'Ego?'

'Haven't you noticed that Karpathy is freaked the fuck out all the time? He inherited his father's job with no warning. Pillars of the group like Alessandra are thinking about leaving. He's had sympathy on his side, but that has a time limit. If he can't convince people that he's ready to take over, ready to lead this community, it's going to collapse around him. Of course he's not going to admit he had no idea what Hannah was doing that night. It makes him look weak and not in control. So he makes something up and sweeps it under the rug.'

'How far do you think he'd be willing to go to maintain that illusion of control?'

'You mean would he murder people who try to leave? What does that achieve?'

'I don't know.' Lane ran his fingers through his hair, tugging gently to try to make himself think. He looked down the hill towards the admin building and the locked shed behind. 'I'm running out of time. I need to look at Karpathy's files. There has to be something there.'

'I should do it,' she said. 'If you get caught in there …'

'I know. I've had enough lectures lately about how I'm trying to make my parole chances go up in smoke. But you can't do it. These people are dangerous. If you're caught somewhere you shouldn't be, you could end up dead.'

Mina gave him a long look. 'So could you.'

CHAPTER TWENTY-FOUR

LANE SPENT THE next few days simply watching Karpathy. He hated to let precious time slip by, but he would only get one shot at this.

He'd always kept one eye on the man's movements, but now he dedicated himself fully to working out his daily routine. While it had seemed like his days were unstructured, paying random visits to farm workers and pitching in on anything that needed doing, Lane soon realised he followed a strict schedule. He appeared at breakfast at 7.15 every morning, made his announcements, disappeared for an hour to do admin, then moved around the farm counterclockwise, visiting each work area and the people stationed there in order.

This week, however, he had added a new element to his routine that would provide Lane's window of opportunity. After Dave had announced the fire danger rating, he and Karpathy would walk the perimeter of the farm together, checking that the firebreaks were in good order, that all the water pumps were working, and that no tree limbs or other debris had fallen and created a hazard.

They'd all developed a fascination with the weather forecast. Each morning they hoped for news of rain, or at least a cool change. At the very least, for a day with no wind instead of the westerlies that blasted the property with hot, dry air and dust. Each morning they were disappointed.

On the fifth day, when Karpathy and Dave left the dining hall after breakfast, Lane slipped out the back through the kitchen. In the morning, that side of the building was in shadow, so he was able to move from there to the shaded side of the admin building without anyone seeing. Then he made his way up the side of the building. He peered around the corner to check that no-one was standing in the open area out the front, and then as quickly as he could, he ran up the steps and slipped in through the door.

He was relieved to find the office door unlocked. He closed it behind himself, then crossed over to the window and pulled the shade down.

This done, he sat in the desk chair and used the desk phone to dial his sister's mobile, putting the call on speaker. If anyone came in, the call would provide some scant cover for being in the room.

'Is everything alright?' Lynnie asked without preamble.

'Yes, I just want to chat.'

Using Hannah's phone and the wi-fi signal, he'd had a chance to look up how many attempts he could actually make on the computer passcode before it locked him out, and he'd discovered he'd been entirely too conservative. If he'd known that, he could have cracked it weeks ago.

Could have, would have, should have. He was here now, and that needed to be his focus. Sitting at the desk plugging in numbers would be time-consuming, so it needed to be his last resort. Every minute he spent in the office was risky.

'You've never called me from this number before,' she said. 'I always call you. What happened to that other phone? Please tell me you put it back.'

'I put it back,' he said. He hadn't – it was more dangerous now to put it back than to keep it hidden. Too much time had passed to pretend it had slipped his mind. 'How's the Albury holiday going?'

He went to the coffee cup for the keys, then unlocked the filing cabinet. He already knew that none of the Karpathy family had a 6 June birthday, but there were other important people.

'The sushi train puts melted cheese on their inari,' she said. 'Otherwise, it's fine. It's not really a holiday. I'm studying, and on standby for when you come to your senses.'

'How's the studying going?'

As she explained how to calculate profit for companies that owned other companies, while paying for goods and services from those companies and also providing goods and services to them, he flipped through the files. Dave's, then Alessandra's, and John's. No, no, no.

'Lane, are you listening?'

'It sounds really challenging.'

Wait.

Alessandra had told him that, right before his death, Karpathy had been in a romantic relationship with Gretel.

What was her last name again? She'd made a joke about it to Sweeney when they met. Sweeney-Todd.

He opened the *S–V* drawer, feeling like he was really scraping the bottom of the barrel now. Would she even have an employee file? But she had babysat the children, and Reggie Karpathy appeared to be a thorough record keeper.

And there it was: Todd, Gretel. Born 6 June 1984.

The year surprised him. He and Gretel were almost the same age, when he'd been sure she had a few years on him.

He went to the computer and punched in 6684.

It unlocked, and he was presented with a screen that was a complete mess. So many files were saved direct to the desktop that they had started to overlap.

He opened the list view, and found the employee files.

Rebecca Goncharov's file was similar to Matilda and Alain's, but there were a few key differences. The application form had been completed online and then saved as a PDF, and the tracking of days worked appeared to have been done using a timesheet application. There was a copy of her change of electoral enrolment form, updating her address to that of the farm. A scan of a cheque and the bank reconciliation. That was a little odd, he thought. Six years ago they were still paying employees with paper cheques?

There was a saved web page of Rebecca's Missing Persons profile, and a zip file labelled 'Inquest Documents'. Apparently the farm had successfully made an application to receive copies of the inquest results, as an interested party. Lane decided not to look at them – time was of the essence, and Mina had been at the inquest. If anything had been revealed there that could have broken the case open, Mina would know about it already.

Finally, he found a file simply marked 'MAP'. It was a Google Maps satellite image, showing a farm that was almost, but not quite, the one Lane knew today. In the north-east corner, in a spot that was bare in the picture but which Lane knew now contained a clump of trees, someone had dropped a red pin.

Lane sat with that for a moment. Visiting the spot marked in Alain's file had yielded nothing, because there was an entire pig enclosure there now. This spot felt more promising, more likely to still show some traces if it was excavated, but he wouldn't be able to convince the police to mount a search with nothing more than an eerie map and a hunch.

He checked Brandon Roby's file and found his days worked had been tracked but there were no payslips. There were copies of his enrolment to vote, his legal will and the medical power of attorney he had signed. Lane was hesitant to invade Brandon's privacy, but he had to check.

A couple of clicks of the mouse revealed Brandon had been telling the truth: the medical power of attorney listed Alessandra and John as his decision makers, not Karpathy.

There was no copy of his Missing Persons file. Perhaps the farm wasn't aware one existed.

Lane hovered the cursor over Hannah's file, and then decided that Mina had been right. He'd been too focused on Hannah for no real reason. The answers lay elsewhere, and he was short on time.

He clicked on the email program, and was prompted to enter a password. Reluctant to embark on a potentially fruitless guessing game, he gave up and went back to the desktop, where he found the icon of an accounting program. Follow the money, right?

The program loaded, and he was immediately lost. The screen filled with charts and line graphs that meant nothing to him.

'Hey, Lynnie, when you look at a business's books for the first time, where do you start?'

'Either the balance sheet or their profit and loss, depending on what they're seeing me for,' she said. 'Why? That's first-year stuff.'

'No reason,' he said, clicking on the balance sheet. Assets, liabilities. It might as well have been in Greek. He switched over to the profit and loss.

That at least he could read. The farm was making a profit. A pretty healthy one. Employee costs seemed a little high. He did a little back-of-the-envelope maths, dividing the total Karpathy was recording per year by the number of people working on the farm. Then he opened up the internet browser and did a quick search for 'average salary of a farm worker'.

To his surprise, the numbers lined up, especially if Karpathy himself, Dave and maybe Alessandra were making the farm manager rates.

Except they weren't, were they? Karpathy held people's money. Technically, Dave and Alessandra didn't cost him anything.

Until they left.

The number one thing Karpathy was determined to stop people from doing.

He addressed Lynnie again. 'Say a business had a deal with their employees that they didn't receive their pay until the end of a job, even if the job took years to complete. How would that work with the tax office?'

'Doesn't sound super legal to me,' she said. 'You'd at least need to be paying people's super and workers' comp insurance. The tax office makes businesses record employee payments with them quarterly. And you'd want to, otherwise you wouldn't get the tax deduction.'

'But theoretically you could record the payment to the tax office without actually making it until the agreed time?'

'Hmm, still sounds pretty illegal. Speaking of, why do I feel like I'm helping you to commit a crime right now?'

'You're not. I'm just taking an interest.'

'Just so you know, William is making frantic "give me the phone" gestures at me.'

'I still have two days left of the week William promised me.'

'Really? Because he told me that agreement was to "extract yourself gracefully", not to go from knee-deep to neck-deep.'

'I'm being graceful.'

'Lane.' Her voice lost all playfulness. 'I'd really hoped we wouldn't have to have this conversation. But I have to be honest. If you don't get parole ... I can't keep coming to see you. It's too hard. If I feel like it's your fault you're there, it's just going to make me resent you.'

'It's always been my fault I'm there, Lynnie.'

She didn't have any answer for that.

'Look, could you just stay on the line for me a little longer? Just wait for me to come back.' He expected her to bark out a no, or hang up on him.

Instead she sighed and said, 'Alright.'

He switched the call to speaker, left the office and walked down the hallway to examine the locked door that led to the shed. He didn't know what he might find inside. Maybe he would turn the handle and all the missing people would come spilling out, like Bluebeard's wives.

Once upon a time he would have had a lock-picking kit to use in a situation like this. However, after a few moments spent examining the lock, he realised he was an idiot.

He returned to the office and grabbed the coffee cup full of keys, then carried it back to the door and started trying them out, one at a time.

'Is there a reason you're trying to break into the plant room?' Karpathy asked.

Startled, Lane dropped the cup, spilling keys across the floor. Karpathy was standing in the open door of the storage room. Lane hadn't heard the outer door open and close. Karpathy must have entered the building while Lane was in the office; in his hurry, Lane hadn't stopped to check the other rooms before he started messing with the door.

'It's this one,' Karpathy said. He crouched down and picked up a ring of keys, selecting a purple one.

'Sorry, I was just, um ...'

Karpathy simply smiled and handed him the key. Not knowing what else to do, Lane took it and unlocked the door.

The room was damp and cool, but smelled fresh and clean. There was a faint buzz of electricity from the grow lights on every rack of shelving that lined the room. On one side stood rows of small glass jars, sealed, with a little green growth in each one. On the other side were racks of mature plants in terracotta pots.

'Pot plants,' Lane said.

Not marijuana plants. Pot plants. Spiky plants, and viny plants, and plants with big glossy leaves striped and spotted with white and pink.

'Why do you keep these in a locked room?' he asked.

'Well, it lowers the contamination risk if we don't have people traipsing in and out whenever. And on that subject, do you mind?' Karpathy pointed to a handwash station by the sink. Next to it, N95 masks hung on a hook.

Feeling like he was going insane, Lane washed his hands and put on a mask.

'I also didn't want you to come in here because I know how important it is for you to keep your hands clean. In a legal sense, I mean – no pun intended.'

Karpathy stepped up to the sink in turn, and also scrubbed and masked up. Then he picked up a pot from a rack near Lane's shoulder and held it out to him. The plant had wide green leaves, covered in a dense white fuzz. 'The angel wing fern,' he said. 'Did you know there was a six-week period last year when one of these could fetch five thousand dollars? Even now this is worth several hundred.'

'Why?'

'Rarity. There are collectors who can and will pay anything to get a new, rare variety.'

'If they're just houseplants, why would I get in trouble?'

'The trouble with these rare collectibles is that there's a cycle. Some new variant pops up, and there's only a handful of specimens around, so they go for top dollar. So people who do manage to get their hands on one start propagating them, and the price drops a bit. Then mass propagation starts, and within a year they're going for twenty dollars at Bunnings. The earlier you can get your hands on one, the more money you can make. Of course that's difficult for the Australian market, when any plant you import is required to spend months in a quarantine facility.'

'You've been smuggling pot plants into the country?'

'Only cuttings. The soil is the riskiest part, you know. There's no real danger. Anyone we send overseas to pick up a specimen knows how to test the plant and make sure it's disease-free. And these plants are destined to sit on a windowsill in a Melbourne penthouse. We're not really risking anything.'

'So rules are for other people, then?'

Karpathy chuckled. 'It's a misdemeanour at worst. And the money it brings in gives us a bit of breathing room to do important things.'

'Is that how you justify everything you do? You're using the money you steal to save the world?'

'Steal?'

Lane felt ridiculous trying to have this conversation through the mask. He stepped back into the hallway and took it off, then moved closer to the open office door, hoping that if Lynnie had stayed on the line as he'd asked, she could be a witness to this conversation – especially if it turned dangerous. Karpathy followed him down the hallway, but gave Lane a few feet of space, like he was trying not to seem intimidating.

'The wages. The people here aren't actually getting paid. Their money only exists on paper. You tell them you're holding it, that they'll have a nice nest egg if they ever decide to leave, but you're actually spending it, aren't you? And maybe you can afford to pay out when people only leave occasionally, or when it's someone who only built up a small amount owing. As long as more people are arriving than leaving, you can cover it. It's almost like a Ponzi scheme, isn't it? But if someone who'd been here for years left, or a bunch of people at once, then your house of cards …' He mimed an explosion. 'Maybe sometimes, to cover the gaps, it helps when someone dies or disappears. You never need to pay them at all.'

Karpathy stared at him. 'Oh,' he said. 'Is this what you've been carrying around? You think my father was a murderer?' He considered this for a moment, then said, 'I can understand, given your own history, why you would jump to that conclusion.'

'You think I'm projecting? You've got a collection of Missing Persons files in your office. Matilda Carver. Alain Serling. Rebecca Goncharov. Where are they?'

Karpathy shook his head. 'I don't know. I wish I did. More than that, I wish they were here. I wish we'd been able to offer them what they needed, because if we had, they'd be safe and well right now. Yes, three missing people is a lot, but over twenty years …'

'That's three that I know of. If I went through every file, would I find more? Would I find people who died mysteriously right before or after leaving?'

'Yes, probably. About three hundred people have lived here at some point in the past twenty years. More, if you count back to when my father first took over the farm. I'm not judging them, but a lot of those people came because they thought they could leave something behind if they moved here. We've had people who struggled with addiction. With their mental health. Relationships with dangerous people. It's not murder; it's statistics.'

'But you're not just some random way station. You don't just employ these people – you rule them. You choose what they eat and where they sleep and what they wear. You work them every minute of daylight, and then they can either hang out together or sit alone in their room in the dark. You control their money. You run their relationships and their family planning.'

'That's how we make this place work. And if they don't like it, they can go. We cut them a cheque and they go.'

'Unless they die or disappear,' Lane pushed.

Karpathy sighed. 'Come with me,' he said, and walked into the office.

Lane glanced at the phone as he entered – the speaker button was still lit up, but if Lynnie was listening on the other end, she was silent.

'I see you've helped yourself to more than one key,' Karpathy noted, sitting in front of the unlocked computer. He navigated to the employee files, and opened Hannah's. 'If someone dies and we owe them money, that debt doesn't disappear. We owe it to their estate.'

'Lucky then that you've got a lawyer on call who's keen to help new arrivals draw up a will. How many people here have pledged all their assets back to the farm if they die?'

'I have no idea,' Karpathy said. 'But I can name one person who didn't.' He pointed to the screen. There was a copy of Hannah's will, leaving all of her worldly goods to a youth homeless shelter in Melbourne. 'I can show you the payment to them in our online banking, if you want. Or you could call them.'

'You're still getting a lot more labour than you're paying for.'

'Sure. And yes, the way we report it involves a bit of fudging the numbers. Show me a farm anywhere in this country that isn't cooking their books a little. Show me one business anywhere whose books are completely accurate. Go outside, gather everyone up, and shout to them that they're working more hours than they're being paid for. They'll laugh at you. Because they know. You realise we could stop paying people, right? We could say to them, *Come. Come help us build something beautiful. We won't pay you anything but you'll always have a safe place to sleep and a roof when it rains and three meals a day and work that you know is making the world better instead of worse.* And they would come.'

'Because you're targeting the vulnerable and desperate.'

'We are providing safety and purpose to people who need it. And they are always free to go. But the world is ending, Lane. This place is a lifeboat, and a lifeboat isn't supposed to be comfortable.'

All at once, the fight went out of Lane. He sat down on a low filing cabinet, his hands on his knees. 'Holy shit,' he said.

Karpathy actually believed his own bullshit.

All this time, Lane had been building every theory on a rotten foundation. He'd started from the assumption that Karpathy was some cold and calculating monster, using cult tactics to twist people into whatever shape he needed. And it was still possible his father had been that person. But Samuel Karpathy had grown up with this as his normal. Hearing the justifications day after day. Seeing the fruit of it.

He believed it.

'Please,' Lane said softly. 'Matilda Carver. She would have lived here when you were around fifteen. What happened to her?'

Karpathy smiled. 'Of course I remember Matilda. She was really pretty. She gave me a Hilltop Hoods CD once. I think I still have it somewhere. She never planned to stay long. She was going somewhere I think – an overseas trip.'

'Czechia,' Lane said. 'But she never got there. Where did she go?'

'That's not my story to tell.'

'What about my lawyer?' Lane asked. 'You've been hiding messages from him.'

That, at last, got a guilty look from Karpathy. 'I did check if it was an emergency, and he said no. New arrivals don't usually get so many phone calls. I didn't expect someone in your position to be so anchored to the world outside. I thought you might settle in better with some space from it.'

'Lane.' Lynnie's voice on the speaker made them both start. 'William called the police.' She sounded panicked.

'We don't need the police,' Lane said. If cops showed up at this point, he was the only one who'd be leaving in handcuffs.

'Good. Because they say unless someone's life is in imminent danger, they're not sending anyone out. The danger rating for your area just went from orange to red. You need to evacuate.'

HE SHUFFLED BACKWARDS *so the door wouldn't hit his knees if it opened. Whoever it was paused at the base of the stairs, and for a moment he thought they might not come in. Then the lock clicked. The key was on the other side? When had that happened? Why?*

Maybe he'd left it there by accident. His head swam so much lately, he could easily have forgotten. But he couldn't have locked it from his side of the door, not without the key. No: they had locked it.

He wanted to leave. He needed *to leave. Were they going to stop him?*

CHAPTER TWENTY-FIVE

OUTSIDE, KARPATHY SHOUTED for Dave, who came bolting around the corner.

'Yes, I know. It's all over the radio.' He pointed across the valley. 'Nobody's figured out how it started yet, but it's six k that way and moving like a motherfucker. The wind's in our favour but we need to get everyone out of here. John's hooking up the stock crate now; there's a farmer on the other side of the bridge who's offered up a paddock for evacuated livestock. That leaves us with just the one ute, so' – he raised his voice to a bellow so the rapidly gathering crowd could hear – 'Natalie's on her way up with the school bus. As soon as it pulls up, we're loading in and heading out. You've got twenty minutes to get your allocated job done and your butt in a seat.'

Lane scanned the faces in the group, but couldn't see Mina. He turned and sprinted to her cabin, but only found her dog, Echo, and her roommate Sarah inside. 'Have you seen Mina?'

'Who?'

'Sorry – Deana.'

'She's helping round up the goats. Are you supposed to be in here?'

He pointed to Echo, who had stood up from his bed and was stretching luxuriously, oblivious to the hubbub around him. 'Come on, boy,' he said, and Echo happily followed at his heel.

He took Echo down to the wash-and-pack shed, where a pile of luggage was growing as people gathered to wait for the bus. 'Sit,' he said.

Echo's butt hit the ground and he looked up at Lane expectantly, his tail sweeping across the grass.

Alessandra held a clipboard. 'Echo,' she said, ticking something off. 'And Lane.'

'Don't mark me just yet,' he said. 'Is Sweeney on your list?'

'No,' she said. 'He said he's made his own arrangements. I explained to him that was a massive violation of his duty of care to you, but he just kind of grunted.'

'That sounds like Sweeney. But you've seen him today?'

When had Lane last seen him? After coming back from the hospital? He'd been so careful to stay out of the guard's way, to keep his ankle bracelet charged and not piss him off anymore, that he hadn't noticed how suspiciously successful he'd been.

Alessandra shook her head and pointed to a satellite phone clipped to her hip. 'We spoke on the phone, I don't have time to run around looking for people.'

'Thanks,' Lane said, turning to leave.

'We're not going to hold the bus if someone's not on it,' she warned. 'Dave will go last and take any stragglers in the ute, but don't take advantage. He's not going to dick around if the wind changes.'

Lane gave her a little salute to show he understood, then jogged away.

He'd wasted every minute he'd been here, trying to figure out what the people here were lying about, completely neglecting the possibility they were telling the whole truth. Who else might believe in what they were saying, and what would it mean if they did?

What did all the missing people have in common? Matilda, struggling with depression. Alain, an asthmatic. Rebecca, a cancer relapse. Hannah, plagued by health anxiety.

He'd been so focused on Reggie Karpathy as a perpetrator that he hadn't even considered how his piece might fit the puzzle if turned another way. What if Karpathy senior, taken suddenly by a heart attack, was a victim?

Karpathy, who had been in a relationship with Gretel.

Gretel, who was so close to Hannah.

Gretel, who had bought the farm next door around the same time people started to disappear.

Gretel, who preached that medicine was poison and that poison was medicine. And what was it she had said to Mina, when she described her mother continuing to undereat even while battling cancer?

Maybe that was your mother's instincts trying to tell her what her body needed to fight it.

He'd seen it in the letters from Rebecca. The ones that had become so short, the handwriting bigger and wobblier. He'd been so quick to assume it was a sign of forgery that he hadn't stopped to consider any other possibilities. Like that it was the handwriting of the same person, experiencing brain fog and weakening grip as she starved herself.

Because Gretel believed that fasting could cure disease.

Gretel, who was now seeing the chronically unwell Sweeney.

Lane had been so happy to have Sweeney too distracted by his new relationship to pay attention to what Lane was up to that he hadn't given it a second thought.

Lane sprinted to their cabin. It seemed oddly still, with the chickens no longer scratching around the yard next door.

'Sweeney,' Lane called, banging on the door to the guard's room.

There was no answer.

He pushed his way inside. Not only was Sweeney not there, there were no signs he was still living in the cabin at all. No bags, no clothes, no papers. The beds were all stripped to bare mattresses.

Outside, Lane flagged down Karpathy, who was headed in the direction of the gate. 'Can you tell Dave that I'm going to find Sweeney? I'll try to get back before he leaves, but don't wait for me.' He pointed up the hill towards Gretel's house, where her car was sitting in the driveway. 'Worst-case scenario, we can leave in that.'

'I'll tell him, but he won't wait anyway. If you're not back by the time he leaves, don't try to leave yourself. Leaving too late can be more dangerous than sheltering in place.'

From his left came a heavy droning, and the buzz of conversation among the farm residents stopped immediately.

An RFS plane sliced through the sky, a spot of white against the pillar of grey smoke. Once it was centred, it unleashed a barrage of red fire retardant, like a gush of blood.

Lane looked at his watch. He still had ten minutes left of the twenty Dave had decreed. He turned and sprinted up the hill.

Gretel's front door was unlocked. Lane didn't bother to knock; he just barged in. Inside, the house was dark and cool. Shockingly cool after weeks without any air conditioning.

'Hello?' he shouted. 'Sweeney?'

'Lane?' a woman's voice shouted back, coming from the front yard. The door crashed open, slamming against the hallway wall, and Mina stood in the doorway.

'What are you doing here?' he asked.

'Sarah says you've got my dog,' Mina said.

'He's on the bus. You need to go – they'll leave without you.'

'They'll leave without you, too. What are you doing?'

'Sweeney!' he shouted by way of answer, heading deeper into the house.

In other circumstances he would have really liked Gretel's kitchen. It was all polished wooden cabinets and slate tiles. A witch's workshop, every surface festooned with bunches of drying herbs and little pots with flowers.

But the effect was ruined by the picture window over the sink, framing the smoke that had grown from a pillar to a grey wall. An edge of red outlined the hills.

'Fuck,' Mina said from behind him. 'It's headed this way.'

Distantly, someone began frantically honking a car horn.

'They're leaving,' Lane said.

'The fire'll slow down once it's headed downhill,' Mina said. 'When it hits the bottom of this hill, that's when we're fucked.'

The house was small. There was a little sitting room, deserted, and a bedroom with an unmade double bed and an ensuite. Sweeney's hoodie was hanging from the towel rack. The bathtub was filled with water, but when Lane touched it, the surface was ice cold.

'They probably evacuated already,' Mina said.

'Her car's in the driveway,' Lane pointed out.

Back in the hallway, Mina said, 'I'm going outside to see if she has a fire cellar.' She turned and grabbed Lane's hand. 'If I don't come back, assume I decided it wasn't safe. Don't come looking for me. If you're outside when that fire rolls over us, you won't burn to death. It'll push a heat front that will boil the marrow in your bones first.'

'Then let me go,' he said.

'You have no idea what to look for,' she said, and was gone before he could argue.

He pulled out Hannah's phone. Even without any reception, he would be able to make an emergency call.

He doubted they could do anything to help, but if things got really bad here, at least he might be able to connect to an operator long enough that the truth about Alain, Matilda and Rebecca wouldn't die with him.

The wi-fi had connected, showing a far stronger connection than near the greenhouse.

Of course. Chalice Well was Gretel's wi-fi. She saw her home as the healing spring.

He found a spare bedroom, the furniture covered in dust sheets, and then at the end of the hallway a door locked from the other side. 'Sweeney?' he shouted, banging on it with his fist.

It opened, to show Gretel standing on a flight of stairs leading down into the dark. She was wearing an N95 mask and a long-sleeved jumpsuit.

'Mina?' he called over his shoulder. 'They're here.'

'What are you doing?' Gretel yelled.

'Where's Sweeney?' he asked.

'He's not feeling well,' Gretel answered. 'He can't be moved right now.'

'What did you give him?' Lane asked.

'Nothing,' she said. 'Some stewed tomatoes. He's just at a delicate stage, the most difficult stage; when it passes, everything will be better.'

'Unless *he* passes,' Lane said.

He pushed past Gretel, rushing down the steps.

'Get out of my house!' she shouted.

'Sweeney?' Lane found a door and rattled the handle. The room plunged into darkness. Gretel must have shut the door leading to the rest of the house.

'He can't be moved,' Gretel repeated. 'You're going to hurt him.'

Lane activated the torch on Hannah's phone. In the weak beam of light, he could see that the door was locked from the outside, the key still in the lock.

'People can get funny during this stage,' she explained. 'The brain plays tricks. Sometimes they panic, think they need to run.'

'Like Hannah did?' he asked.

It all made sense. People who were experiencing starvation often had a final burst of euphoric energy: the body's last-ditch attempt to save itself. In a moment of clarity, Hannah must have realised her mistake, fled Gretel's house and run down the hill. Called the only person she could think of who might be able to come pick her up. Could she trust Dave or Karpathy to drive her to safety? Lane wouldn't have taken that risk in her shoes.

But Natalie hadn't answered her call, and with the threat of the floods closing the roads any minute, Hannah had taken her life into her own hands: she'd stolen the ute and tried to drive to town, even when she realised she didn't have enough petrol. Then she'd lost control, flipped the ute, and her already overtaxed body couldn't handle it.

She hadn't even been sick. Gretel had killed her with a cure for illnesses that were all in her mind.

'Exactly,' Gretel said. 'If I'd locked her in, for her own protection, she would be fine now. Once you get past this stage, it's so beautiful. The body is finally clean of everything the world uses to destroy it. He'll be able to heal, properly, and be so much stronger than before.'

'Or he'll die. Like Rebecca?'

Gretel's voice sounded sad. 'Rebecca came to me way too late.'

'So Rebecca is dead?' Even as he'd put the pieces together, some part of him had held out hope there could be some other explanation. That he could bring someone home alive.

'Yes. Her body had been through so much – all of those poisons they pumped into her when she was just a little kid. Even then, maybe if she'd come to me as soon as she knew she needed help instead of sitting on the fence ... I've discovered that sometimes people need a little push, for their own good.'

'Like a little extra seasoning in their soup, to open up their minds?' A thought struck him. 'Or perhaps engineering a situation you can rescue them from, so they trust you more?'

He couldn't see her expression in the dark, and that unsettled him. 'You weren't ever in any danger. I only put a handful of fuel in the kiln, it would have burned out before making enough smoke to kill you. But a brush with death can be a clarifying experience.'

Upstairs there was a thump. Someone was trying to open the door. Gretel must have locked it behind her.

'What about Alain? And Matilda?' He swung the phone around, the torch still lit, so he could see Gretel's face when he said their names.

Her expression darkened. 'I was young, and stupid. I thought I knew more than I did. I've learned a lot since then.'

There was a sound of cracking wood, and light rushed into the room, blinding Lane for a moment. Mina stood at the top of the stairs, looking at the split doorjamb with an expression of surprise at her own panicked strength.

'It's coming,' she said. 'Can you hear it?'

They all fell silent. Somewhere close by – far too close by – the beast roared.

Lane took advantage of Gretel's distraction to edge down the hallway. As he turned the key in the door, Gretel shrieked, 'Leave him alone!'

The room was little more than a long narrow cupboard, only wide enough for a single bed pushed against the far wall, with blankets piled over a lumpy human shape. The floor was old polished wood, and there were no windows. There was a horrendous smell, old sweat and sickness mixed with something metallic.

The bandage on Sweeney's arm. The scars observed on Hannah's body.

'Have you been bleeding him?' he asked.

'Fasting alone doesn't work anymore,' Gretel said. 'There's toxins in our body now that we can't filter out by ourselves. The only way is to get the bad blood out.'

'Jesus. Mina, help me,' Lane called, his voice rising to a shout. 'I don't think Sweeney can walk.'

'No!' Gretel's feet pounded on the stairs, and she tried to push the door shut in Mina's face. 'You're the ones who are putting him in danger.'

'Leave her alone!' Lane shouted. He ran up the stairs behind Gretel.

Mina managed to grip the edge of the door, and he saw Gretel tense, ready to slam it shut even if it smashed Mina's fingers.

He reached up and grabbed Gretel's ankle and yanked. She lost her footing and slid down the stairs, her chin connecting with the top step with a crack. Lane stepped over her and pushed the door open. 'Come on,' he said, grabbing Mina's hand. He pushed the door shut behind them, paltry shelter that it would be against the coming inferno.

All three of them stumbled down the stairs, Gretel sobbing and clutching at her face.

'Is this a fire cellar?' Mina asked.

'It's mudbrick,' Gretel said.

'I don't know if that's going to be enough.'

'The kiln,' Lane said. 'You make pottery, right?'

'You're right,' Mina said. 'A kiln is designed to keep extreme heat in. It will keep it out. How big is it?'

'You'd fit,' Gretel conceded. 'But it's not necessary. We're safe down here.'

'I'm not risking it,' Mina said.

Lane held up his phone torch, illuminating the corners. There it was: a little smaller than a walk-in freezer. There were racks inside to hold the pots as they were fired, but Mina yanked those out and tossed them to the side, clearing a space that would just fit them all.

'Help me with Sweeney,' Lane said.

Gretel tried to object, but Mina pushed her aside.

Lane gently lifted Sweeney's wrist, searching for a pulse. His skin was reassuringly warm under Lane's fingers, but felt papery and fragile.

He couldn't feel a pulse.

'Try his neck,' Mina said, leaning past him to press two fingers under Sweeney's chin. 'The pulse is weaker in the extremities.' She let out a wobbly breath. 'He's alive.'

Sweeney wasn't asleep; he was unconscious. He didn't even stir when Lane put a hand on his shoulder and tried to shake him awake.

Mina positioned herself at the foot of the bed, ready to help lift him.

'Careful,' Lane said, remembering how Hannah's heart had given out on her. 'Use the sheet.'

He put his hands on either side of Sweeney's head and grabbed fistfuls of the sheets. Mina did the same near his feet, and they used the sheet like a sling to lift Sweeney up and then lower him gently to the floor. Together they slid him out of the death room and into the kiln, where Mina put him in the recovery position.

'In or out?' Lane said to Gretel.

She stepped in after them, and pulled the door shut. It was a tight squeeze, and Lane was glad he wasn't claustrophobic.

Mina lay down next to Sweeney. 'You should lie face down,' she said to Lane.

'Is that likely to help?' he asked, cramming himself in next to her.

'It will make it easier for them to identify the bodies,' she said.

'I've missed our talks,' he said, and she laughed.

'It's cold comfort, but at least I get to say I told you so,' she whispered. She found his hand in the dark and squeezed. 'No survivors.'

CHAPTER TWENTY-SIX

THE FIRE WAS so loud, even dulled by the walls of the kiln and the cellar. Upstairs, Gretel's smoke detectors screamed and then fell silent as their batteries melted. Every now and then there was a bang. Inside the kiln, someone was crying softly.

Over the top of it all, the roaring.

Then, silence.

Lane didn't know what to do. Was it like a hurricane, where a sudden silence meant only a reprieve? Perhaps it had changed direction briefly, but would change back again. Perhaps the fire crews had beaten it back only temporarily. Perhaps it had gone completely over the top and rolled on, burning everything in its path and carrying on in search of more.

Perhaps it was over.

He could hear breathing, but he didn't know if it was the sound of four people, or his own breath echoing back to him in the tight space.

'Mina?' he whispered. 'You still here?'

'Stop talking,' she said. 'Oxygen thief.'

The tightness in his chest loosened. He still had the phone. He woke it up, so they could have the light of the screen instead of lying in the darkness.

Somewhere above, an engine rumbled. A door slammed, and then heavy footsteps echoed.

Huh, he thought. The house was still up there.

Whoever it was had boots on, because they thumped on the stairs as they descended.

'We're in here,' Lane called, sitting up.

Light washed over them as the kiln door opened. Standing there, her orange search and rescue jumpsuit streaked with soot and her hair soaked with sweat, was Natalie Matthews.

•

At the hospital, Lynnie barrelled into him like she was trying to knock him to the ground. 'You arsehole,' she shouted into his ear, wrapping her arms around his neck.

'Fair,' he said, hugging her back. Without letting go, he turned to watch the ambulance bay doors. They crashed open to reveal two paramedics pushing a gurney with Sweeney strapped in. Lane couldn't get much of a read on his condition, but he supposed as long as there wasn't anyone kneeling on the gurney, trying to resuscitate him while they moved, it was the best he could hope for.

'I called Carver,' William said. He reached past Lynnie to clap Lane on the shoulder.

'Why?'

'I figure whatever conversation is about to happen between you, me, the police and the governor of Albury Correctional Centre, it should be as much his problem as yours.'

An ER doctor arrived to whisk Lane away before he could ask where Mina and Gretel were. The three of them had been judged well enough to ride in the SES truck down to Georges Bridge, where they were met by two patient transport vehicles. Sweeney had stayed on the hill under Natalie's care until a full ambulance could arrive. Lane had been placed into one vehicle, accompanied by a large male SES volunteer who was happy to be deputised as a temporary guard, while Mina and Gretel rode together in the other.

As he followed the doctor through the ER, he noticed Natalie standing at the front desk, talking to the triage nurse.

'Can I have a moment?' he asked the doctor, who looked annoyed but shrugged and stepped aside.

'Natalie,' Lane said.

'It's so good to see you,' she said. 'When Dave rolled into the place of last resort without you three, we thought you were dead. The situation changed like that.' She snapped her fingers.

'I'd really love to talk to you properly,' he said, 'but we don't have time now, and I don't want you to come face to face with him by accident, before you're ready. Your father is on his way.'

CHAPTER TWENTY-SEVEN

LANE WAS ADMITTED for observation. An officer from Albury Correctional Centre was dispatched and took up residence outside his room. A few minutes later, there was a rap on the door, and Lane called out for whoever it was to come in, hoping it would be someone with news about the others.

It was a uniformed police officer, her hat tucked under her arm.

'Hi, Lane. Do you feel up to giving a statement, while it's all still fresh in your mind?' she asked.

'No,' he said. 'I don't.'

'Fair enough. How about just one question? I'm getting some muddled stories, so it would really help to clear up one thing. Gretel Todd suffered some injuries during the fire. Ms McCreery says she pushed on the door, and that made Gretel lose her footing and fall down the stairs. That's not what Ms Todd says happened. Do you remember?'

Her supervisor needed to explain to her why it was a really bad idea to tell one witness what another witness had said.

'Is my sister still here?' he asked.

'Yes, she's in the family lounge.'

'The man with her is my lawyer. He can help you with scheduling an interview time.'

If Gretel tried to press charges against him for assault, that could be very bad. But he suspected Gretel had a world of hurt coming her way, and he didn't have the energy to worry about himself.

The officer let herself out, and Lane caught a flash of orange in the hallway.

'Natalie?' he called. This he did have energy to worry about.

She came in, looking wary. She'd unbuttoned the jumpsuit and tied the sleeves around her waist, and put on a clean white t-shirt.

'Do you want me to keep calling you Natalie, or should I switch to Matilda?' he asked.

'Natalie. It would feel weird to change now.' She sat heavily in the chair beside his bed. 'How did you figure it out?'

'When you searched for us, you walked straight from the front door to the door to the stairs without a moment's hesitation. Mina and I had to go all over the house before we noticed that door. So you'd been there before.' He picked at his blanket. 'I get the impression the only people Gretel lets in her house are those she's hoping to put through her ... regimen.'

Natalie looked stricken.

'Then, once I had the suspicion … well. You've changed pretty dramatically these past twenty years, but I can see it now.'

'You mean I've doubled in size. You can say it.'

'It's more than just your weight. The shape of your face, your hair, it's all different.'

'Have you told my parents?'

He shook his head. 'I told them that if I found you alive and you didn't want them to know, I wouldn't tell them.'

She nodded, looking down at her hands.

'It's none of my business, but I'd love to understand why.'

She hesitated, still looking down, then took a deep breath and met his eyes.

'I killed Alain Serling.'

Lane glanced at the door, hoping the police officer was well out of earshot. 'You killed him? Why?'

She sighed. 'Alain and I were at the farm together. We were friends, I liked him a lot. I think he liked me a little more. He trusted me.'

'So you convinced him to trust Gretel?'

'I was … I think I was one of her first converts. At the time I was struggling really badly. I thought that travelling, some space from my family, would make me feel better. It didn't. But being at the farm, that helped somewhat. What really helped was being around Gretel.'

Lane wondered how much of that was influenced by Gretel's free hand with the mushrooms.

'We were practically the same age, but she was so together compared to me. She'd buckled down, saved up all that money, and bought her own little house and farm. I was just bumming around, mad at my parents. Living on the farm, I learned so much about how the world could work, and I'd found it all so mind-blowing that when Gretel started throwing in her two cents, I was primed to be gullible.'

'Susceptible,' Lane suggested.

'What she said made sense. Food is so processed, you never know what's in it, and people seem to be sick all the time. Switching over to fresh whole foods had made me feel better, and when Gretel suggested I needed to cut certain things out, it seemed to be working. Then she started suggesting fasts – to detox.'

'People often do feel good when fasting,' Lane observed, recalling his theory about Hannah's final moments. 'There's a euphoria.'

'The fasts got longer and longer. I felt worse and worse, but she told me that was a good sign. It was proof I was healing. Then she suggested I leave the farm and come live with her.'

'Is that how it works? When she has someone hooked, she convinces them to tell Karpathy they're leaving and then sneaks them over to her house? Why?'

'Well, not everyone "understands the process".' She made air quotes with her fingers. 'Why waste energy trying to make them understand? In a few weeks I would return to the farm as living proof it worked.'

'But you didn't go back.'

'Well, technically it did work – in the sense that I survived, and let her convince me that I felt better. I was healed and could eat anything I wanted, as long as all I wanted was stewed tomatoes or a soup made from a teaspoon of barley and a cup of water. Everything else made me throw up. Just before I was ready to make my triumphant return to the world, Gretel told me Alain was moving in.' She squeezed her eyes shut. 'He was ready to try it. He'd struggled all his life with asthma, and she'd told him that it was linked to food allergies. And I told him her method worked, that I had never felt better.'

'That doesn't make it your fault.'

'That's not the part that was my fault. Well, it was. But it gets worse. Alain started the process. It was so much worse for him. My body was perfectly healthy at the start; I just had the bloody morbs. He needed medication to breathe, and he stopped taking it. He lost so much weight, and all his strength, and I just kept telling him, it works. Then the moment of panic came. He wanted out. He wanted to leave. And I asked … I asked if there was someone I could call who would help him. I knew there wasn't; he had a garbage family. It was me. I was the person who could help him. And instead I convinced him to stay and die.'

'What happened when he did?'

'I freaked out. Gretel freaked out. I had a complete breakdown – it's all a blank. I slipped out in the middle of the night and walked along the road until a trucker picked me up and gave me a ride to Albury. He probably thinks he picked up a cryptid, the hysterical skeleton woman of Hill Road.'

'He never reported that to police?'

She shrugged. 'Some people like to mind their own business. I went to the hospital and didn't tell them anything. I asked them not to contact my family, and I was an adult, so they didn't. I was treated for refeeding syndrome, diagnosed with an eating disorder, and spent six months in an inpatient program.'

'You didn't tell anyone what happened to Alain?'

She shook her head. 'You have to understand. I don't even know if what Gretel did was a crime. Convincing someone to starve themselves to death? And if it *was* a crime, I was guilty too.'

'Why didn't you contact your parents? They'd have understood.'

'My parents would have understood? My father, who runs a prison, would have understood me killing a man?'

'You didn't kill him. You made a mistake. Gretel is the only person responsible for these deaths.' He paused, aware that he was about to say something very cruel. 'You realise that if you'd spoken up at the time, Rebecca Goncharov would still be alive?'

That tipped her over, and she began to cry. 'I know,' she said. 'Until then, I thought Gretel had been scared back to her senses, just like I was. And to be on the safe side, I kept watch from town. Made sure that any newcomers to the farm knew they had other options – that they could reach out for help, and I would find them a place to go. I thought it was working. She went nearly fifteen years before she killed Rebecca.'

'Why didn't you speak up then?'

'Speak up how? Walk into a police station and say I'm pretty sure this missing person died because Gretel Todd convinced her to starve herself to death? How do I know? Oh, because

I helped her do it to someone else and then covered it up for fifteen years. I'd also have to answer questions about how I'd been living under a false identity all that time, which involved little things like getting paid under the table so I didn't have to file a tax return.'

His mind boggled at the logistics. It was almost funny. Samuel Karpathy had known, when Lane brought up Matilda's disappearance, that she was barely a stone's throw away. That Lane had already talked to her at least once.

But that was one thing the farm residents could be trusted to do. If Matilda Carver had asked to be called Natalie Matthews from now on, they would all do it no questions asked. If she asked them to stonewall anyone who asked about Matilda Carver, they would.

Natalie grabbed a tissue from Lane's bedside table and dabbed at her eyes. 'I know it was selfish. If I could go back to the day Alain died, I'd do everything differently. But Rebecca's death couldn't be undone, and I convinced myself I could make it the last one. After that, Nadya came on board, helping me to keep watch. It was unethical, but if she knew someone at the farm was seriously unwell she'd let me know, so I could talk to them before Gretel got her claws in. Over the past six years, I've steered away four people.'

Perhaps that was why Dave believed no-one ever got seriously ill on the farm. Natalie and Nadya spirited them away.

'Did you share your suspicions with Nadya about what really happened to Rebecca?'

'No. It wouldn't be fair to burden her with that.'

'Well.' Lane didn't know what to say to that. 'For better or worse, it's all going to come out now. And I think you're going to deal with some pretty serious judgement from people. But if it helps, I don't think your parents will be among them.'

She laughed bitterly. 'I don't know if you know my parents at all, but they're not exactly open-minded, forgiving people.'

'The parents you knew weren't the ones who spent twenty years searching for their daughter.'

THE DOOR SWUNG inwards, revealing Matilda, who flinched with surprise when she saw him so close. 'What are you doing?'

'I want to go,' Alain whispered.

She crouched in front of him, like a mother soothing a toddler throwing a tantrum in the cereal aisle. 'Go where?'

Talking was hard. He needed to choose his words carefully. 'Home.'

She looked genuinely confused. 'And that's not here?'

'I need to go,' he said. He closed his eyes. 'I'm scared.'

'I know. I was scared too.' She put her hands on his shoulders and he collapsed a little, hunching closer to the floor. She quickly took them away. 'Where's home, Alain?'

Nowhere. She knew that. There was no door in the entire world that he could knock on and be welcomed in. There was no-one who would wrap their arms around his aching body and pull him close. He missed the time when he thought he'd found that. He missed the time when he'd trusted her.

'Is there anyone you could call who would help you?' she asked.

He stayed silent. He was tired. He needed to sleep.

'I'll help you back to bed,' she said, and her voice was so kind.

CHAPTER TWENTY-EIGHT

THE SHIRTS IN Albury Correctional Centre were just as itchy as the ones in the Special Purpose Centre back in Bowral. Lane found himself missing the years-worn softness of the shirts at the Karpathy farm.

A guard led him through to the visitors room where Sam Karpathy waited, still wearing those familiar work pants and a button-down.

'Thanks for agreeing to see me,' he said.

'I'm just curious about why you're here,' Lane replied.

That wasn't entirely honest. It was fucking lonely in here, and a visitor was a visitor. At least he could be sure Karpathy wasn't here to try to get him to join a church or a pyramid scheme.

'I just wanted to check how you're doing.'

Lane spread his arms out, as if to say, *See for yourself.*

Frankly, Karpathy seemed to be doing worse. He appeared shrunken, somehow, from the man who had ruled the farm.

He didn't sit up as straight, and Lane doubted he was sleeping well.

'How's the rebuild going?'

'Good,' Karpathy said, without smiling. 'We lost a lot of mature fruit trees, but the orchards protected most of the buildings. The pig shed was seriously damaged, but …'

The pig shed would have been demolished by the police anyway, looking for Alain's remains, Lane thought. He understood why Karpathy didn't want to say it.

'The important thing is no lives were lost.'

'The farm is back up and running?'

'In a way. Some people, uh … well, you know, because we were evacuated, everyone qualified for an emergency payout from the government. A few people decided that the payout, along with their farm wages, would be enough for a fresh start. Some decided to move to the BlazeAid camp, which is great.'

Lane nodded. BlazeAid was an organisation that moved into areas hit by bushfires, setting up camp for months or even years while volunteers rebuilt fences and other structures that had been lost.

'How many are left?'

'Maybe ten,' Karpathy admitted. 'Dave says he's not going anywhere. I think Alessandra is just waiting until the crisis has passed before she peaces out.'

'Why are you here?' Lane asked again. 'You have to know I'm not interested in being resident eleven.'

'I do know that. But … do you believe me? That I didn't know what Gretel was doing?'

'Shouldn't you be more interested in whether the police believe you? The courts?'

'The police believe me.' Karpathy didn't sound entirely confident about that.

'She buried them on your land. She marked the locations in your files.'

'She did all the filing herself. Even before she and my father got together. After my mum left, she took over a lot of the farm admin work. It's sexist, I know, but it's the traditional farm-wife stuff.'

'Alright. You didn't know. I absolve you.'

'But you think I should have known.'

Lane stared at him.

Oh.

'*You* think you should have known.'

Karpathy grimaced. 'Of course I should have. Multiple people disappeared and we thought it meant nothing. Natalie was so traumatised by the experience of living on our farm that she devoted her whole life to offering people an escape route. My own sister joined her. They saw through it and I couldn't.'

'Okay,' Lane said.

Karpathy deflated. 'Do you hear from Natalie at all?'

'Not exactly. We're all trying not to incriminate ourselves any further, which makes casual chats impossible. I think she and her parents are trying to work things out. My lawyer says she's not going to be charged, but her story isn't getting a lot of public sympathy. William's not even sure they'll make a murder charge stick on Gretel. Alain and Rebecca chose to stop taking their medication. They chose to stop eating. William thinks that the most dangerous thing for her is that she admitted to helping Rebecca hide her location from her family. That suggests Gretel knew what she was doing was going to kill Rebecca and tried to hide her tracks.'

Gretel had admitted to that part when was interviewed. It couldn't even accurately be called an interrogation. With the cheerful openness of someone convinced they were in the right, she'd admitted to everything. Just like she'd convinced Matilda to lie to the farm residents about where she was going, she'd convinced Rebecca too. But, almost certainly because of what had happened to Alain, she'd gone a step further.

Rebecca had asked Dave to take her to the train station, only to get off the train ten minutes later at Wodonga and into Gretel's waiting car. Hours later, back at Gretel's, she'd called her mother claiming to have arrived in Melbourne.

'But no matter how much Gretel manipulated Rebecca,' Lane went on, 'she still chose to do what she did. Gretel will definitely do time for hiding their bodies, but that's nothing compared to everything else she did.' He looked Karpathy in the eye. 'They chose to do that because they trusted her. Your father deliberately built a community of lost, vulnerable people, and a monster used that as a hunting ground. He set out to bind them to him, to win their absolute trust, and then told them they could trust her too. You inherited that, along with everything else.'

'What can we do?' Karpathy asked. 'Shut our doors to the people who most need a home?'

'I can't give you advice on how to make Karpathy farm less culty,' Lane said. 'Get therapy. I've heard it works.'

CHAPTER TWENTY-NINE

WHEN LANE THOUGHT about it, he had always imagined getting his *Shawshank Redemption* moment. He would sit in front of the parole board and wow them with his speech about how he had learned, and grown, and was ready to be a better man. If they let him, he would go out there and be a contributing member of society.

But the New South Wales State Parole Authority was not particularly concerned with what was cinematic. Instead, it happened like this ...

A few weeks after Lane returned to Albury Correctional Centre, his application to be transferred back to the Special Purpose Centre in Bowral was granted, on the grounds that being closer to his sister, who had just graduated and started a new job in Sydney, would help the process of reintegrating into the community. He dropped out of his agriculture course, which he had found was not to his liking, but did complete a correspondence course on the theoretical components of search and rescue training.

One day, when 11.59 pm ticked over to midnight, a Corrective Services computer system automatically added his file to a list of those eligible to be considered for parole. A date was set for a closed-door hearing. Letters were sent to his registered victims, Evelyn Holland and Mina McCreery, advising him that he was being considered for parole and they were entitled to provide a statement in opposition or support.

Letters were sent.

The meeting was held.

And a decision was made.

•

Which was how Lane found himself standing at the gates of the Special Purpose Centre, wearing a hideous shirt he'd bought at a Salvos many years ago because it fit. It didn't fit anymore.

Lynnie and William were waiting for him. For some reason, Lynnie had brought flowers. She dragged him into an enormous hug. He held on for as long as she would let him, trying his hardest not to cry. When she finally let go, she pushed the flowers into his left hand, and William shook his right hand firmly.

'Just so you know, I'm resigning as your lawyer effective immediately,' William said. 'I'm wearing one hat only from now on, and if you get up to any more nonsense, make it some other lawyer's problem.'

'No more nonsense,' Lane promised. He looked at the flowers, a tight bouquet of red roses. They smelled lovely, but he didn't quite know what to do with them.

They walked to William's car, which Lane was relieved to see had dark-tinted windows. He doubted there would be much press interest in his release, but he didn't want to worry about being photographed.

'Shotgun,' Lynnie said, as if he would have fought her for the front seat of her own fiancé's car. Lane opened the door, and slid into the back seat.

Mina was in the other seat, wearing a pair of dark sunglasses and a nervous smile.

'Hey,' he said.

'Hi,' she said.

'Bleach and ammonia?' he asked.

She shrugged. 'We survived, didn't we?'

Somewhere a guard pushed a button. The car park gates opened, and they drove away.

ACKNOWLEDGEMENTS

I would like to acknowledge the Traditional Owners of the lands I lived and worked on while writing this book. At various times, this book was written on Wiradjuri, Wurundjeri and Waywurru country. I pay my respects to their Elders past and present.

Georges Bridge is a fictional town in a real part of Australia. Albury and Wodonga are real places, but Albury Prison is fictional. The sushi train is also real. Please don't ban me.

Special thanks to the volunteers of the Tallangatta SES, both for fact-checking help and for giving up their own time, unpaid, to keep people safe over a staggeringly large geographical area.

Thank you to:

Everyone at Hachette.

My editors, Rebecca Saunders, Emma Rafferty, Ali Lavau and Rebecca Hamilton.

Alex Ross, @alexrosscreative on Instagram, for a beautiful cover, and a belated thank you for the incredible *RIPPER* cover too.

My agent Sarah McKenzie.

Freya Marske, and the sprinters of the Word Camp. Without the motivation, accountability and sympathy you provide, this book would be 100 words long.

My friends and family. Any characters named after you are either an accident or intended as a compliment.

Most of all, the readers who have followed Lane to this point. The last three years have been a masterclass in maintaining a poker face, as several of you predicted the last page of this book beat for beat. Many others had an entirely different interpretation of the story so far, and this book is not intended to prove you wrong. Every time a reader picks up a book a new version of the story is created, and that has been one of my favourite parts of putting my work out into the world.